DARK
DECEPTION

Books by Nancy Mehl

FINDING SANCTUARY

Gathering Shadows
Deadly Echoes
Rising Darkness

ROAD TO KINGDOM

Inescapable
Unbreakable
Unforeseeable

DEFENDERS OF JUSTICE

Fatal Frost
Dark Deception

DARK DECEPTION

NANCY MEHL

BETHANYHOUSE

a division of Baker Publishing Group
Minneapolis, Minnesota

© 2017 by Nancy Mehl

Published by Bethany House Publishers
11400 Hampshire Avenue South
Bloomington, Minnesota 55438
www.bethanyhouse.com

Bethany House Publishers is a division of
Baker Publishing Group, Grand Rapids, Michigan

Printed in the United States of America

Library of Congress Cataloging-in-Publication Data
Names: Mehl, Nancy, author.
Title: Dark deception / Nancy Mehl.
Description: Minneapolis, Minnesota : Bethany House, a division of Baker
    Publishing Group, [2017] | Series: Defenders of justice ; 2
Identifiers: LCCN 2016056194| ISBN 9780764230349 (hardcover) | ISBN
    9780764217784 (softcover)
Subjects: LCSH: Witnesses—Protection—Fiction. | Murder victims' families—
    Fiction. | GSAFD: Suspense fiction. | Christian fiction.
Classification: LCC PS3613.E4254 D37 2017 | DDC 813/.6—dc23
LC record available at https://lccn.loc.gov/2016056194

Scripture quotations are from the King James Version of the Bible.

Cover design by Dan Pitts
Cover photography by Mike Habermann Photography, LLC

Nancy Mehl is represented by The Steve Laube Agency.

17 18 19 20 21 22 23   7 6 5 4 3 2 1

This novel is dedicated to Peter Marsh.

If I could talk to you one more time, I'd tell you how smart, funny, and special you were.

If I could talk to you one more time, I'd tell you that I still remember your great smile.

If I could talk to you one more time, I'd tell you how much it meant to me when you'd leave the other boys playing outside so you could come in just to visit with your friend's mom.

If I could talk to you one more time, I'd tell you how much you were loved.

If I could talk to you one more time, I'd wrap my arms around you and never let go.

If I could talk to you one more time, I'd tell you that one of the worst moments in my life was telling my son that you were gone. I'd tell you that we both cried. That we still cry.

If I could talk to you one more time, I'd tell you that God can turn any situation around. That life is never, ever hopeless. If only you'd talked to us one more time.

But now there's an empty spot in the world where you should be. No one will ever fill it. No one else can. It will always belong to you.

We can't talk to you one more time in this world, but we're praying that someday we'll get to talk to you one more time . . . forever.

We love you, Peter.

PROLOGUE

Playing dead was harder than she ever could have imagined. Despite the pain and the warm blood that surrounded her, she fought to lie perfectly still. It was quiet. Too quiet. There was no doubt in her mind that if he thought she was still alive, he would come back and finish the job.

How could this be happening? Only two hours ago she and Kelly were at a party, celebrating. Then they'd come home to find a man hiding in the bathroom. Kate hadn't known anything was wrong until she'd found him with one arm around Kelly's neck, his other hand holding a knife to her throat. He'd looked shocked to see her. As if he hadn't known Kelly had a sister.

"Back up," he'd ordered. "Or I'll slit her throat."

Kate wanted to stop him. Wanted to free her sister, but she couldn't find a way to do it. If she angered him, she was certain Kelly would die. So she stayed where she was, praying he would leave.

But he didn't. Not until Kelly was dead, and Kate wished she could join her. She lay on the floor until she was absolutely sure he was gone. Then she crawled over to the phone and dialed 911.

When the dispatcher answered, all she could do was cry.

CHAPTER
ONE

Icy rain pelted the windows of the St. Louis courtroom, given strength by a stiff wind that shrieked and moaned, eerily echoing the sounds of the serial killer's victims. The city was under a tornado watch, and if the watch became a warning, the courtroom would be emptied and everyone would be directed to the building's basement. Seated a couple of rows behind the defense table, Deputy U.S. Marshal Tony DeLuca shivered, even though the room was abnormally warm. The old courthouse smelled of sweat and despair. Its polished floors had been trod upon by thousands of feet. Its marble pillars had seen many criminals pass through the doors while their victims waited inside its walls, praying for justice.

There was complete silence as twenty-year-old Kate O'Brien walked slowly up to the front of the room and took the stand. She held up her hand as she was sworn in. Tony could see her body tremble, and he wished he could stand by her side and comfort her as she faced the man who'd tried to take her life. Deep down inside, Tony believed she'd be okay. Kate's fragile beauty belied her inner strength. She was determined to conquer the monster who had brought so much destruction into her life.

She took her seat, purposely looking away from Alan Gerard, who stared at her brazenly, as if trying to destroy her confidence. Kate had vowed to ignore Gerard until the moment she was forced to identify him. After that, she'd made it clear he would never take up space in her head again. Tony admired her bravery, but he doubted if anyone could so easily banish the demons that lurked in the dark.

He looked carefully around the packed courtroom. There had been several threats made against Kate from delusional people who considered themselves fans of the demented serial killer. Although some in law enforcement had chalked up most of them to individuals who would never carry out their warnings, Tony took each one seriously. Several of the letter-writers had been tracked down and found to be harmless, but there were a dozen or so who couldn't be traced. One in particular bothered him. The verbiage used was educated and succinct. Although the writer was obviously delusional, he had reasoned out his insanity in a way that kept Tony awake at night.

Everyone has a destiny. Every step we take only brings us closer to the inevitable. There is no way to change what must happen. Kate O'Brien's course is ordained, and there is nothing anyone can do about it. Accepting this truth is the only thing that can free our souls.

Although Tony believed in destiny too, he refused to accept that there was no deliverance from evil. He was determined that Kate would find happiness in a world that had been so unkind to her.

Tony had talked to her about witness protection, but she didn't want anything to do with it. She was ready to leave her aunt's house and start a new life—on her own terms. Even though Tony had assured her they would work to provide her with the kind of lifestyle she wanted, Kate's mind was made up. Tony could only hope that after Gerard was sentenced, the crazies would find some other vicious killer to worship. Still, he felt unsettled. On guard. As if his gut was trying to tell him that Kate was in danger.

As District Attorney Matthew Gibbons stood up and headed her way, Kate searched the gallery until she spotted Tony. She'd asked him to stay where she could see him. She'd told him she felt more secure knowing he was there. Tony hoped she'd be able to keep herself together as she faced Gerard in court. The pressure of living through that awful night again—of coming face-to-face with the monster . . . Well, talking about it and actually going through with it could prove to be two very different things.

Tony kept his gaze steady as Kate stared back at him. If he could send her additional courage through sheer will, she would have all she needed.

After Kate was sworn in, Gibbons asked her to recount the events of April twenty-third of last year. She began with the birthday party. She and Kelly were turning nineteen—getting ready for college, moving into their own apartment. They should have started a year earlier, but Kelly had been injured in a car accident with her boyfriend. Scott had walked away with a mild concussion, but Kelly had broken both legs and shattered her right arm. Recovery and rehabilitation had taken so long, starting school was impossible. Kate had decided to wait for her sister rather than begin without her. Sharing an apartment and going to college together was something they'd looked forward to since they were children.

"Where was this party held?" Gibbons asked.

"At McGoogles. Near the campus."

"So this was a happy occasion?"

"Yes, very. Kelly was doing well after her accident, and we were both looking forward to our first year in college."

"How late did the party last?"

"We shut it down around midnight. Even though Kelly was much stronger, she still tired easily. I wanted to get her home so she could get some rest."

"And where was home?"

"We'd just found an apartment near the college. We'd moved in two weeks earlier. That's where we went."

"You're talking about the apartment on Delmar?"

"Yes."

The assistant D.A. cleared his throat. Tony knew the testimony that would follow was important. Even though there was DNA at the crime scene that linked Gerard to the attacks, it was only a small amount of evidence—a spot of blood in one location, found after the scene was initially processed. The defense claimed the DNA had been planted. That no one who had committed such a brutal murder could have left such a small amount of blood behind. They also contended there were no marks on Gerard's body—no cuts that could have produced blood. There was nothing under the girls' nails, no fingerprints that matched Gerard's, and nothing else to link him to the murders—except for Kate's eyewitness testimony. She'd recognized him as a maintenance worker at the college. Her identification had led to his arrest.

The lack of physical evidence was highly unusual, but not for Alan Gerard. He was suspected in a long string of other murders. In almost every case, just like this one, there was nothing left behind linking him to the killings. In addition to that, only one body had ever been recovered. Tony couldn't quite understand why he'd left Kelly and Kate behind. Maybe he'd been thrown off from his usually well-timed, thoroughly planned procedure because he hadn't realized Kelly was a twin. He'd thought his victim would be alone. Thank God Kate had survived and could describe her attacker.

Even though the prosecution believed the DNA was enough to get a conviction, Kate's testimony would make the case a slam dunk for the state.

"Tell me what happened when you got home," Gibbons said gently.

Kate took a deep breath and once again looked at Tony. He nodded slightly and smiled. She shifted in her chair as if trying to find a more comfortable position, but there was no way to make this any easier. The words she must say were horrific. Impossible. Tony realized he was holding his breath and forced himself to slowly breathe out. The entire courtroom was as silent as a tomb except for a large clock on the wall *tick-tick-ticking* away the seconds. Now it was here. The moment Kate had prepared herself for. Tony fought an urge to take out his gun and shoot the clock. The sound was driving him crazy.

"We . . . uh . . ." She locked eyes with Tony, her face pale but her expression determined. "We got home around twelve-fifteen. Everything seemed fine. We entered the apartment, and Kelly went into the bathroom. I had some leftovers from the party and put them in the fridge."

Gibbons nodded. "And then you heard a noise?"

"Objection," the defense attorney said loudly. "Leading the witness."

Gerard's lawyer had a reputation for getting guilty people off. He was sleazy with a capital *sleaze*. Tony had no respect for the man. Darwin Branford was a third-generation lawyer who had followed in his father's and grandfather's footsteps. His grandfather had dropped dead two years ago under suspicious circumstances, and his father was serving five years in prison for attempting to bribe a judge.

"Sustained," the judge said. "You know better, Mr. Gibbons."

"Sorry, your honor," Gibbons said. "What happened after you put your food in the refrigerator, Miss O'Brien?"

"I heard a noise. I wasn't sure what it was, but it concerned me. I went over and knocked on the bathroom door to see if Kelly was all right."

"And then what?"

"I . . . I heard her scream. I tried to open the door, but it was locked." Kate reached up and brushed away a lock of crimson hair that had fallen across her forehead.

Her bright red hair and startling blue eyes were disquieting. Unfortunately, it was her eyes that had drawn the Blue-Eyed Killer to her and Kelly. Truthfully, Tony hated the inane names the press loved to tack onto low-life murderers. Especially this one. The title didn't even make sense. Correctly used, it would mean that the killer had blue eyes—and Gerard's eyes were brown. But it had stuck and it wasn't going away. In this case, however, at least it had alerted potential victims that the killer was looking for women who had blue eyes. There were other similarities among the victims, though. His first known victim, Tammy Rice, had been in her thirties and was the oldest. Most of them were younger. In their twenties.

At first, authorities hadn't recognized that they were looking for a serial killer. Tammy had a son who was briefly suspected of killing his mother, but a solid alibi had cleared him. When Ann Barton, the second victim, disappeared and the same song sheet that was left with Tammy's body showed up at Ann's house, officials began to look in another direction.

Besides having blue eyes, all of his victims also had long hair. Hair color changed from victim to victim, but the killer never deviated from eye color and long hair. So far, profilers hadn't figured out who he was actually trying to kill. Gerard's mother was a lovely lady who couldn't believe her son had committed such heinous crimes. She had short brown hair and hazel eyes. And there didn't seem to be any past girlfriends who fit the description. Gerard wasn't talking, so it was possible they might never understand his predilections. Tony didn't care. He just wanted Gerard locked away forever.

Gibbons nodded at Kate again. She clasped her hands together for a moment and looked away. Gibbons moved closer to her and effectively blocked Tony from her line of sight. The silence from the stand told Tony Kate had noticed. Would she let Gibbons know he needed to move? Or was the prosecutor so focused on her answers he'd forgotten her request to keep Tony in her field of vision?

He was just about to get up and move to another location when suddenly Gibbons stepped back a few feet and glanced back at Tony. Obviously he'd realized his faux pas. Tony frowned at him.

"Could you tell us what happened next?" Gibbons said quickly, trying to reestablish Kate's concentration.

Kate met Tony's gaze once again. The relief on her face was evident. "Yes. Suddenly the door burst open. There was a man with my sister. He had one arm around her neck and he held a knife up to her throat with his other hand."

"Did this man say anything to you?"

She nodded and then realized her mistake. "Yes. He told me to back up or he'd kill Kelly."

"And what did you do?"

"I moved away, into the living room." She blinked several times. "I . . . I wanted to run out the front door and get help, but I was afraid. Afraid he'd hurt Kelly. Maybe if I had . . ."

"That's okay, Miss O'Brien. Let's stay focused on the facts, okay?"

Tony tensed a bit. Gibbons's response seemed harsh. As soon as the thought came, he dismissed it. Gibbons's job was to keep Kate's testimony centered around the facts that would send Gerard to his justified reward. He couldn't take a chance on coddling Kate right now. If he did, she might fall apart—and his case with her.

"I . . . I'm sorry." She clasped her hands together again and clearly fought to gain control of her emotions while Gibbons waited for her. "He told us to sit down on the couch," she said finally. "I sat down first, and then he pushed Kelly next to me."

"Did you say anything to him?"

"Yes. I told him he could take anything he wanted. Our computers, our TV, jewelry . . . I even told him about the extra cash we had hidden in the bedroom."

"You thought he was there to rob you?"

Again she started to nod before she caught herself. "Yes. There had been quite a few robberies in the neighborhood. I just assumed that's what he wanted."

"And when did you realize he was there for . . . something much different?"

Kate's eyes widened and she gulped. When she opened her mouth, nothing came out. Tony smiled at her and nodded again. He felt so helpless. He wanted to get out of his chair and wring Gerard's neck. Put an end to this. After a few seconds, he noticed a slight dip of her chin.

"He . . . he started singing. Softly."

"And what did he sing?"

"I didn't know what it was then. I found out later it was a song from the eighties. 'Blue-Eyed Angel.'"

Even though he'd tried to force that stupid song out of his mind, the words ran through his thoughts as if they had a life of their own. *She has a heart as cold as ice. Frozen kisses that take my breath away. Blue-Eyed Angel who sees into my soul and somehow makes me whole.* It hadn't been popular when it was released, but now that the song had become part of the Blue-Eyed Killer's repertoire, the stupid thing was played nonstop on television and radio. The group that had released it, Brain Dead Zombies, had soared to fame. Their notoriety wasn't based on their talent—just on a bloodthirsty murderer's bad taste in music.

"Then what did he do?"

Tony brought his attention back to Kate, aware that his mind had wandered for a moment. Hopefully, she hadn't noticed. She didn't seem to. Her large blue eyes still sought his. Although he kept his gaze steady, the account of the terrible acts that had left Kelly dead and Kate barely clinging to life were too awful even for him. Even though he was only twenty-seven, his stint in law enforcement had already forced him to see things no human being should ever see.

Kate took a deep, shuddering breath and bravely repeated the words she'd rehearsed so many times. Her tone was almost robot-like, but Tony knew it was the only way she could get through it.

The entire courtroom was silent as the words dropped like toxic bombs, fouling the air and the atmosphere around them. Several people in the gallery got up and left. Quiet sobbing came from different parts of the room. Tony glanced over at Kate's aunt, but Miriam had her usual stoic expression firmly in place. Kelly and Kate were only six years old when their parents died in a motorcycle accident. Miriam was the kind of person who took her responsibilities seriously, and she'd taken in the twins. Unfortunately, she wasn't really the motherly type. She'd done an admirable job of raising her nieces, and she had great affection for them, but there was no deep love between her and Kate. Kate was pretty much on her own without Kelly.

Finally, Kate stopped talking. Even the defense attorney looked stunned. After a few seconds, Gibbons walked over to the side of the courtroom, next to a sour-faced guard who glared at him.

"Miss O'Brien," he said, his voice smooth and controlled, "is the man who attacked you . . . who killed your sister . . . in this courtroom?"

"Yes. Yes, he is," Kate said.

"Will you please point him out?"

This was it. The moment of truth. Tony nodded at Kate as her eyes bored into his. Then she turned her head to focus on the sorry excuse for a human being who had torn her life to shreds. Tony waited for the words he knew were coming. But instead of Kate pointing at Gerard to seal his fate, something happened that momentarily froze Tony to his seat.

Without warning, the prison guard, who day in and day out had escorted Gerard to the courtroom, pulled out his gun and shot Gibbons. Then he approached Kate with a crazed look on his face. Kate leapt up and put her hands out in front of her, as if somehow she had the ability to stop bullets.

Tony's momentary shock disappeared as his training kicked in. He pulled his weapon and ran toward the front of the courtroom. The guard was yelling something about retribution, but Tony didn't pay any attention to his words. His eyes were glued to the man's trigger finger. There was one slight movement, but it was the last voluntary action the guard's body ever made. Tony's bullet struck the guard's temple, killing him instantly. As a horror-struck courtroom began to come back to life, people pulled themselves up off the floor, many of them running for the doors. Tony hurried over to Kate. She stepped out of the witness box and threw her arms around him, her body shaking and her voice a whisper.

"I don't understand," she said. "I don't understand."

But when Tony turned around and looked at Alan Gerard,

he understood. He understood perfectly. Gerard stared back at him, his eyes narrowed and his mouth twisted into a half smile. Even though he was under arrest, kept in a cage, Gerard had just taken two more lives—and tried to complete his deadly plans for Kate.

CHAPTER
TWO

In Garden City, Kansas, Police Sergeant Leon Shook hung up the phone, a frown on his usually jovial face. He turned around to stare at his friend, Officer Kevin Kennedy. "That was odd. Another tip from a *concerned citizen.* This one is really nuts." Leon's emphasis made it clear he didn't put much stock in information phoned in by people who didn't care enough to give their names. He could run the phone number in an attempt to find the identity of the caller, but almost all these *tips* came from burner phones. No way to trace them.

"What was it this time?" Kevin asked. "Another alien body in a cornfield?"

"Nope. Ann Barton's body is in Valley View Cemetery. Look for Dorothy."

Kevin snorted. "Sure. And maybe we can check with the Wizard while we're there. How many of these crazy calls have we gotten over the years?"

"Hundreds. Along with all the letters and emails. Give some scumbag killer a nickname and the loonies come out of the woodwork. Can't believe they still contact us after all this time."

"I guess some of those people were really trying to help."

Leon laughed. "Yeah, and some of them were just off their rockers. Especially the so-called psychics. Like the one who told us we would discover Ann's remains in a storm drain on Main Street."

"Found a drowned rat," Kevin said with a grin. "I guess her psychic antenna was a little off-kilter."

"She still calls every few months or so, wanting to know if we've found the body yet. As if Ann is going to suddenly pop up after a heavy rain."

Kevin shook his head. "I don't think Ann's in Kansas. My guess is Gerard took her over state lines. The FBI went through this area with a fine-toothed comb. If she was here, they'd have found her."

Leon sighed. "I know, but I really wish we could locate her body. I'd love to give her parents some closure. Henry doesn't even ask for updates anymore. I think he's given up."

Henry and Beth Barton were good people. The loss of their daughter Ann had devastated their lives. Then, six years ago, Alan Gerard, the Blue-Eyed Killer, had confessed to murdering her. He was finally convicted two years later and had been in jail the last four years. But he still wouldn't tell anyone where Ann was. Leon couldn't imagine how the Bartons felt. How they had survived. *"Day by day,"* Beth had said once. *"You just put one foot in front of the other. You can't worry about tomorrow because it's too much to handle."*

"So what now?" Kevin asked.

"You know what?" Leon stood up and grabbed the jacket

that was draped over the back of his desk chair. "Let's go. We have to do everything we can, no matter how ridiculous the lead seems."

Kevin started to say something else but Leon silenced him with a wave of his hand. "I know it doesn't make sense, but it's for the Bartons."

"Maybe we should just follow the yellow brick road," Kevin grumbled. Without saying another word, he got up from his own chair, grabbed the keys to the squad car, and the two men headed out the front door, telling the chief's personal assistant where they were going. Chief Henderson was speaking at a meeting of the local Kiwanis Club. If Leon had felt the tip was important enough, he would have interrupted the meeting. But law enforcement had been following bad leads about the Blue-Eyed Killer for almost twenty years. Bothering the chief with another one could get an officer stuck on desk duty until he had been sufficiently punished. Especially a lead as goofy as this one.

The two men got into their squad car and drove toward the cemetery, stopping briefly to get breakfast from the Garden City Coffee Shop. Their omelets would keep until they got back to the office. Since Leon was certain this trip would be a waste of time, he wasn't worried about being gone too long. If it took longer than he anticipated, they could always nuke their food in the office microwave.

When they reached the cemetery, they pulled over to the side of the road to figure out their next step. The Valley View Cemetery was rather infamous. The bodies of the Clutter family, murdered by Richard Hickock and Perry Smith and immortalized in the book *In Cold Blood*, were buried there.

The irony of looking for the victim of a serial killer in the same place the Clutters had been laid to rest wasn't lost on Leon. Even with its rather ominous history, Valley View was actually a lovely place, peaceful and well-maintained. Leon and his wife, Linda, lived nearby and frequently took walks through the cemetery when the weather was nice.

"So how do we do this?" Kevin asked.

"Let's head over to the office. Ask about graves that belong to women named Dorothy."

"Sounds good."

Leon started the car and drove over to the cemetery's office. The director was at lunch, but his administrative assistant, Bonnie, was sitting at her desk. Leon told her what he wanted, and although she looked at him oddly, she didn't ask any questions.

"Give me a minute to pull up that information," she said.

She began tapping her keyboard and a few minutes later had a list of women named Dorothy buried in the cemetery. She printed it out and handed it to Leon. "Wanna tell me what this is for?"

Leon shook his head. "Not really."

Bonnie rolled her eyes. "Fine. I'll probably sleep better if you keep it to yourself."

"We're running down a lead that's most likely a dead end. Telling you would be a waste of my time and yours. I've got breakfast from the coffee shop in my car. I don't want to be here any longer than I have to."

Bonnie winked at him. "Totally understand. Knock yourself out."

Leon and Kevin said good-bye and stepped outside. Leon

studied the list for a moment. "Nine names and locations here. I guess we'll start on one side and work our way to the other."

They got back in their car, and Leon drove while Kevin gave him directions. Although they had trouble finding a couple of the graves, one by one they crossed names off their list. Leon couldn't help but notice how lush and beautiful the cemetery was. Their reason for being there seemed almost profane in the lovely, peaceful setting.

At the seventh grave Leon voiced his frustration. "What the heck are we doing? I'll bet some of the local teenagers set us up. They're probably hiding somewhere watching us. Getting a big kick out of this." Even though he didn't put much stock in the anonymous tip, the voice on the phone hadn't sounded like a kid's. And there had been a serious tone to it that made it hard for Leon to dismiss it out of hand. But maybe that was because he wanted so badly to bring the Bartons some peace. To let them bury their child.

"Like you said, it's for the Bartons," Kevin reminded him. "Only two more and we can head back to the station. I'm hungry."

"Yeah, yeah. Let's get this over with."

They got back in the car and drove to the eighth name on the list. As soon as Leon got out, he noticed something lying on the grave. As they got closer, he realized someone had stuck a stake through a piece of paper and jammed it into the ground next to the headstone. "What in the world . . ." Kevin started to pick it up but Leon grabbed him before he could. "Don't touch it. Call the chief."

"I don't understand."

"It's sheet music." Leon turned toward Kevin, his eyes wide. "It's that song. 'Blue-Eyed Angel.'"

As Kevin dialed the police chief, Leon's heart pounded in his chest. Was someone playing a really cruel joke, or had they finally found Ann Barton?

CHAPTER
THREE

Richard Batterson, Chief Deputy U.S. Marshal for the District of Missouri's U.S. Marshals' Office, stared at his deputy Marshal for a full minute without saying anything. Tony DeLuca was one of his best deputies. The district attorney needed to talk to Kate O'Brien, one of their witnesses. A subpoena lay on the desk in front of him. The DNA evidence that had pointed to Alan Gerard as the man who attacked Kate and killed her sister six years ago had been thrown out. Gerard's conviction had been overturned by the appellate court, and he was out of prison.

Batterson was furious. An investigation by a group dedicated to freeing innocent prisoners had proven that the seal on the vial of Gerard's blood was broken. An evidence clerk admitted that she noticed it not long after Gerard was arrested. She reported it to the M.E., and he resealed it after telling her not to notify anyone about the breach. Afraid of losing her job, she'd kept quiet about it, even though the detail had bothered her.

Now a retired crime-scene tech had come forward and

admitted he had opened the vial and taken some blood, placing it at the crime scene. At the time, he'd believed strongly that Gerard was the Blue-Eyed Killer. The tech wanted Gerard stopped before another woman died. The fact that his own daughters had long hair and blue eyes had ignited his decision to betray his department's code of ethics.

Although everyone knew Gerard had killed at least fifteen women, he was suspected of many more. But right now, all they had was Kate O'Brien's eyewitness testimony in the death of her sister. Without the forensic evidence, she was the only hope they had to send Gerard back to prison.

The knowledge that he was free horrified Batterson. More women would die before he was arrested again. That was a given.

Originally, the subpoena had been delivered to the Marshals' office in the area where Kate currently lived, but she'd refused to cooperate. Although initially she'd turned down the offer to go into the WITSEC program, after the second trial she'd changed her mind. Now that she was settled, she had no desire to uproot her life again. Who could blame her? The D.A. was insisting that the St. Louis office handle the situation. They knew DeLuca had been close to Kate. Batterson wanted to say no, but he couldn't. Besides, the look on his deputy's face made it clear he was determined to go. The question was, could he afford to be without DeLuca at a time like this?

Although his office, in league with the local police, had recently shut down a major cartel, there were more blood-thirsty cartels waiting in the wings to take its place. In addition to dealing with that dangerous threat, neighborhood gangs were spreading death throughout their communities. Police weren't getting much help from those in government. Several local politicians were more concerned about staying in office than stopping the bloodshed. Rogue judges were tossing dangerous criminals out on the streets rather than putting them away. Law enforcement and the public paid the price for their carelessness. The Marshals backed up the police on cases involving federal fugitives and criminals who crossed state lines, and they were currently engaged in a violent war for control of their city.

Batterson stared at the old coffee rings on his desk before speaking. "Okay," he said slowly. "Go there. Talk her into coming back. Touch base with the local Marshals when you arrive. They've already arranged to have a special deputy accompany you back to St. Louis." It was standard procedure for two Marshals to accompany a witness, at least one of them being female if the witness was a woman. "After that . . ."

"After that she's the D.A.'s problem," DeLuca finished for him.

Batterson watched as DeLuca's shoulders visibly relaxed. What was it about Kate O'Brien that made his deputy so tense? He looked down at the case file again. Then he slowly pushed it toward DeLuca. "Here's her information. It goes without saying that you can't share this with anyone else, right?" A bad experience the year before had made Batterson paranoid about files and privacy.

DeLuca nodded. "Of course, Chief."

Generally, only Washington knew the location of witnesses in protection, but Batterson was confident DeLuca would protect the witness with his life—if it called for that.

"Weird case," Batterson said. "Never saw anything like it before. The first time O'Brien testified she almost died."

"The guard was manipulated by Gerard," DeLuca said. "He was in the middle of a messy divorce, and his wife had threatened to take his kids. Ruin him financially. The guy was on the brink, and Gerard pushed him over the edge. Convinced him that Kate was just like his wife. A liar trying to send an innocent man to prison for something he didn't do. In the guard's mind, killing Kate was striking back at his wife. Stone-cold crazy. Too bad Gerard couldn't be charged with his death as well as Matthew Gibbons's. He might just as well have pulled the trigger."

"Lucky for Kate O'Brien you were in the courtroom. Anyone else might not have reacted quickly enough to save her."

DeLuca shook his head. "But not fast enough to save Gibbons. I regret that."

"Don't. No one could have anticipated what happened."

"Maybe not. I was there because some of Gerard's *fans* had threatened Kate. I was already watching the gallery, but I never expected the threat to come from . . ."

"Someone who was supposed to be protecting her?" Batterson finished.

"Yeah."

Batterson cleared his throat. "Quite a few people think another one of Gerard's minions is behind the mess-up with the DNA evidence. I know some crime tech took responsibility, but I have to wonder if Gerard had something to do with it."

"I don't know. That group . . . the one that got Gerard's conviction overturned? What are they called?"

"The Freedom Project."

"Right. They uncovered several other inconsistencies with evidence in different cases. I know Gerard has a group of bloodthirsty groupies who revere him, but I don't think any of them are smart or sophisticated enough to break into a guarded evidence room and tamper with a blood sample. Makes more sense that the crime tech told the truth. That he wanted Gerard stopped and did what he could to bring that about. He may have actually saved a few lives."

"It's entirely possible . . ." Batterson said slowly. "Whatever happened to the guy who ran that website? What was it? BEKlives.com? So far no one's been able to find him. Or discover who he was. He may have been nuts, but he wasn't stupid."

"Still can't believe the FBI never tracked him down."

"They might have, but a month or so after Gerard went to prison, the site disappeared. Never heard from him again." For some reason, Batterson couldn't get the guy out of his head. His postings were nothing more than Bible verses, most of them taken out of context. Batterson still remembered the first one. *The righteous shall rejoice when he seeth the vengeance: he shall wash his feet in the blood of the wicked.* Although the guy who ran the website was obviously a worshipper of the Blue-Eyed Killer, sometimes it was almost as if he had been the maestro behind the evil orchestra of death played out by Gerard. Some of those who followed serial killers seemed more entranced by the website than by the person the site publicized.

"There was a scripture before every disappearance," De-Luca said. "Verses full of vengeance and judgment. As if B.E.K. was God's hand of revenge."

Batterson nodded. "I was just remembering that. Every time there was a new post, law enforcement braced for another murder."

"Yeah. The website would disappear sometimes, but it always came back. Different IP address and impossible to trace."

Batterson grunted. "Whoever ran the site was a computer genius. Still not sure how it's related to B.E.K., though. Never thought Gerard was smart enough to pull off something like that."

"Yeah. The FBI decided it was someone else. A wacky fan."

"But how would he know B.E.K. was getting ready to kill again?"

Tony shrugged. "I have no idea. The scriptures were released randomly. In between times, most of the postings were just wild stories about B.E.K. or some other serial killer. A lot of boasting about how the police couldn't find the Blue-Eyed Killer. Until Gerard was caught, that is. There were some weird poems, too. Crazy, rambling writings that talked about revenge and justice. They didn't make much sense. The FBI couldn't get anything from them that pointed to the identity of the killer. And they tried."

"If the murders matched the verses, there should be around twenty victims," Batterson said. "Toward the end, before the website shut down, there were verses posted but no new murders that followed. That we know of, anyway. Maybe he didn't take credit for all of them."

"It's possible."

Batterson sighed. "When Gerard was captured, it was like some kind of victory. As if revealing his identity was the ultimate goal. Unfortunately, putting a name and a face to the list of terrible crimes the Blue-Eyed Killer committed turned him into a legend. The website stayed up through the trial with postings about what was happening. But when Gerard went to prison it disappeared for good. Good riddance as far as I'm concerned." Batterson pushed the thoughts about the website guy out of his head. He didn't have time to worry about one insane man who would most probably never be heard from again.

"So I guess the people from the Freedom Project believe Gerard is innocent?" DeLuca said. "How do they explain Kate's testimony?"

Batterson shrugged. "Gerard worked as a maintenance man at the college. They say she saw him there and somehow substituted his face for the killer's. They have some head shrinker who backs them up. They believe Gerard took credit for the killing because he was insecure and wanted attention."

DeLuca snorted. "That's ridiculous. Why would she pick the janitor? Had she been to McDonald's recently? Maybe she saw Ronald McDonald kill her sister."

Batterson was silent for a moment. "I asked Dr. Abbot about it. You know, the gal we use when you guys go squirrely?"

Tony smiled. "Yeah, I know who you mean. And what was her opinion?"

"She says trauma can definitely cause false memories. In other words, after the event, Kate can't remember the attacker's face so she replaces it with another one. In this case, Alan Gerard. She convinces herself he's the killer because she desperately needs to bring closure to her situation."

"And you believe that?"

Batterson frowned at his deputy. "I'm not sure. I like Dr. Abbot. She seems to know what she's talking about, and I certainly don't understand what makes some people tick. If she can help us, I'm open to listening. That's why she's on the payroll."

"I guess . . ."

"Anyway, now we're looking at a new trial." He pushed back the thick black glasses that sat on the bridge of his nose. Then he leaned back in his chair, causing it to squeak. His administrative assistant was always trying to oil the old chair, but he wouldn't allow it. For some reason, he found the sound comforting. "Trust me, the D.A. is just as unhappy about this as we are. I was surprised O'Brien was willing to sit through a second trial. Now they're asking her to testify a third time. Doesn't seem right. I don't blame her for saying no."

"She never hesitated when it came to the second trial. She wanted Gerard behind bars. No matter what. She'll come through this time, too."

Batterson chewed on his bottom lip, a bad habit he'd tried to break over the years. However, stress kept bringing it back. DeLuca seemed to think this woman was superhuman, but she wasn't. She was a person who'd been through an ordeal most people couldn't imagine. "I can understand why she wouldn't be willing to tear her life to shreds again."

DeLuca didn't say anything at first, but he sniffed. Batterson almost smiled. Whenever DeLuca didn't agree with something, he'd sniff as if smelling something putrid. Batterson found it amusing. Tony's sniff was his only tell. Batterson always knew when DeLuca was upset about an assignment— or when he thought his boss was full of baloney.

"Now that the DNA evidence has been thrown out, Kate knows she's the only person who can I.D. the killer," DeLuca said. "She won't allow him to walk away. The local Marshals must have handled her wrong. I won't have any problems."

"I hope you're right." Batterson sighed. "This affects all of us. We're going to be revisiting the past for a while. The Freedom Project brought six more cases into the spotlight. Unfortunately, any case where DNA nailed the suspect probably won't be tried again if the tech who messed up the Gerard case was anywhere near it. Some of them involved violent criminals. These people will probably hit the streets—and put the public at risk. The only thing that can keep Gerard behind bars is Kate O'Brien." He reached for the file he'd given DeLuca and flipped it open. "Excuse me, Emily Lockhart. Hmm. She doesn't look like an Emily to me." Batterson studied his deputy. "You sure you can handle this in a professional manner? If you can't, we'll go another direction."

DeLuca nodded. "Of course. You know me better than that, Chief. The job comes first."

Batterson didn't argue. It was true. DeLuca always put his duties before anything else. In fact, Batterson wasn't even sure if DeLuca had a personal life. He would occasionally join Batterson and some of his other deputy Marshals when they went out to a local pub on Friday nights, but he didn't stay long—and he didn't drink much. One beer and no more. Of course, DeLuca's lack of a social life meant any time Batterson needed him, he was available. Batterson felt a little guilty about relying on DeLuca so much, but the deputy didn't seem to mind. In fact, he appeared to thrive on work.

DeLuca never talked about a girlfriend, although plenty

of women around the office had shown interest in him. His shaggy dark blond hair and deep green eyes seemed to appeal to women. But Batterson had never seen any feminine pursuit end in success. DeLuca's love was his job, and there didn't seem to be time for much else.

When he was younger, Batterson had felt the same way. But the past couple of years he'd been rethinking his priorities. All he really wanted was the kind of relationship his folks had, but he'd begun to doubt that he'd ever have that. Was it fair to bring this kind of evil into a marriage? Besides, these days spouses were disposable, and commitment only lasted as long as both partners were entertained. Even though Batterson had never experienced the deep and lasting kind of relationship he dreamed of, he felt the urge to keep looking. Keep hoping. Even after three failed marriages.

Batterson shoved the file back toward DeLuca. "When will you leave?" he asked.

"Tomorrow morning. I have some work to finish up today. I'll pack tonight and head out at first light." He flipped open the file. "Where is she located?"

"A small town in Arkansas. Not far from Hot Springs. It's a fishing resort."

DeLuca's eyebrows shot up. "A fishing resort? Really?"

Batterson smiled. "Yeah. When I say *resort*, I mean a few cabins for really dedicated fishermen. Guys who don't mind roughing it. I guess O'Brien runs a diner there."

"A diner?"

"Yeah. I was surprised, too. She had a choice between this place and a larger metropolitan city. Still small compared to St. Louis, but with more options. More excitement. She chose the hole-in-the-wall." Batterson shrugged. "Anyway, get on the road, and keep in touch. O'Brien needs to understand that the D.A. can force her to testify if necessary. This isn't actually a choice."

DeLuca let out a quick breath of air. "Seems like it should be."

"It's the law," Batterson said matter-of-factly. "We have to support it."

DeLuca grabbed the file and stood. "I understand." He stared down at Batterson. "Any new threats? Anything to be worried about?"

"Not yet, but we need to act as if there will be. Make sure she's safe, and get her to court. We'll protect her while she's here and get her back to her life as soon as possible. You'll have to be very careful. This thing will be all over the news. We need to keep her new identity under wraps the best we can. Moving her again is to be avoided at all costs. The trouble and expense is extreme."

"Got it, Chief."

DeLuca left the office, closing the door behind him. Batterson still had some concerns about sending him to Shelter Cove, but he knew he'd have a battle on his hands if he tried to send someone else. Tony DeLuca wasn't the kind of man to back down. He was tough when he needed to be, and gentle when it was necessary. Batterson recalled a raid on a drug house that had happened the year before. The local Marshals joined the police to find and bring down a major supplier. When they hit the house, the dealer was gone, leaving behind his victims—two parents who were so out of it they didn't realize their baby was near death. The drug dealer had left the parents and the baby behind because he knew the police were on to him. His actions were especially heinous because the woman was his sister and the dying child his niece. But family didn't mean much when drugs were involved.

DeLuca had gently cradled the child in his arms all the way to the hospital, talking softly to her. Encouraging her to live. And he'd visited every day until she was released. Thankfully, little Keisha was now living in a wonderful home with a loving family. DeLuca still dropped by from time to time to check on the little girl. Batterson figured the same compassion he'd shown to Keisha was what drove him now. He cared about Kate O'Brien and wanted to be there for her. Maybe Batterson was giving in to DeLuca's gentler side, but in the end it was DeLuca's commitment to the Marshals that decided it for Batterson. If he had any agent who deserved the benefit of the doubt, it was Tony DeLuca. If DeLuca was convinced he needed to do this, he probably did.

Batterson rubbed his temples with his fingertips. He could feel the beginnings of a tension headache. His headaches were a portent. Always had been. He had a bad feeling that this situation was going to get a lot worse before it got better.

CHAPTER
FOUR

Kate started the coffeemakers and began wrapping utensils for the tables in the Shelter Café. She could hear Bella in the kitchen, belting out "Bringing in the Sheaves" while she plopped dough into hot grease. The smell of fresh doughnuts filled the small restaurant. Another day had dawned in Shelter Cove, Arkansas. Usually Kate felt a sense of relief—and thankfulness for the life she'd found in the small town. Here she wasn't Kate O'Brien. She was Emily Lockhart. The horrible trail of death and destruction left behind by Alan Gerard seemed far away. Or had until recently, anyway.

Without meaning to, Kate slammed the utensils down on the table harder than she should, causing Bella to pause in her enthusiastic but off-key version of the old gospel favorite. It was clear that thinking about the past could still trigger Kate's anger. She took a few deep breaths to calm herself and waited until her cook began her spirited caterwauling once again. Bella loved her Lord and didn't care who knew about it. As awful as her tone-deaf renditions were, Kate enjoyed listening to her in the mornings. It stirred something in her soul and helped to get her day going in the right direction. And today she needed all the help she could get.

Hearing from the U.S. Marshals Service last week had dredged up old memories, forgotten and buried. She had no desire to revisit the horror. Why couldn't they just leave her alone? She'd sent the local Marshals packing, but she knew they'd be back. They had a subpoena. Not something she could ignore. She'd worked so hard to get her life back to normal, and now once again, someone had messed up—and they wanted her to pay the price for their incompetence. She couldn't believe they were asking her to testify a third time. How many trials would it take before Gerard was locked away for good?

The news that he was out of jail had hit her hard. The first night after the Marshals left, fear and panic had overwhelmed her. She'd prayed for hours, crouching in a corner of the bedroom, jumping over every noise, every movement outside. Springtime was noisy in Shelter Cove. The wind whipped around and through the town as if trying to prepare everyone for the rain and storms that would inevitably come. It had shown no mercy that night—every sigh, every breath of wind taking Kate back to that horrible night, Gerard panting in excitement as he'd carried out his evil intent. Kate's hand went automatically to the scars on her chest. The reminder of his act of terror. If the knife had gone a little deeper, she would have joined Kelly that night. She'd wondered many times if that outcome wouldn't have been better, but now, when the thoughts came, she pushed them away. She didn't want to go back to the dark place she'd fallen into after she'd first come to Shelter Cove. For some reason, she was still alive, and she intended to live not only for herself, but also for the sister who'd had her future so cruelly ripped away.

When Kate was younger, she'd searched for her calling, but she'd never found it. Enrolling in college had been a confusing exercise. She'd finally decided to be an English major because she loved to read. It was her passion. She'd considered sharing her love of reading as a teacher. She really liked spending time with children, and even though the idea of a teaching career didn't appeal to Kelly, who was driven by a yearning to make her mark on the world, eventually it began to feel right to Kate. However, after Kelly died, she lost all interest in college. For now she was satisfied running the café.

Kelly had known what she wanted to be since she was five years old. She'd started building things with blocks and construction sets when she was three. Her favorite word was *architect*. As she got older, her plan never changed. She wanted to design buildings. All kinds of buildings. Kate still had the plans she'd drawn up for an incredible house—the house Kelly had planned to live in someday after she got married. But that would never happen. Kate wondered what her architect sister would think of the Shelter Café.

A smile tickled Kate's lips as she gazed around the cozy restaurant. Blue checkered tablecloths, white tables, and chairs with small blue flowers hand-painted on the backs. The polished wooden floors gleamed, and the bright white walls, decorated with old-fashioned kitchen utensils and ceramic plates, gave the room a feeling of home. The large white ceiling fans clicked as they whirled. Kate walked over to the jukebox in the corner and selected the songs for today. Her customers weren't interested in rock music. John Denver, The Carpenters, Johnny Cash, and some mellow Elvis were favorites. Kate started the song "Superstar," and Karen Carpenter's honeyed tones oozed out into the room. Kate loved this song. Boy, Kelly would laugh if she saw her sister enjoying these old tunes. Music had been important to them. In Shelter Cove, Kate had discovered a whole new world of music that she not only enjoyed but that didn't remind her of the past. Well, *her* past anyway. Songs she'd shared with Kelly brought back too many memories. Too much pain.

In the last couple of years, Kate had been content in Shelter Cove, and she'd finally begun to feel safe. But that was only because Gerard was locked up in prison. Now that he was out, she couldn't stop looking around every corner. Checking out anyone new in town. Afraid every unidentified noise in her house was Gerard coming for her. She knew it was silly, that he had no idea where she was. And even if he did he'd never risk approaching her again. But fear was usually devoid of common sense. And it was more powerful than she liked to admit.

She'd just placed the last wrapped utensils on the final table when a knock came at the front door. Kate peered down at her watch. Five-thirty. The diner didn't open until six. She decided to ignore it, but the knocking came again. This time more insistent.

"You gonna get that, honey?" Bella called out.

Kate sighed deeply. Everyone in town knew when they

opened. Must be a tourist staying at the resort. Couldn't they see the *Closed* sign on the door?

"I'm getting it, Bella," she yelled. Kate hurried over to the door and pulled up the shade that covered the glass on the upper portion. She gasped at the face staring back at her. Dark sandy hair, too long for the job he had, and deep green eyes that seemed to look right through her. Even though she'd been expecting him, seeing his face again sent something like a shock of electricity through her. She slowly unlocked the door.

"I wasn't sure you'd come," she said, her voice higher than normal.

"You didn't leave us much choice. Dragging you out in handcuffs might make your friends and neighbors wonder."

She stared past him for several seconds, her mind trying to process what was happening. In the end, she couldn't. She'd wanted to see him again, prayed he'd come, but now that he stood in front of her, her thoughts were jumping around like sausages on a hot griddle. She'd spent a lot of time lying in bed at night, trying to picture his face. Now he was here. Her imagination had been spot-on. He was just as handsome as she remembered.

She swung the door open. "You might as well come in."

Tony chuckled. "Hey, I'm thrilled to see you, too."

He ambled into the Shelter Café, wearing the same smile on his face that would jump into her mind at the strangest moments. She'd forgotten, however, how tall he was, and that he had a presence you could feel. His expression made you suspect he was just one step away from pulling off the greatest practical joke ever conceived. He never actually did anything, he just made you think he could if he wanted to.

"Nice place," he said, looking around the small diner.

"I can't talk to you now," Kate said quickly. She didn't want to be rude, but seeing him again had shaken her to the core. She needed time to regroup. "I'm getting ready to open. Lots to do still."

"Can't I get some breakfast?" he said with a crooked smile. "I'm starving."

"How could you get here so early? It's at least a seven-hour drive."

Tony shrugged. "I couldn't sleep last night. Decided I might as well hit the road. Less traffic."

"You must be tired."

"A nap wouldn't hurt."

Kate pointed at a table. "Sit down. I'll order something for you. Then you can get some rest. Where are you staying?"

Tony slid into a chair at the table Kate indicated. "Nowhere yet. Figured I'd check out the cabins at the resort."

Kate nodded. "Tell Bobby I sent you. He'll give you a good deal."

"And when can we get together?"

Kate crossed her arms over her chest and stared at him. "I've got a gal who can cover for me this evening. I'll call her. Why don't you come to my place around six? I'll make supper."

Tony cocked his head to the side and grinned at her. "You cook, too? Is there anything you can't do?"

Yeah, save my sister. Kate gulped at the words that slid

into her head. She shoved them away. "I run a café. Kind of a clue, isn't it?"

"Not necessarily. I have a friend in St. Louis who owns a successful restaurant. Can't boil water for an egg, but he knows how to hire people who can do what he can't."

Kate managed a small smile. "Well, I can boil water, but I don't actually do the cooking. I've hired an exceptional cook."

"I hope she's better at cooking than she is at singing," Tony said with a grin.

"If she wasn't, I wouldn't be in business for long." She started to ask him if he wanted coffee but suddenly remembered his near addiction to caffeine. During the two trials, Tony was always looking for hot coffee. Thankfully, there'd been a shop near the courthouse. "You take your coffee black, as I remember."

He flashed his boyish grin again, and something inside Kate's chest lurched. She'd missed him more than she'd admitted to herself. Even though she'd only been nineteen when they first met, she'd had a huge crush on him. But she was a child then, and now she was an adult. Too old for puppy love.

"Yeah, black and strong. Thanks."

"Do you want to see a menu?"

Tony shook his head. "Nah. I'm a bacon-and-eggs man. Over hard. Wheat bread."

"Okay. You got it. I'll be back."

Kate walked toward the kitchen, taking deep breaths, trying to tamp down all the feelings that bombarded her. It was ridiculous. She hadn't seen Tony in four years. Why was she reacting like some kind of love-sick teenager?

"I need a Sunrise Platter," Kate called out to Bella when she walked into the kitchen. "Over hard with wheat."

Bella, who'd been belting out "The Old Rugged Cross," stopped and stared at her. "The sun movin' a little faster in the sky today?" The confused look on her dark face made Kate want to giggle. Bella was the kind of person who liked everything done in order. She had a certain routine every morning, and God help anyone who interrupted her plans.

"A guy came in early, and I told him we'd serve him," Kate said. "I can take care of him if you want."

"Nah, honey, I'll do it," Bella said with a deep sigh. She immediately began to prepare Tony's food. Although she muttered under her breath, within minutes she'd start singing again. Whenever she got upset, it never lasted long. Kate loved her to pieces. Even though Bella didn't know the truth about Kate's past life, she seemed to understand that there were secrets hidden behind her boss's smile. Once Bella had discerned that the past was something Kate didn't want to talk about, she'd dropped the subject. Somehow she always knew when to talk and when to listen. She was Kate's best friend. In truth, a mother figure.

Kate quietly left the kitchen and went back out into the café. She got Tony's coffee and brought it to his table. "I've got a few more things to do before we open," she said.

"Go ahead," Tony said after taking a sip of the steaming coffee. "Don't let me disrupt your routine." He put down the cup. "How do you plan to explain who I am?" he asked quietly.

"Well, Bella knows I don't have any siblings. Would you like to be a distant cousin?"

Tony nodded. "Sounds good. Cousin Tony."

She nodded. "If you say so."

"I do, Emily."

Kate sighed. "I don't think I look like an Emily."

Tony laughed. "My boss said the same thing. So what does an Emily look like?"

Kate paused and bit her lip as she thought. "I think Emily is girly and sweet. I'm not that."

"No, you're not that." He stared at Kate for a moment. "I like the hair, by the way. It fits you."

Kate had cut her vibrant red hair not long after she'd moved to Shelter Cove. Gerard had liked long hair, and she just couldn't keep anything that reminded her of him. Her bangs were longer, but the sides were short. Easy to take care of and much more suited to her lifestyle. She reached her hand up to check her hair before she realized what she was doing. Kate felt her face flush. The last thing she needed was for Tony to think she was primping. If he ever found out about the feelings she'd had for him, he'd think her childish and silly.

"Thanks. Makes getting ready in the morning a lot easier." She suddenly realized she hadn't put salt and pepper shakers on his table yet. Kate walked over to a nearby table where all the shakers were lined up and grabbed two of them. Then she carried them over to Tony's table and put them down in front of him. "I'll have your breakfast in a little bit. Then I'll see you tonight."

He nodded but didn't say anything. Kate was momentarily startled by the guarded look in his eyes. What was that about? As she went back to preparing her diner for another busy day, her heart raced with anticipation . . . and something else. Something she hadn't felt in four years. A warning. A stirring beyond the barrier she'd created to keep out the vile whispers that waited in the dark. As if something malevolent had been awakened.

CHAPTER
FIVE

Batterson felt a rush of annoyance at the knock on his door. He had a few hard and fast rules, and one of them was to leave him alone when his door was shut. If it was an emergency, visitors were supposed to check in with his administrative assistant, who would call him before anyone was permitted to cross the threshold. And it was well known that the emergency better be dire, or else a tongue-lashing would probably be the result of disturbing the chief's quiet time. Sometimes he just needed time to think. Life as a U.S. Marshal was fast-paced, and many decisions were made quickly and without much time to consider all the consequences. A few times a week, he liked to sit in his chair, stare out the window, and contemplate. Cases, people, and situations. This was the only time he allowed himself to be totally unavailable.

Outside of work he had only one other rule, but it was set in stone. Without it, he wasn't sure he could face his job. The mind goes off at home. A few beers, fast food, some TV, and sleep. If he allowed the pressures of his job to follow him out the office door, he'd eventually lose his mind. Many times he watched normal people driving home at night and wondered what it would be like to do something else. To have a life that didn't include gangs, drug dealers, violence, and death. Most people had no idea of the awful things that happened in the shadows while they ate dinner with their families and complained about their boring jobs. There was another world. A dark world based on deception. One that operated outside of civility and kindness. Even though a part of him longed to experience life without the horrible things people did to each other, he knew he wasn't built for life in the light. He was called to the darkness, and there was no way out for him. Of course, his mother disagreed. A strong Christian, she believed he was called to fight evil. "You are the one God sends to people during the worst moments of their lives," she'd told him. "He knows you're strong enough to overcome the darkness. One day you'll know it, too."

"Come in," he barked, glaring at the door.

The knob turned and Deputy U.S. Marshal Mark St. Laurent came in. Batterson relaxed a bit. Mark was not only a top-notch deputy Marshal, he was a friend. And he'd never break Batterson's closed-door rule unless it was absolutely necessary.

"What's going on?" Batterson asked.

Mark shut the door behind him and sat down in one of the chairs in front of Batterson's desk. "Something's up, Chief," he said. The look on Mark's face made Batterson's chest tighten. "Just got a heads-up from Tally Williams."

Williams was a lieutenant with the St. Louis P.D. He was

friends with Mark and Mark's fiancée, Mercy Brennan, another one of Batterson's deputies. Tally worked closely with the Marshals. When the police couldn't find dangerous perps, sometimes the Marshals joined forces with them. It could be a slippery slope—ego could get in the way. But with Tally's help, the local police and the Marshals had formed a great partnership. Together they stood against the violent crime that infected the city.

"And?"

"Police in Kansas passed along some information. About a week ago, they found a body buried in Garden City, Kansas."

Batterson's eyebrows shot up. "Garden City? What are you saying?"

Mark took a deep breath before speaking. "They found Ann Barton."

"Ann Barton? Gerard's second victim? That's great. I mean, as long as they can tie him to it." Even though the news seemed good, Batterson could tell something was wrong. He sighed. "Okay, spit it out."

"Her remains were in a cemetery."

Batterson stared at Mark as if he'd just told him all the gangs in St. Louis had become friends and were holding hands and singing "Kumbaya" under the Arch. "What are you talking about? In what cemetery?"

"Someone else's grave." Mark pulled a piece of paper out of his pocket and quickly looked it over. "A Dorothy Fisher."

Batterson shook his head. Mark wasn't making sense, and Batterson's temper was starting to flare. "You need to explain this so I understand it. Now. Don't leave anything out."

Mark took a deep breath. "Okay. Sorry, Chief. The police

in Garden City got a phone call. A tip about Ann Barton. That she was in Valley View Cemetery. With Dorothy." He held up his hand to stop Batterson from letting loose a stream of expletives. "That's all they said, Chief. So the cops went there, looked for every burial site that belonged to a Dorothy. One of them had a copy of the song 'Blue-Eyed Angel' staked on top of the grave. They got a court order to exhume the body. About a foot away from the vault that holds the coffin, they found the remains of Ann Barton. She was wrapped in several layers of plastic."

"How in the world did they know it was her?"

"Well, their first clue was a necklace in the dirt. Not with the body, but about a foot above it. It was Ann's. When she disappeared, Ann's mother showed everyone a picture of the necklace. I guess Ann never took it off. Then they took the remains to the M.E. He checked the dental records and says it's definitely Ann."

"So Gerard stashed the body there all those years ago? Clever for a psychopath. So now we can charge him with Ann Barton's murder."

"Not so fast, Chief."

"What? Please tell me we've got some kind of evidence this time."

Although the body of Gerard's first victim, Tammy Rice, had been discovered years ago in Kansas, the only DNA found was never identified. They tested her son, but it wasn't a match. After Gerard was caught, his DNA was tested as well, but it didn't match either. Authorities concluded it probably came from a friend of Tammy's. Some kind of accidental transfer. Although Gerard had refused to give details of the killing, he'd accepted responsibility. Case closed. He was never tried for that murder since there wasn't any direct evidence, but it was okay since they had him for Kelly O'Brien's murder. That was supposed to be enough to keep him behind bars the rest of his life. Unfortunately, it hadn't worked out that way.

Mark cleared his throat. "There was a fingerprint. On the necklace. I think the killer accidentally dropped it. Probably planned to take it as a trophy."

Batterson frowned. "Tell me it was Gerard's fingerprint."

Mark slowly shook his head. "It belongs to a man named Malcolm Bodine."

Batterson felt his face get hot. They needed something solid so they could arrest Gerard again. His brow furrowed. "Bodine. Why does that name sound familiar?"

"You've got a good memory. His body was found in an alley almost six years ago. He'd been beaten and robbed. No one ever claimed his body."

Batterson nodded. "I remember. I think it stuck in my mind because of his name."

"It *is* unusual."

"That's not why. I grew up next to a family named Bodine. I was afraid it was one of them, but thankfully it wasn't." He leaned back in his chair and stared at Mark. "I take it there's more?"

"I would say so."

Mark paused for a moment, and the look on his face made the hairs on the back of Batterson's neck stand up.

"They matched the DNA from Tammy Rice's body to Malcolm Bodine. Or should I say the man who called himself

Malcolm Bodine. Turns out the real Bodine died when he was young. This guy took over his identity. We have no idea who he really is."

Mark's words hung in the air like odd, empty bubbles. It took a few seconds for Batterson to understand what he'd said.

"I don't get it. How can that be?"

Mark rubbed his face with his hands as if trying to wake himself up.

Batterson knew he wasn't tired. He was as shocked as his boss.

"It means Gerard isn't the Blue-Eyed Killer, Chief. It was this Bodine guy."

Batterson suddenly found himself standing up, even though he didn't remember getting out of his seat. "But that's not possible."

Mark also got to his feet and faced him. "It's too much of a coincidence. Bodine couldn't have just happened to know both victims. And remember that the blood evidence that linked Gerard to Kelly O'Brien's murder has been discounted. The only thing left is her sister's testimony. Weigh the memory of one terrified girl against DNA and fingerprints. Either Kate O'Brien got it wrong or Gerard was a copycat."

"Where was Bodine when the O'Brien girls were attacked?"

"In St. Louis. His body was discovered a few days after that. He could have done it."

Batterson plopped back down in his chair like a ragdoll, which was appropriate since that was exactly how he felt. "So now what?"

"I don't know. There will be a detailed investigation. I'm

not sure how this will affect Gerard. Until recently, he's always claimed to be the Blue-Eyed Killer. Of course, now that he thinks he's going to walk, he says he didn't kill anyone. Says he confessed because he was coerced by the police."

Batterson slammed his fist on his desk. "No one forced him to confess. He couldn't wait to take credit for all those deaths. And I hate that stupid moniker. The press attaches names to monsters and makes them seem human. I blame them for Gerard's fan club—and for that prison guard who tried to kill Kate."

Mark didn't say anything, just stood there and waited.

"Tony's supposed to be bringing Kate O'Brien back to testify at a new trial," Batterson said. "Now I wonder if there will even be one."

Mark sat down again, too. "It will take some time to figure that out. We'll need to hear from the D.A."

"I suppose they're trying to figure out who Bodine really is."

"Sure, but so far no luck. His fingerprints and DNA aren't showing up on any database. At this point, we may never know his real name. Maybe that doesn't matter. I don't know."

"What's Gerard saying about all this?" Batterson asked.

"Nothing. This is brand-new information. He couldn't have heard about it yet. I'm sure you'll be briefed at some point by our friends at the FBI, but Tally thought you might need the information sooner than later. Keep it to yourself as long as you can. I don't want him to get in trouble for breaking protocol. The press is already sniffing around. Even if they find out about Ann Barton, the FBI is keeping Bodine's name to themselves. They just don't know enough about him to go public."

"I will. Thanks for bringing this to me."

"You're welcome."

As Mark got up to leave, Batterson had to remind himself that his deputy was getting married soon. Life couldn't be all about what happened in the shadows. There were other things. "Got a date for the wedding yet?"

"Yeah. We're going for September. Gives us time to get ready, and we both like the fall. Frankly, Mercy and I would be happy to elope, but Mercy's mom wants to see her daughter married with all the usual pomp and circumstance."

"How's her mom doing?"

Mark smiled. "Good. After years of estrangement, she and Mercy are getting along pretty well now. It's not something Mercy ever expected, but she's starting to enjoy the changes. Took a while for her to trust it, though. We're still taking it one day at a time."

"That's all you can do." Batterson almost winced at his lame encouragement. What did he know about relationships?

"You want the door closed?" Mark asked.

Batterson nodded and watched as the door swung shut. He sat at his desk for a while, trying to figure out what to do next. Finally, he picked up the phone and called Tony.

CHAPTER
SIX

After breakfast, Tony drove over to the Sheltering Arms Fishing Resort. The name sounded like it belonged to a nursing home rather than a place where fishermen gathered to search for "the big one."

Tony was no stranger to fishing. His grandfather, called Nonno by his grandchildren, had taught him to fish. Nonno was a great fisherman. Patient, hopeful, and successful. When Tony was younger, going out on the lake with his grandfather was a chore, something he did because his parents insisted. However, as he got older, he began to look forward to his outings with Nonno. He found that it was one of the few times he could completely relax. After throwing your bait in the water, there was nothing else to do. You had to wait for a tug on the other end, and you couldn't work for the results. It was out of your hands. But the anticipation of that tug kept you in your seat, determined to experience the thrill of conquest. Man over fish. He was past due for a vacation. Maybe after this assignment, he'd take some time off, grab his fishing pole, and go somewhere like this. Someplace peaceful.

When he got out of his car, Tony stopped and took a deep breath of fresh air. The fishy scent coming from the lake made him feel as if Nonno were standing right next to him. He felt a rush of emotion. He missed his grandfather. His entire family felt the man's absence. More than anything, Tony wanted to be the kind of man who could impact his family in the way Nonno had. His love of family, his faith, and his example of what a man should be had shaped the DeLuca family for generations. What a legacy.

The small resort looked clean and well kept. Only six cabins. If it had been much bigger, Kate probably wouldn't have been relocated here. The Marshals tried to keep their witnesses in places without much traffic. It was safer. That worked great for people who loved solitude, but not so well for those who enjoyed life in the big city.

Tony went inside the small building with the sign overhead that read *Office*. A tall, skinny man sat on a stool behind the counter, reading a book. He reminded Tony of something his mother used to say about some people. *"They look like they've been rode hard and put away wet."* She meant they appeared to have had a hard life. Her description would certainly fit this guy. He looked to be in his fifties, but Tony guessed he was only in his late thirties or early forties.

When Tony got a little closer, he glanced at the book the man was holding. It was written by one of Tony's favorite authors. Top-notch detective fiction. Great reading. At least the guy had excellent taste in literature. After a few seconds, the man looked up from his novel. "Can I help you?" His nasally voice fit his weather-beaten, hangdog face.

"Got any cabins available?"

The man put the book on the counter after carefully sliding his bookmark between the pages he'd been reading. "Yep. How long you gonna be here?"

"Tonight. Maybe tomorrow."

"That'll work. We got a big group coming in on Thursday."

Tony held out his hand. "I'm Tony DeLuca. Glad to meet you."

The man smiled and shook Tony's hand. The smile reminded Tony of his sister Sophia's baby. More of an indication of gas pain than a real smile.

"Nice to meet you. I'm Bobby Wade. Gonna do any fishing while you're here?"

The guy had a pronounced lisp. Tony immediately felt sorry for him. Unattractive and a lisp. Didn't seem fair somehow. "Not this time. Wish I could. I'm here to visit my cousin, Emily Lockhart. Do you know her?"

Bobby's dull eyes took on new life. "Emily from the café? Sure." This time his smile seemed heartfelt.

"You're friends?"

Bobby blushed. "Well, kind of. I mean, everyone in Shelter Cove knows each other. We're a pretty small town. Emily's just . . . well, she's special. Always nice to everyone."

Seemed like Bobby had a crush on Kate. "You lived here long?" Tony asked.

"Nah. Used to live in Phoenix. Got tired of the heat. Bought this place about three years ago. The guy who owned it got sick and wanted out. Been here ever since."

Tony would have asked if Bobby was married, but he was pretty sure what the answer would be. A glance at his ring finger confirmed his suspicions.

"Need your driver's license," Bobby said.

Tony took his license out of his wallet and pushed it across the counter. Bobby picked it up and copied some information into a ledger. This place sure wasn't high-tech.

Bobby gave him back his license. "How you wanna pay?"

Tony noticed an old credit card machine on the counter, the kind where you had to slide the contraption across the card so it would make an impression on a carbon receipt. He hadn't realized they were still around. He handed Bobby his card. After processing it on the ancient machine, Bobby gave it back to him.

"Cabin six is close to the dock. Cabin two is closer to the office. Which one ya want?"

"Six sounds good."

Tony loved the water, but frankly, having some space between him and Bobby sounded like a good idea.

Bobby turned around and took a key from a large wooden board nailed to the wall. He handed it to Tony. "If you need fresh sheets or towels, see me. I've got everything. Cleaning lady comes on Mondays, Wednesdays, and Fridays. She's already cleaned your room."

"Sounds perfect. Thanks, Bobby."

Tony took the key and went back to his car. Cabin six was the last one in the row. It was more like a small tract house than a cabin, but as long as it was clean, Tony didn't care. He'd once had to guard a witness in an abandoned bunkhouse on a military base. It had been filthy. He and two other deputies worked like crazy to clean it up so it would be livable, but even after all their hard work, Tony still felt dirty.

Tony grabbed his suitcase and carried it over to the cabin's door. He stuck the key in the knob and turned it. The door opened into a neat but plain room. On one side were a couch, two chairs, and a small entertainment center with an old TV. An ancient blue Formica kitchen table and matching chairs sat in a corner across the room. A gas stove sat on one side of a sink, with a small fridge on the other side. At the back of the room was a bed. Full size, no headboard. A large maple armoire stood next to the bed.

Tony put his suitcase on top of the dark blue chenille bedspread. A quick look around convinced him the room was as clean as he could hope for. The extremely small bathroom was basic, but it would work. Again, the fixtures were outdated, but they'd been scrubbed. The scent of bleach reassured him somewhat. Nevertheless, he unzipped his bag and got out the spray can of disinfectant he carried with him any time he had to travel. He sprayed the bedspread, the bathroom, the phone, the TV remote, the doorknobs, and the faucet on the kitchen sink. Afterward he felt better.

People liked to kid him about his apartment. He'd had some guys from work over to watch football once, and they'd laughed at how clean and neat he kept his place. "You'll make someone a great wife," one of them had said, making everyone laugh. Tony's mom had raised him to pick up after himself, and he felt better when his surroundings were tidy. He wasn't embarrassed by the guys' comments. In fact, he'd had a great time. He kept telling himself he needed to ask them over again, but his job kept him so busy he'd never found another chance. He'd gotten invitations from some of them, but he'd turned most of them down. After a while, people quit asking. It wasn't something he was proud of, but his work came first. Always.

He hung up his clothes in the armoire but kept his underwear and personal items in his suitcase. Much more hygienic.

After getting settled, he thought about taking a quick nap, but he was still buzzed from the coffee he'd had at the diner. He decided to check out the town a bit before eating lunch. Then he'd be ready to catch a few winks in the afternoon. Although he was certain Shelter Cove was a safe place, it always made him feel better to make sure his surroundings were secure. It had become a habit he couldn't break.

He changed his shirt and slacks, choosing something more causal. Jeans and a sweater seemed appropriate. The spring air was nippy, and Tony knew from experience it was always colder near water. After he changed, he prepared to leave, but first he removed Kate's file from his suitcase. He slid it under his mattress, then put the *Do Not Disturb* sign on the door. Even though Bobby said no one would be cleaning today, he didn't want to take any chances.

He grabbed his black leather jacket and had just walked out the door when he noticed a green sedan parked on the road in front of the resort. Although he couldn't see the driver, as soon as Tony stopped to look his way, the car took off. The vehicle was too far away for him to read the license plate. It was probably nothing, but somewhere inside Tony's head, alarm bells rang. Was there really something to be concerned about or was it his overprotective nature rearing its head? He'd erred on the side of caution more than once.

He didn't consider it a weakness, but still, he didn't want to overreact.

He sighed as he got into his car. Tony tried hard to listen to his gut, yet everything seemed fine in Shelter Cove. So why did he feel so uneasy?

CHAPTER
SEVEN

Kate walked through her day like a person in a trance. She'd hoped Tony would come. Now he was here.

She smiled as she remembered the day Tony bought a birthday cake and brought it to the hotel where they'd put her up during the trial. She'd just turned twenty. He and another deputy, a really nice guy named Randy, sang "Happy Birthday" and gave her a couple of CDs. They knew she loved TobyMac. She still listened to the CDs and had even kept the candles from her cake. It was on that birthday that she'd decided she was in love with Tony DeLuca.

Ben Kramer, owner of Shelter Cove's only grocery store, held up his coffee cup, signaling his desire for a refill. Kate grabbed the pot and headed for his table.

"How are you today, Ben?" she asked as she poured the steaming hot coffee into his cup.

"We're doin' just fine, Emily," he said with a smile. "Margie's been tryin' to get over the flu, you know. Last night she felt well enough to fix supper. Good thing. Wasn't sure how much longer we were gonna last on my cookin'."

Kate grinned. "You sell food but you can't cook it? That's hard to believe."

"Well, Joe at the pharmacy sells laxatives, but he ain't always constipated."

Kate laughed and lightly slapped Ben on the back. His jokes were pretty bad, but he was always in a good mood, and he had a way of making everyone feel better.

"I heard you have some family in town?" Sheriff's Deputy Warren Killian, who sat at the table with Ben, held up his cup, too.

Kate motioned for him to put it down on the table. When he did, she filled it up. "You know everything that happens in Shelter Cove, don't you?"

"It's my job. Like to know about any new people hanging around."

"In case we're infiltrated by terrorists committed to taking over the town?"

Warren shook his finger at her. "No. But many folks don't realize small towns are a good place for criminals to hide out. They think no one will find them."

"Well, I can guarantee you my cousin isn't a criminal."

"I thought you told me you didn't have any relatives," Ben said. "Must have misheard."

"No *immediate* family," she replied. "He's a distant cousin. Haven't seen him in years. He was in the area and stopped by to say hello."

"He looks like a nice guy," Warren said.

Kate frowned at him. "When did you see him? You weren't here this morning when he came in."

"Over by the cabins. I was driving by and noticed him."

"And you knew right away he was related to me?"

Warren chuckled. "You sure are suspicious, Emily." He shook his head. "Betty from the hair salon saw him in here earlier. She told me what he looked like. 'Course, it wasn't hard to figure out. Most of the folks who stay at the cabins are fishermen. Not slicked-up, good-looking city types."

Kate nodded. "You're right about that. Tony certainly stands out in a crowd."

Although she felt she should say more about her *cousin*— come up with something that made it sound as if she actually knew him—her mind was blank, shut down by anxiety. She needed to snap out of it and focus. She was trying to stay calm about Gerard's release, but something deep in the dark recesses of her mind reached out from time to time and grabbed her by the throat, making it hard for her to breathe. Even though Ben and Warren certainly didn't pose any kind of threat, before she'd gone into the protection program, Tony had drilled it into her head that she could never take a chance and reveal the truth about herself. Never make a slip. She'd taken his warnings to heart. As time went by, she'd begun to relax some. Until recently, she'd felt any real threats against her had ended long ago. There was that one crazy guy with a website who'd worshipped Alan Gerard and tried to convince a few other deluded, sad people that their allegiance to him made them special somehow. The site had disappeared after Gerard went to prison, and there had been no hint of any threats toward her since then. But now Gerard was free. Her mind battled between her fear of him and her desperate belief that he couldn't find her even if he wanted to.

"So how was your vacation?" she asked Warren, forcing

herself to say something so her silence wouldn't seem suspicious. "First time I remember you taking time off since you've been here."

"Needed to get away for awhile," he said. "Went home. Visited family and friends."

"Good for you. Hope you enjoyed yourself."

Warren shook his head and gave her an odd smile. "Well, it was certainly . . . interesting."

Ben laughed. "Sometimes that's the best you can get with family. All in all, interesting isn't too bad."

Warren smiled. "You've got that right."

"You goin' to the church supper Sunday after service?" Ben asked Kate.

"I'm not sure," she said slowly. "Tony asked me to take a trip with him. To see some other cousins. I'm seriously thinking about it."

Ben slapped the table with his hand. "Good for you. Have you taken a day off since you started this café?"

"Just when I was too sick to come in," Kate said.

"'You deserve a break today.'" Ben sang the slogan softly.

Kate smiled and shook her head. "You're a mess. You know that, right?"

"But I'm *your* mess, isn't that so?"

She grinned. "Yes. You're my mess. You need anything else?"

"Why don't you wrap up a couple of Bella's cinnamon rolls for me? I'll take them home to Margie. That should make her happy. Just put it on my tab."

Kate patted his shoulder. "I'd be happy to send a couple of rolls to her. And no charge. She should get a lot more than cinnamon rolls for putting up with you."

Ben laughed heartily as Kate walked away. She glanced up at the clock. It was almost eleven. Seven hours until she saw Tony again. It felt like an eternity.

Tony's tour of Shelter Cove didn't take long. It was a typical small town. Several small businesses, a grocery store, a bakery, a burger place, a tiny library, a post office, and a city hall where town leaders could gather and argue about whether or not to put up a new streetlight on Main Street. Tony loved pastries and chose a couple of cheese Danishes for lunch. The bakery also sold coffee, so he bought a large cup to drink with his extremely unhealthy meal and headed back to the resort. He'd devoured one Danish and was starting on the other one when his cell phone rang. It was Batterson.

"Hello, Chief," he said into the phone, trying to quickly swallow a mouthful of pastry and cream. Almost choking, he struggled to catch his breath. It didn't really make any difference. All he could hear was a crackling noise on the other end. After several attempts to make out what Batterson was saying, he spoke into the phone. "Chief, I just can't hear you. Might be the reception here. Let me call you back." With that he hung up.

Tony gulped down most of the coffee, wrapped the rest of the Danish in the paper bag from the bakery, and stuck it in the fridge in his room. He'd have to finish it later. Then he grabbed his phone and hurried outside. He walked across the street and plodded up a small hill that stood between the resort and the rest of the town. When he dialed the chief, the call went right through.

"Sorry about that, Chief," Tony said. "The reception stinks out here. Can you hear me now?" Immediately, Tony was reminded of an old TV commercial where the actor kept asking everyone, "Can you hear me now?" Tony had wanted to smack the guy. Of course, violence against some random guy in a commercial probably wasn't in keeping with the public's perception of a deputy U.S. Marshal.

"Much better," Batterson barked through the phone. "I need to be able to reach you when it's important."

"You can," Tony said. "If you call and I don't answer right away, give me a minute to call you back. I'll find out where the reception is best and return your call as quickly as I can. And you can also call the motel." He rattled off the name of the resort and his cabin number. "I'm sure the landline is much clearer."

Batterson grumbled a little. Tony wasn't sure what he was actually saying, but it was best to be quiet when the chief had a burr under his saddle.

"We have a problem," Batterson said loudly, causing Tony to jump.

Tony listened as Batterson explained the turn of events in Gerard's case. When Batterson finished, it took Tony a few seconds to process what the chief had said.

"I don't understand," he answered finally. "Are you saying that Gerard isn't the Blue-Eyed Killer? That's impossible. Kate saw him."

"She says she did," Batterson said in a low voice. "Maybe she was wrong. Maybe the defense was right all along. She saw Gerard at the college and thought he was the one who attacked her and her sister. Look, the FBI has already tied two of the murders to this guy who called himself Malcolm Bodine. Murder number one and murder number two. It's not a coincidence, Tony. Not accidental transfer. Bodine is our guy."

"But . . ."

"I know it's hard to take in, but until I get some direction here, stay put. There's no reason to bring Kate this way unless we have to."

Tony shook his head, trying to destroy what felt like cobwebs obscuring his thoughts. "So if this guy . . . Bodine . . . killed Kelly O'Brien, why did Gerard say he did it?"

Batterson sighed through the phone. "Who knows what makes these nuts tick? Dr. Abbot says someone like Gerard feels weak . . . impotent. Taking credit for the attack on the O'Brien girls made him feel important. Powerful. Gave him the kind of attention he couldn't get on his own."

"I just can't believe Kate got it wrong. Does this Bodine guy look anything like Gerard?"

"No, not even close. It's not a case of mistaken identity, Tony."

"Then Gerard must be a copycat. It's the only thing that makes sense."

"I know. That was my first thought, too. But what about the song? We found a copy of it at the crime scene. That detail wasn't released to the public until the trial. How could Gerard know about that?"

"Maybe there was an accomplice. Someone fed him inside information."

"There's no proof of that. At least not now."

Tony couldn't argue with Batterson. Frankly, something

smelled wrong about the whole thing, but as the chief often said, evidence doesn't lie. Tony's number-one concern right now was Kate. How would she take this news?

"I guess I'll hang out here until you tell me what to do next."

"There's not much you *can* do. I don't want to uproot our witness and bring her here if the D.A. decides not to try the case again. I hate to leave you stranded, but right now there's no choice. I contacted the local office and told them we were on hold."

"I understand." Tony paused for a moment to think. "How do I explain this to Kate?" he asked finally.

There was silence for a few seconds before Batterson said, "Don't tell her anything yet. Just say there's a delay. Cook up some excuse. Finding out that it might not have been Gerard after all . . . Let's wait until I have more information."

"Okay." The idea of lying to Kate made Tony uncomfortable, but he had his orders.

"I'll get back with you as soon as I can. And Tony . . ."

"Yeah?"

"Be careful. I know this case got personal for you. But you need to keep your distance."

"Of course, Chief. You don't have to worry about that."

Tony hung up but stared at his phone for a while before putting it back in his pocket. Was what he'd told the chief true? Was there really nothing to worry about? Although in his mind Tony wanted to believe he could treat Kate in a professional manner, his heart seemed to be saying something quite different.

CHAPTER
EIGHT

He stared at his image in the mirror. Even his own mother wouldn't recognize him. Not that she would care. He hadn't heard from her in years. Not surprising since he'd told her to leave him alone. He didn't hate her. He had no feelings for her at all. In fact, he felt nothing for anyone. Not even his father, the man who thought he could "beat the devil" out of his son. He was seventeen when he struck back. The memory of the look on his father's face when he hit him with a baseball bat still made him laugh. That was the last time the old man ever touched him. He left home a few months later.

The shrink he'd seen when he was young had called him a sociopath. He'd looked up the term. Actually, it seemed about right. He was constantly in trouble as a teenager, stealing, lying, attacking kids weaker than himself. When he got older, he'd taken it further. Killing had consumed his mind. It was the ultimate test of control. Knowing he could end someone's life had given him the kind of rush nothing else ever had, and he intended to keep at it. But before he began again, he had a loose end. Something that had to be fixed.

Nothing else mattered to him now except finding and killing Kate O'Brien.

Tony knocked on the door right at six o'clock. The smells coming from within the attractive bungalow made his mouth water. He only got home-cooked meals when he went home for a visit. His mother was an amazing cook, and his sisters weren't half bad, either. Sitting down for dinner with his family was like eating at a fine Italian restaurant—with unlimited refills. He usually left with an extra couple of pounds to work off in the gym.

The door swung open and Kate stood on the other side. Her face was slightly flushed, and her incredible blue eyes stared into his. She wore jeans and a soft-looking dark blue sweater that emphasized her eyes. For a moment he couldn't speak.

"Come on in," she said, waving her hand behind her.

"Thanks," he choked out, trying to regain his composure. Why did he feel like an awkward kid around her? What was wrong with him?

He looked around Kate's neat and comfortable house. Polished wood floors with Oriental rugs, a large beige couch with colorful throw pillows, and two light blue overstuffed chairs near a large white-brick fireplace. The paintings on the walls were interesting. Outdoor scenes. Colorful and tasteful. It wasn't what he'd expected. When he'd arrived in Shelter Cove, he'd still envisioned Kate as the wide-eyed, timid nineteen-year-old girl who'd endured horrors no one should ever face. But she'd changed. She was twenty-five now. A woman. Someone with style. Someone who knew what she liked.

"This is nice," he said with a smile.

"Thank you. I enjoy decorating."

She gestured toward the kitchen. "I'm just finishing up. Are you thirsty? I've got iced tea, lemonade, water . . . milk, if you're a milk drinker."

"Lemonade sounds good."

"Have a seat. I'll get it for you."

"Let me take care of it. You're busy."

She smiled at him. "That would be great. Follow me."

He walked behind her into the kitchen. "Great kitchen. Love the island."

She bent down to look in the oven and then grabbed some potholders. "Thanks. I redid it after I moved in. The previous owners were stuck in the seventies." She took a large casserole dish out of the oven and placed it on top of the stove. "I painted the cabinets white, replaced the old linoleum floor with tile, put in the stone countertops, and installed the island."

"I'm surprised. Where did you learn to do that?"

Kate turned around to gaze at him, a look of amusement on her face. "I read up on it. The internet is a pretty handy tool for someone like me. When I got stuck, I called Jim Mason over at the hardware store. He came over and helped." She pointed at one of the cabinets. "Glasses in there. Lemonade's in the fridge. Pour me a glass too, okay?"

"Sure." Tony got the glasses and put them on the counter near the refrigerator. "That looks awesome," he said, gesturing toward the casserole dish. "What is it?"

"Sausage manicotti. I figured since you're Italian I couldn't go wrong."

Although Tony was pretty sure it wouldn't compare to his mother's manicotti, it looked delicious. "I love manicotti. One of my favorite dishes."

"Good."

While Kate finished tossing a salad, Tony got the pitcher of lemonade out of the refrigerator. He poured both glasses and added some ice cubes from the freezer. He'd started to carry the glasses to the small kitchen table near the window when Kate called out his name.

"We're eating in the dining room," she said. "It gives me an excuse to use my good china."

"Okay." Tony carried the glasses into the adjoining room, which was also tastefully decorated. The table was already set. He put the glasses down and picked up one of the plates. "These are beautiful."

"They were my mother's," Kate said as she carried the large glass salad bowl into the room and put it on the table. "Kelly had dibs on them, but after she . . . Well, I took them. This is the first time I've used them since I've been here."

"Really? Wow. I'm honored."

She shrugged. "I don't have much company. I'm always afraid I'll reveal something I shouldn't." Her brow furrowed. "You know, after Gerard went to prison, it seemed a little silly. I felt pretty safe. Even his followers seemed to drift away."

"And now he's out." Tony shook his head. "Look, I know our rules might seem ridiculous, but as you can see, it turned out to be the best thing you could have done."

Her eyes widened. "Do you think he'll try to find me?"

"Doesn't matter. The truth is, you don't have to worry about him because we're good at what we do. Sometimes what we ask of you might sound extreme, but it's because we don't take chances."

Kate's expression relaxed a bit. "I guess so, but it's just hard sometimes, you know? Living around people and not being honest with them."

"I understand. But at least you're safe. And you seem happy here." He chuckled. "Running a café? I wouldn't have guessed that."

"Have a seat. I'll tell you about it while we eat."

"Can I help with anything else?"

"No. I'm fine."

She tossed him a smile before slipping back into the kitchen. She'd been a beautiful girl, but she'd certainly grown into a captivating woman. Tony felt his throat tighten. He quickly reminded himself that she was a witness and he was a deputy Marshal. They would never be anything else. Even if their professional relationship didn't make anything beyond that impossible, he was seven years older than Kate. A huge difference for someone as young as she was.

"Hope you like this," Kate said as she carried the casserole dish to the table. "It just dawned on me that I might be competing with your mother. Didn't you tell me once she was a fabulous cook?"

"She is, but no comparisons. I'm just happy to be eating something besides fast food."

"Only burger place in Shelter Cove is Archie's Grill down the road. He makes great cheeseburgers, but if you want it speedy, he's not your guy. Archie likes to talk. I think he holds your food hostage just so you have to listen to him."

Tony laughed. "Thanks for the warning. Maybe I'd better stock up from the grocery store. I had some great Danish for lunch, but I can't eat that way every day."

"You can always come to the café." Kate slid into the chair across from him. "You'll get good food there."

"I'm trying to get in and out without drawing too much attention. Not sure hanging around your café is the way to do that."

"You're supposed to be my cousin. Frankly, it might seem stranger if you stay away."

Tony didn't want to argue with her. Usually when a Marshal had to transport a witness, they arrived one day and took off the next. Staying longer was highly unusual. But in this case, he didn't have a choice. "I guess you have a point."

"Do you mind praying over the meal?" she asked softly.

Tony nodded. She knew he was a Christian. He'd prayed for her during the trials—on his own and twice with her in the courtroom when she seemed to be struggling. Even though it had been a couple of years since he'd gone to church, he still remembered how to pray. "I'd be glad to." He bowed his head and asked a blessing on the food. Then he thanked God for keeping Kate safe. When he was done, he said, "Amen." He looked up and found Kate staring at him. The look on her face surprised him. "Did I say something wrong?" he asked.

Kate's expression instantly relaxed and she laughed. "No, not at all. Sorry. You're the only person besides me who's prayed in this house. It just struck me as odd."

Tony frowned. "Don't you have a church here? Friends?"

Kate picked up her napkin and carefully placed it in her lap. "I have Bella. You know, my cook. And there are a few others. Several people who come into the café. They look after me. But I don't invite anyone here." She shook her head and wagged her finger at him. "Get that worried look off your face. I've been to other people's houses—even attended gatherings at the church. I just keep this place for . . . myself. It makes me feel . . . safer. More in control."

Tony grabbed his fork. "Don't folks in Shelter Cove find that a little odd?"

"If they do, no one's ever said anything. It's not like I refuse to allow anyone to cross my doorstep. Plenty of people have been by to drop off something or to pick me up for an event. I've just never asked anyone over for dinner—or had a party." She shrugged. "If I want to eat with someone, I do it at the café. Much easier. Remember, the café's open every day of the week. I'm almost always there."

"I'd say you're trying to hide out in that place."

Kate took a bite of her manicotti before responding. Tony noticed the pink spots that appeared on her cheeks. Obviously, he'd hit a nerve.

"So you're a psychiatrist now?" she asked after swallowing.

"No. Just concerned about you." Not wanting to anger her further, he scooped a big forkful of manicotti into his mouth. The flavors exploded on his tongue, and his eyes widened. "Wow, Kate. This is . . . incredible. I can't believe I'm saying this, but it might even be better than my mom's."

The tightness in her face softened. "Really? I remember how you used to talk about her cooking. That's a real compliment."

"I pity the man who marries you. If everything you cook is this good, he'll end up weighing five hundred pounds."

"Not sure I'll ever get married, but thanks anyway."

"Why do you say that?"

Kate wrinkled her nose. Tony had forgotten about her habit of doing that when she was on the spot. He thought it was cute. Not that he'd ever tell her that. Especially now.

"Let's see . . . 'Hey, honey, you might want to know that my real name isn't Emily Lockhart. I was once the target of a crazed serial killer . . . and by the way . . . I had a twin sister but she was murdered. . . .'" She frowned at him. "Oh, wait a minute. I can't tell him that. In fact, I'll never be able to be honest with my own husband. Sounds like a real solid basis for a marriage."

Tony watched as she took a quick bite of manicotti. She stared down at her plate, refusing to meet his eyes.

"I know it's hard," he said gently. "Something like this takes a long time to deal with, and you're never really the same again."

Kate put her fork down with force. The sound of metal hitting china sounded like an alarm in the quiet room. "I'm fine. I had a hard time the first year, but I dealt with it."

Tony cleared his throat, trying to snag a moment to think. Why was Kate so combative? It felt as if everything he said upset her. He wasn't sure what to do. His job was to protect her. He wasn't her friend, and he had no business getting into her personal life. Even though a voice in his head told him to leave it alone, he just couldn't.

"You know, sometimes we think we've dealt with something, but the truth is, we've only buried it."

To his surprise, Kate stood abruptly and pushed back her chair. "I think we're done here." She said the words with angry precision. "Tell the local Marshals I'll let them escort me back to St. Louis. I'm not going with you."

With that, she stomped out of the room, leaving Tony alone and confused. He stared at her empty chair. Why had she reacted so violently to what he'd said? Should he leave, or should he stay and try to find a way to fix this?

CHAPTER
NINE

As soon as she entered her bedroom and shut the door behind her, Kate was sorry for her reaction. Why had she blown up at Tony? He was only trying to help. But pushing the past into a closet and locking the door had taken every ounce of strength she could muster. As much as she cared for him, she couldn't allow anyone to rattle that door. If it opened, she felt as if it would destroy her. It was the monster under the bed. The bogeyman in the closet.

She'd given up everything to come to Shelter Cove. Her past, her life, her very identity. When she'd arrived in the small town, she was lost in a dark abyss of pain and grief.

She pulled up one of her long sleeves and pushed back the silver bracelet she always wore. It had belonged to Kelly. Kate stared at the scars on her wrists. It seemed like such a long time ago. Somehow she'd survived. Little by little, she'd started to heal, but only by shutting the past away where it couldn't touch her anymore. In the end, moving to Shelter Cove had saved her. The deaths of her parents, Kelly's murder, the attack by Alan Gerard—they all existed in St. Louis. Not here. Not in this town. Why couldn't Tony understand that? He was probably disappointed in her. He'd told her several times during the trials that he admired her strength. But she wasn't strong. Not then, not now.

She stared at the doorknob, wanting to turn it. Wanting to go back out there and apologize, but she couldn't. She listened for the front door to open and close, letting her know Tony was gone, but she didn't hear anything. Was he still out there? What should she do? She waited for what seemed like an eternity but according to her watch was a little over fifteen minutes. Finally, she took a deep breath and got up from the bed. She slowly opened the door and made her way back toward the dining room. Tony was still there, just finishing up his meal.

"I helped myself to seconds," he said. "I hope that's all right."

Kate put her hands on her hips and glared at him. "You don't know how to take a hint, do you?"

Tony gave her a sideways grin, and her anger lessened.

"I really don't," he said. "It's one of my weaknesses." He pointed at her chair. "My job is to protect you, and that's what I intend to do. Even if I have to protect you from yourself."

Kate felt a cold hand of fear grasp her heart. He wasn't going to leave this alone, was he?

"Look," he said, obviously noticing her distress, "let me talk for"—he glanced at his watch—"ten minutes. That's it. Then I'll shut up. About the past. About all of it. After that we'll only talk about what's in front of us. The upcoming trial and how to prepare for it. Can you at least give me ten minutes? After all, I saved your life."

"I can't believe you're holding that over my head."

Tony chuckled. "Hey, I'm not above using anything that will give me a chance to make you listen to reason." His smile slipped some and she could see the seriousness behind his attempt to lighten the tension between them. "Please, Kate. Just ten minutes."

She sighed and sat back down at the table, picking at her food, which was cold now. Before she could react, Tony reached over and grabbed her plate.

"Let me heat that up for you," he said. "Then we'll talk."

Kate frowned at him. "You didn't say I had to talk. You said all I had to do was listen."

"Fine. But if you feel like talking, you can. Let's leave it at that, okay?"

Without saying another word, he left the dining room. As Kate sat there, it felt like the butterflies in her stomach had turned into frightened birds chased by a deadly predator. But it was stupid to be afraid of whatever it was Tony wanted to say. They were just words. She didn't have to agree with them. She didn't have to even take them in. So why did she feel almost frozen by fear? As if Alan Gerard stood over her again, his leering smile mocking her pain. For just a moment, she considered making Tony leave. Shutting this down before it went any further. Yet it bothered her that she was so terrified. If she really had a handle on the past, why did she feel like this? There was a part of her that wanted to face the demon. At the same time, a different voice whispered warnings to her. Telling her she couldn't allow herself to become vulnerable. That she had to protect herself and her sanity at all costs. She shook her head in confusion. What was wrong with her? She felt as if it had been only a few days since Kelly died. Not six years.

"Here you go." Tony came over and put her plate in front of her. She realized she hadn't told him not to put her mother's dishes in the microwave, but when she touched the plate, it was obvious he hadn't. It surprised her that a man would take the time to figure out how to protect good china. Tony was always surprising her. During both of Gerard's trials, it was as if he could climb inside her head. Whenever she needed encouragement, he picked up on it, knew just what to say. He was different from any man she'd ever met. Not that she had a lot of experience with men. Then . . . or now.

As he stood next to her, she could smell his cologne. It was the same scent he'd worn back then. Somehow the memory of it had stayed with her all these years. There had been times she was certain he was near because she'd gotten a whiff of that cologne. But it was just her imagination. Until now. He was really here, and for some reason all she wanted to do was push him away. It didn't make sense.

"Thank you," she said quietly. She waited until he sat down again. "You don't mind if I eat while you talk?"

"No. In fact, I think keeping your mouth full might be a good idea."

Kate felt her face grow hot. "Look, Tony. You grew up in a perfect family. Your parents love you, and you've got brothers and sisters coming out of your ears. My folks died in an accident when I was six, and my sister was murdered in front of me. Do you really think you can relate to me?"

She was shocked to see tears spring to Tony's eyes. She'd never seen him get emotional—over anything. Even when he'd shot that guard, he seemed to take it rather nonchalantly. When she'd asked him if he was all right, he'd said, "I don't want to shoot anyone, but when you're in law enforcement you have to be prepared to do whatever it takes. I was just doing my job." That seemed to explain everything. At the time she'd wondered if he'd suffered more than he let on, but since he never mentioned it again, she'd assumed he was all right.

"Kate, everyone has pain. Even if you can't see the scars, no one gets through life unscathed."

"I know that," she snapped. "But I dealt with what happened after I moved here. You weren't here. You don't know what I went through, and you have no right to judge me. It's been four years, Tony, and I'm doing fine. Really."

Tony sighed. "If you weren't hurting, you wouldn't react every time I say something that touches a sore spot." He paused and peered deeply into her eyes. "You know it's true. You're wondering right now why you felt so defensive about what I said."

Kate was startled by his words. Once again, it was as if he were psychic, reading her mind. She didn't say anything, just took a bite of manicotti. Even though she knew it was good, at that moment it tasted like cardboard in her mouth.

Tony took a long drink of his lemonade and then put the glass down on the table. "Look, it's true. I grew up in an awesome family. My mother and father are my greatest supporters. They made sure all of us kids went to church, and all of my brothers and sisters are Christians. But we've had our share of trials. One of my sisters had a miscarriage, and my dad had a cancer scare. Thank God he's in remission. Has been for ten years. There have been other things—nieces and nephews in trouble—one nephew was in a terrible accident, but thankfully he recovered."

"None of that comes close to what I've been through," Kate said. "Except for your sister. I can't imagine losing a child."

"Yes, you can," Tony said. "It's like losing a sister. Except we never got to see what Angela—that was her name—would have been. She never got the chance to accomplish anything in this life. Kelly did. You're fortunate to know that she was a remarkable young lady, and that she's in heaven, waiting for you."

"Angela's in heaven, too."

Tony smiled. "I know. My sister reminds herself of that all the time."

Kate put down her fork and leaned back in her chair, crossing her arms. "Your ten minutes starts now. I'm listening."

Although she intended to hear Tony out, she really wanted to run away. Or tell him to leave. She'd lived with fear for a long time, and until Alan Gerard was released, she'd felt she'd conquered it. But sitting here in her own dining room, with a man she liked and trusted, she was hit with a wave of apprehension that rivaled her worst nightmares.

CHAPTER
TEN

Tony cleared his throat and then took a deep breath. As he slowly exhaled, Kate could see the uneasiness on his face. Whatever he was going to tell her was difficult for him. That was obvious. She had a strange urge to tell him to forget it. To keep his personal demons to himself. But that was selfish. Tony had been there for her when she needed him. The least she could do was listen to him now.

"Just now, when I told you about my family, I left someone out. My brother Jeremy. He was a great kid. Two years younger than me. Followed me everywhere. Looked up to me. Tried to be like me. Sometimes he got on my nerves. Probably the same thing all big brothers go through."

Kate noticed he'd used the word *was*. She sat up straighter in her chair, dreading the rest of his story. Even though she'd been angry at Tony for pushing her, she didn't want to see him in pain. She noticed that he'd turned pale, and she tried to brace herself for what was ahead.

"In a large family, you have to work to get attention,"

he continued. "Eventually Jeremy quit trying. His grades dropped, and he started spending a lot of time alone. In high school, I played football. Dated the head cheerleader. Little by little, Jeremy got lost in the shuffle. I noticed something was wrong, and I tried several times to reach out to him. My parents were worried about him, too. Took him to a therapist. Tried to help him. He kept telling everyone he was okay. But when he was thirteen . . ."

Kate wanted to find a way to keep the next words from coming out of Tony's mouth. Apprehension skittered through her. The scars on her wrists began to itch like crazy, and she had to bite her lower lip to keep from scratching them.

He gulped a couple of times and began again. "When he was thirteen, he killed himself. My mother found him hanging in his closet." He blinked back the tears in his eyes. "We found out later that a neighbor we'd trusted had been molesting him." Tony locked eyes with Kate. "If he'd told someone—faced what was happening—he'd be alive today. Instead, he buried it. I guess he thought ignoring the damage inside would keep it under control. It's the same thing you're doing, Kate, and I don't want to watch you self-destruct the way Jeremy did."

Tony got up and crossed over to where Kate sat. Before she could move, he grabbed her arm. "I know what these scars mean, Kate. I have no intention of standing by while someone else I care about drifts away."

Kate felt as if she'd stopped breathing, and she realized tears were flowing down her cheeks.

Tony let go of her arm and sat down in the chair next to her. "When Jeremy died, it felt as if part of me died with him. I blamed myself. If only I'd paid more attention to him. If only I'd helped him when he needed it." Faint furrows of concentration wrinkled his forehead. "For the first time in my life, I realized why people take their own lives. When depression overtakes them, they're not thinking about anyone else. Not because they don't want to. It's because they can't. The pain is so powerful, it encompasses everything. And in that moment, making it stop is something you have to do because you can't find a way to bear it anymore. I don't judge anyone who makes that terrible choice. I've felt the draw of it. Honestly, it's like realizing you're on fire and you have to put it out yourself because no one else can. The only way I got through it was one step at a time."

"One breath at a time," Kate whispered.

"What?"

"One breath at a time." Kate ran her hand through her short hair. "After Kelly died, I remember thinking people didn't take their own lives because they couldn't face the next day. It was because they couldn't face their next breath." She shook her head. "When I first got here, I felt so alone. Kelly was gone. Being a twin is . . . different. It's like you're two parts of a whole. Half of me was gone and the other half was dying. I was stranded in a strange place by myself without a friend. Without anywhere to go for help. It was terrifying. One night it just seemed too much. I grabbed a sharp knife and . . . Well, you can see the results." She pulled up both sleeves so he could see the twin scars. She couldn't help but feel exposed in front of him. Almost naked. With great effort, she forced herself to continue. "Thankfully, I didn't cut deeply enough. When my wounds healed, I promised myself I'd never do anything like that again." She sighed so deeply it felt as if it came from the deepest part of her soul. "You know, a few days before I did this, I heard a soldier talk about suicide on TV. He compared killing yourself to being a suicide bomber. Once the bomb goes off, it leaves an empty spot where the bomber stood. An almost perfect circle. But what lies beyond that circle is devastation. Death, carnage, bodies blown apart." As she looked at Tony, her eyes felt hot with the tears she tried to blink away. "He said suicide doesn't just destroy you—it demolishes those around you. Those who love you." She nodded her head. "His explanation made perfect sense. One death affects so many other people. The people in your life are horribly injured—possibly forever. His intent was to make people think about the damage they could cause by their actions. But when I heard him say these things, all I could think was . . . there's no one in my life who would miss me. Who would be injured by my death. That realization was the final straw."

Tony's eyes sought hers, and she knew he understood.

"At some point, if you really know God, you realize there's a way out," he said. "A way to live again. He'll walk you through it if you let Him. I had to give everything to Him after Jeremy died. Everything. I couldn't handle life on my own. And He was faithful."

"I believe that," Kate said emphatically. "I prayed. Turned it over to God. I'm doing okay now. I really am." She hated the sound of desperation that pierced through her words.

"I know you believe that, but deliverance isn't denial, Kate. And it isn't delusion. God wants to heal you, but you have to be honest with Him . . . and with yourself."

"I . . . am. I'm not hiding."

Tony sighed and gazed into her eyes. "Maybe I'm wrong, but to me it sounds like you're hiding in your house. And in the café. And why do you wear your sister's bracelet? Are you trying to remind yourself of her death?"

"No," Kate snapped. "I wear it to be closer to her."

"It's just a piece of jewelry. It isn't Kelly. You might think you're wearing it to honor her, and someday you might be able to do that. But right now? I'm afraid it's just a reminder that you lived and she died. And it makes you feel guilty."

"So what if you're right?" Kate asked, her voice quivering. "What do you want me to do? If I have a breakdown, will that satisfy you?"

Tony leaned forward until his face was only inches from hers. "Of course not. But you've got to face the pain, Kate. The fear. The loss. No matter how hard it is."

Kate wiped away her tears with the back of her hand. "I . . . I can't, Tony. I can't. I tried. It was like dying, like I was drowning in deep water and couldn't fight my way back to the surface. This is the only way I can make it. I know it. You've got to leave me alone. If you don't . . ."

"If I don't, you'll go on like this until the day comes when your mind can't protect you any longer. And when that happens, it will be worse than you can imagine, and I'm afraid you won't have anywhere else to hide. You might not escape next time."

Kate forcefully blew out a breath of air. "I'm not turning into one of those people who lives the rest of their lives as a victim. I can't stand being around people like that."

"I understand that. I'm not talking about people who find

their identity in their problems. I want to see you free to be the person you were always meant to be."

"I'm not trying to hang on to my pain. I'm really not."

He reached over and took her hand. His grip was warm and reassuring. "I believe you. But you've got to grieve, Kate. To honestly grieve. Even if it scares the heck out of you. And you've got to forgive yourself for . . . surviving. It will be hard, but I know you can do it."

Kate shook her head. "After Kelly died, everything was about making sure Gerard was punished. I spent hours and hours with the police, the D.A. and his people. Going over what happened. Identifying Gerard. Rehearsing my testimony. And then came the trial. And then the second trial." She stared at Tony for a moment. "There wasn't any time to even think about what I'd lost. How I felt. My whole life was about finding justice for my sister. I know you thought I was strong, Tony. Determined. But I was just focused. When I got to Shelter Cove, I had to concentrate on blending in. Finding a new life. When the grief started to come, I . . . I couldn't accept it. I'm sure what I did . . . what I tried to do . . . happened because I didn't know how to deal with those feelings by myself. Facing it alone almost killed me, but I made a choice to live. I'll never hurt myself again. I'm certain of that."

Tony let go of Kate's hand and leaned back in his chair. "After Jeremy died, I did the same thing. Pushed my pain and confusion into a dark place and tried to ignore it. My family needed me, and I wanted to be strong for them. And then one day the past came flooding in. And when my emotions surfaced, they exploded with a vengeance. Thankfully,

I had another brother who recognized what was happening. Vinny got me to someone who could help me. The therapist helped me to see that acknowledging the damage in my soul wasn't weakness. It was strength. Strength faces the truth, Kate. And seeks real healing. It doesn't run from it."

Although she could understand what he meant, Kate felt the bars around her bruised psyche go up, protecting her from facing the shadows that whispered her name.

"I . . . I'm sorry about Jeremy," she said softly. "And I appreciate what you're saying, but . . . I need time to think. Please. I've listened. Now give me time to process everything."

"Fair enough." He got up and went back to his original chair across the table. Then picked up his glass and drained it.

"Can I get you some more?" Kate asked, trying to keep her voice steady.

"Thanks. I'm fine."

The look of concern on his face made Kate's pulse pound. "I need to pack and make arrangements for someone to cover the café," she said. "When are we leaving for St. Louis?"

"Not right away. There's been . . . a development."

"I don't understand. What kind of development?"

Tony drummed his fingers on the table for a few seconds. Kate could tell he was upset about something.

"The D.A. doesn't have all his ducks in a row. He wants us to wait a bit. If we go now, you'll just have to cool your heels in a hotel room for a while. Wouldn't you rather wait here?"

"Yeah, I would." She frowned at him. "Everything's all right, isn't it?"

He stood up. "Everything's fine. Don't worry." He looked at his watch. "It's getting late, and we need to get some sleep.

We'll talk more tomorrow. You still haven't told me how you got involved with the café, and I'd really like to hear about it." He hesitated for a moment. Then he turned his head to stare at her. As she met his eyes, her breath caught in her throat.

"I would be injured, Kate," he said, his voice low and soft. "If anything happened to you, I would be injured."

It took her a moment to understand what he meant. Then she nodded and watched him leave. She sat still and listened to his car start and then drive away. Part of her wanted to run after him, beg him to come back. But another voice in her head warned her that Tony DeLuca was dangerous. If she got too close, there was a good chance she'd slip back into the darkness. But this time she might pull Tony in with her.

CHAPTER
ELEVEN

As soon as he stepped outside, Tony began to second-guess himself. He'd talked to Kate about facing the truth, and then he'd been dishonest. Hadn't told her about the new evidence. He wanted Kate to trust him, but he was trained to obey orders. In this situation, he could either risk his relationship with Kate or he could risk his job. There had never been a question of his loyalties—until now. His only option was to go back to Batterson. Get permission to tell Kate what was really going on. He decided he had no other choice. He'd convince Batterson that she shouldn't be left in the dark. Then he'd talk to Kate. If he handled it right, maybe she'd never know he'd kept something from her.

Ever since Batterson had told him about Malcolm Bodine, Tony just couldn't accept the idea that Kate's identification had been wrong. He believed she really had seen Gerard that night. That it was Gerard who killed Kelly and attacked Kate. It wasn't that it was impossible for a victim to become confused about an attacker, but in this case, he trusted Kate more than the supposed *facts* that cast doubt on her eyewitness account.

Tony drove back to the resort. When he pulled up in front of the cabin, he got out, intending to go inside. But the lure of the lake and the sight of the sun sinking down below the horizon, the sky streaked with reddish hues, drew him out onto the long dock that stretched out over the water. Tiny lights along the sides of the dock helped him see where he was going.

As he walked, he breathed in everything. The water lapping against the dock, the sweet evening air whispering lightly against his cheek, the cacophony of birdsong and bullfrogs and all the other night sounds that surrounded him. He loved all of it, and being here brought a sense of rest to his troubled soul.

As he stood at the end of the dock, Tony felt as if God was all around him. He stared out into the darkness, the lake like black ink, and he prayed. He hadn't meant to leave God behind—he'd just allowed his job to become . . . everything.

"I'm sorry, God," he said quietly. "My mom's right. I need You more than I need anything else. If You'll give me another chance, I'll do better. Put You first. And if You could help me with Kate, I'd really appreciate it. I don't know what to do." He sighed into the night. "I lost Jeremy. I don't want to lose her."

It was only at the last minute that he heard the boards on the dock squeak behind him. Before he had a chance to turn around, someone put an arm around his neck. Then there was a quick sting—like a bee's.

And everything went black.

"Mr. DeLuca? Mr. DeLuca, are you all right?"

Tony forced his eyes open. They felt as if they'd been sealed with wet sand. His head hurt so badly he could barely move it. As he looked around him, he realized he was still on the dock, but the sun was coming up. Could it really be morning? How long had he been lying here? He struggled to sit up. Bobby, the guy from the office, put his arm around Tony to support him.

"One of our fishermen came down here a little while ago and found you. He ran and got me. We've called the doctor."

"No . . . I'm all right. I . . ." Actually, the world swam around him, making it look as if he was sitting at the bottom of the lake instead of on the dock. "I . . . I think something stung me."

"Are you allergic to anything?" Bobby asked. "Bees? Wasps?"

Tony shook his head. "No. Nothing like that."

"Do you have heart problems? Any kind of physical disability that might cause you to faint?"

"No. I passed my last physical with flying colors." Tony tried to get to his feet, but he immediately slumped back down. He put his hand up to his neck. Sure enough, it was sore. He moved his head toward Bobby. "Can you see anything here?" he asked, pointing to the spot that hurt.

"Sorry. Not in this light."

Once again, Tony attempted to get to his feet. With Bobby's help, he succeeded this time but felt wobbly and out of control. "Could you help me back to my room?" he asked. His tongue seemed too big for his mouth. What had happened? Was this really caused by some kind of insect, or had he been attacked by something more . . . human? Suddenly he remembered someone grabbing him right before he felt the sting.

"Don't you think you should wait for the doctor?" Bobby said. "Maybe we shouldn't move you."

Tony shook his head. "I don't have any kind of spinal injury. This is something different. Please, I need to get to my room."

A man Tony didn't know stepped out of the shadows. Tony hadn't noticed him before. He looked to be in his twenties, dressed in old jeans, thick boots, a plaid shirt, and a khaki vest. His hat was decorated with different lures. Must be the fisherman who'd discovered him.

"I'll help," he said. The man and Bobby got on each side to support Tony so he could get down the dock and back to his cabin. Although his legs felt like overcooked spaghetti, little by little he began to gain control of his gait. By the time they reached his door, he was ready to try it on his own.

"Thanks, guys," he said, disengaging himself from his helpers. "I'm feeling a lot stronger." He studied Bobby and the other man. Were they really there to help him, or could they have had something to do with what had happened? Was he in danger even now?

"The doctor will be here soon," Bobby said. "Please let him check you over."

"Okay. Just send him here when he arrives." The two men seemed to be truly concerned about him. If they'd wanted to hurt him, they could have done it anytime. They appeared to be harmless. "Thank you. Both of you. I really appreciate it." He held out his hand to the man with the fishing hat. "I don't even know your name."

The man smiled. "I'm Steven. Hope you get to feeling better." He shook Tony's hand and then addressed Bobby. "I'll be out for a while. Probably have the boat back before noon."

Bobby nodded at him, and the man walked away.

Then Tony shook Bobby's hand. "Thanks. Really. Sorry for the trouble."

"Not a problem. Just hope you'll be okay. If you need anything, just call me."

"I will, but I think I can take it from here."

As Bobby walked away, headed toward the office, Tony waited by the door to his cabin. When the office door closed, Tony walked a few feet away, hoping he could get a good signal on his phone. He dialed Kate's number. Thankfully, she answered after only a couple rings.

"Sorry to be calling so early," he said. "Just checking up on you. Everything okay?"

There was silence for a moment, then Kate said, "Well, except that you woke me up, everything's fine."

"I thought you had a restaurant to run. Figured you'd be up at the crack of dawn."

A buzzer sounded in the background. "Good timing. There's my alarm. Too bad I set it. I had no idea you'd be taking its place this morning."

"Funny." Tony could feel himself swaying a bit. He needed to sit down. "Hey, why don't you wait for me? Let me drive you to the café?" He felt so out of control he didn't wait for a response. "Gotta go," he said thickly, before hanging up. He slowly made his way back to the cabin, everything around him rolling and making his stomach turn over. When he reached the porch, he grabbed the wooden railing, trying to steady himself. Once the world around him stopped moving on its own, he looked up at the sky. Although it was still early, it seemed unusually dark. Sure enough, black clouds gathered over Shelter Cove. Storm clouds.

Tony unlocked the door to his cabin and went inside. He immediately grabbed his suitcase and dug around for some pain reliever. He always kept some strong stuff with him because of occasional severe headaches. He had one now that was awful, but he suspected it was because of whatever he'd been dosed with. He quickly swallowed several pills. "Not the best answer to prayer I've ever had, God," he said softly. If his head didn't hurt so much, maybe he would have found the situation a little funny. Ask God for help and you get coldcocked. But why would someone want to drug him? He'd just picked up his phone to call Batterson when he heard a knock on his door.

Stifling an urge to curse, Tony yanked it open. An older man stood there, a black medical bag in his hand.

"Mr. DeLuca? I'm Doc Henderson. Bobby called to say you were sick. Maybe injured?"

Tony pulled open the door. "Wow, a doctor who still does house calls. I'm in a hurry, but I do need to talk to you."

The doctor came into the room and put his bag on the bed. "Can you tell me what happened? And how you're feeling now?"

"I'm not sure what happened. How do I feel? Like I'm standing still and you're doing the twist."

The doctor stared at him. "Is there something I should know?"

Tony sat down on the bed, next to the doctor's bag. "Like what?"

"Like what your relationship with Emily is. I doubt you're her cousin. Does your being here have anything to do with her being in witness protection?"

When Tony started to protest, the doctor shook his head. "I don't know all the details, but I do know a little bit. After she got here, she . . . hurt herself. I stitched her up. She didn't tell me much, but I know she is in the protection program." He held up his hand like a traffic cop directing cars. "Don't tell her I shared this with you. You should know, though, that she was in bad shape for a while. She's a lot better now, but I keep an eye on her." He pinned Tony with a hard stare. "I'll do anything I can to help her, and I won't tell anyone about her . . . or you. You can trust me. Now tell me what really happened."

Tony hesitated a moment but finally decided to come clean. Maybe it was because the room was still spinning, but he didn't feel like playing games with the doctor. He took out his wallet and showed the doctor his I.D. card. "Doc, I'm a deputy U.S. Marshal on assignment. I expect you to keep that information to yourself."

Doc Henderson's eyebrows shot up. "Is the town in any danger?"

Tony put his wallet back in his jacket. "No, I don't believe so. I'm here to transport Emily. As I said, it's very important you don't share this with anyone. I'm trying to keep her safe. Like you."

The doctor, who reminded Tony of a picture he'd seen of Albert Einstein, nodded. "I understand."

Although he'd just met the man, Tony's gut told him the doctor was on the level. "Someone else was on the dock last night. They came up behind me. I think they injected me with something." Tony turned his head so the doctor could see his neck. He pointed to the sore spot. "Right here."

Doc Henderson got a small flashlight out of his bag and looked closely at the spot Tony indicated. "Yep," he said softly. "That's an injection site."

"What kind of drug would knock someone out for about eight hours and leave them feeling fuzzy and weak? Oh, and give them a really bad headache?"

"Could be several things. Propofol would do it. It has a short onset of action, about forty seconds. Of course it could be Haldol or one of the benzodiazepines."

"I think the guy put his arm around my neck first. Cut off my air. I probably passed out from that and then the drug kicked in."

"That's entirely possible."

"Any permanent damage with the drugs you mentioned?"

The doctor shook his head. "No. But if someone injected you with something like that, you need to be careful. Next time the results could be quite different. Too much of that stuff can kill you."

"Trust me, Doc. I won't give him another chance." Tony grabbed his checkbook from his suitcase. "What do I owe you?"

"Don't worry about it," Doc Henderson said, closing his medical bag. "I didn't do anything. Just watch yourself." He seemed to study Tony for a moment. "Do you need something for your headache?"

"Thanks, I took something. I'm already feeling better."

He took the doctor's arm and guided him to the door. He needed to contact Batterson right away. And even though Kate seemed to be okay, he wanted to get over to her place as soon as possible. He intended to stick close to her today. Thankfully, his mind was beginning to clear and he was starting to feel like his old self again. He was determined to find out who'd drugged him—and why.

After Henderson left, Tony grabbed his phone and found that Batterson had tried to call him several times. Then he noticed the light on the phone in his room flashing. Although he wanted to use the room phone since he felt a little drained, he worried about the line not being secure. Tony took his cell phone and left the room, walking toward the same spot where he'd called Kate from a few minutes earlier. He tapped Batterson's number. His boss answered immediately.

"Where have you been?" he bellowed. "I've been trying to reach you for hours."

Tony briefly described his attack the night before and his visit with the doctor. "But I'm fine now, Chief. What's going on?"

There was a brief silence from the other end of the line, and Tony's stomach clenched. Something was wrong. Wrong in Shelter Cove—and wrong in St. Louis. He waited for Batterson's next words. When he heard them, he wasn't completely surprised.

"I got a phone call late last night," Batterson said. "Alan Gerard has disappeared."

CHAPTER
TWELVE

"I . . . I don't understand. Wasn't he being watched?"

"Of course he was, but he slipped away. He disappeared sometime late yesterday afternoon."

"You think he's here?" Although Gerard was the first person Tony might suspect of attacking him, it didn't make sense. "If he's not the Blue-Eyed Killer, why would he come to Shelter Cove? And besides that, how would he know where Kate was?"

"You're asking a lot of questions I don't have answers for. Look, the guy who ran that website? BEKlives.com? He was a computer tech extraordinaire. I'm going to tell you something, but you've got to keep it between us. The office in Washington was hacked not long after Gerard's second trial. The intrusion was caught and shut down. Washington waited for fallout, but it never came. Or so they thought."

"You're telling me Gerard's computer fan might have found Kate's location? Why wasn't she moved?"

"Because no one was sure who the hacker was or what

he wanted. There was nothing to indicate he was targeting Kate. The hacker could have looked at all of our witnesses. We couldn't possibly have relocated everyone. Our Washington office works under the direction of the Department of Justice. Unfortunately, back then funding was tight. Too tight. They decided to wait to see if any further action was required. In the end, they decided it was a one-time deal with no lasting consequences."

"So you don't know if our witness was compromised?"

"No, not for certain," Batterson said. "But I suspect it now."

"You should have told me about this. Kate could be in real danger."

"Like I said, at the time there was no reason to think the breach had anything to do with her."

"But is there reason to think that now?"

"Well, the website's up again."

Tony was stunned by this news. "Wait a minute. Gerard's crazy computer groupie is back? Why? Especially since it looks like Gerard isn't B.E.K. How would this guy even know what's going on?"

"The story's out. Someone leaked it. The media's jumping all over it this morning. Pulling the trial apart. Kate's image is all over TV. They know Gerard was released, but they don't know he's missing."

"What's the message on the website?"

Batterson sighed. "Just a verse. Like always. *The revenger of blood himself shall slay the murderer: when he meeteth him, he shall slay him.* It's from Numbers."

"That's odd. A little different than the other ones."

"I don't think you can tell much from the ravings of a madman."

"We don't need this, that's for sure." Tony thought for a moment. "We've got to take it as a warning, Chief. We've got to move Kate. Now. The news is gonna reach here eventually. This is a small town, but they have computers and television. Someone's gonna recognize Kate. If Gerard wants to find her, it's gonna get easier real quick."

"I don't know, Tony. Like you said, if Gerard isn't the person who attacked Kate and killed her sister, why would he be looking for her?"

"I still think he's the guy who killed Kelly O'Brien, and I have a hunch your gut's telling you the same thing. We need to be proactive. Protect our witness with the information we have. Maybe the evidence linking this Bodine guy is wrong. I'm not sure we should just accept it without more information. Besides, someone attacked me this morning. Why?" Tony felt an overwhelming sense of urgency to get over to Kate's. "I need to sign off, Chief. I want to check on Kate."

"All right. You get her ready. I'll contact the office near you and tell them we're on the move." Batterson sighed into the phone. "You need backup. You should have called for it immediately, Tony. Before meeting with the doctor."

"You're right, Chief." Tony was silent after that. He couldn't argue. It should have been his first action. True, whatever he was dosed with had dulled his mind at first, but his training should have taken over.

"I'm gonna let it pass because you weren't yourself. But next time, if you ignore procedure, there will be consequences. Do you understand?"

"Yeah, I get it. Any idea where we can take Kate?"

"We have to bring her here. Don't have any other choice. We can protect her in St. Louis until we can figure out our next move. I'll have the local Marshals contact you directly. You can work out the details with them. Keep me updated."

"I will. Gotta go."

"Tony?"

"Yeah?"

"One more thing. You should know that the media also have a story about Gerard not being the Blue-Eyed Killer. That there's another suspect. They don't know who it is, though, and we're taking steps to make sure they won't find out. We're not sure how the media got hold of it, but if Kate listens to the news this morning . . ."

"She'll know I didn't tell her the truth."

"That was my call, not yours. She'll understand."

Tony wasn't too sure she would, but he didn't say anything.

"Stay alert and be careful," Batterson said.

"I will, Chief."

Tony slid his phone into his jacket pocket. Then he hurried back to his room. After quickly washing his face and combing his hair, he got into his car and headed over to Kate's. He knocked on her door several times. When she didn't answer, he decided she'd ignored his request for her to wait for him and had already gone to the café. He quickly drove over there, pulled up next to the front door, and got out. There was a car in the parking lot he assumed was hers. He peered through the café windows, but it was dark inside. He tried the front door and found it locked. After banging on it several times, he went around to the side of the building.

A door next to the trash bins was open so he went inside. Why were the lights off?

"Anyone here?" he called out. "Kate?"

There was no answer. Tony felt his shoulders tense, and he pulled out his gun. "Kate, are you here?" he said again. Still nothing.

He was in some kind of hallway. The only light came from outside, and the clouds weren't helping. He could barely make out shelves along the walls, loaded with supplies. He slowly pushed open a door at the end of the hallway and found the kitchen. It was outlined in shadow. He could smell something familiar, and it wasn't food. It was blood. His free hand felt the wall next to him and discovered a light switch. As he held his gun in front of him, his heart racing in his chest, he clicked on the light.

There wouldn't be any more off-pitch hymns echoing through the Shelter Café. Kate's cook, Bella, lay sprawled on the floor, her eyes open and unseeing, a large knife sticking out of her chest.

Deputy Warren Killian rushed to the Shelter Café after getting a call from Tony DeLuca. He found Bella's body and searched the rest of the building, but no one else was there. He called for assistance and waited for backup to arrive. When DeLuca had told him he was going to see if Kate was okay, he'd made a mistake. Hadn't used the name Emily. As far as Warren knew, no one else was aware of Emily's real identity. Would DeLuca realize his slip? Would he say something? Warren decided to confront the situation head-on. It was the only way. It might keep him from saying something that would draw DeLuca's attention. If DeLuca ever found out the truth, his presence in Shelter Cove would become suspect—and so would he. And he couldn't afford that.

Tony drove like a crazy man back to Kate's. Was she all right? Was she alive? He pulled into her driveway, his tires squealing on the concrete. He ran over to the garage and looked inside. There was a car. Kate had never left her house. He pulled out his gun, went up to the front door, and found it locked. He took a step back and then kicked it in.

"Kate?" he yelled. "Kate, where are you?"

A quick look around the living room, the kitchen, and the dining room revealed nothing. Then he went into Kate's bedroom. Her bed was unmade, the sheets pulled almost completely off the mattress. A bedside table was overturned, and a lamp lay shattered on the floor. Tony looked closer, being careful not to touch anything in an effort to leave evidence undisturbed. There was blood on the carpet. Not a lot, but enough to make it clear someone had been injured. As he looked around the room, he could come to only one conclusion.

Kate had been abducted by Alan Gerard.

CHAPTER
THIRTEEN

Tony called Batterson and brought him up to date.

"You stay put," Batterson said grimly. "Reinforcements are on the way. I'll notify the FBI. We'll find her, Tony."

Tony listened to his boss's instructions but wasn't certain he could follow them. Where was Kate? Gerard had tried to kill her during the trial. Was he trying to finish the job now? Was it already too late?

He mumbled something to Batterson and disconnected the call. Not quite sure what to do, he got in his car and drove back to the café. Additional cars from the sheriff's department had arrived, along with several police vehicles. Tony quickly found Deputy Killian and pulled him aside.

"Emily's gone," he said. "There are signs of a struggle. Some blood. She's been abducted."

Killian's eyes widened. "Isn't Gerard still in St. Louis?"

Tony frowned at the deputy. "Gerard? What are you talking about?"

Killian sighed. "I'm not an idiot, Tony. I know Emily is

Kate O'Brien. I've known it for a long time. Hard to hide her anywhere. The Blue-Eyed Killer case was all over the media."

Tony stared at Killian for a moment. "Is there anyone else in town who knows who she is? Who could have given away her location?"

Killian was quiet for a moment. "I honestly don't know," he said finally, "but if I could figure it out, someone else could have, too. Trust me. If I think of anything that could help, you'll be the first to know."

"If it is Gerard . . ."

Killian shook his head. "Let's pray it isn't. No matter what, I'll do whatever I can to help find her."

Tony thanked him and walked away, intending to call Batterson, but before he could grab his phone, someone called out his name. When Tony looked up he saw Bobby waving at him, indicating he wanted Tony to come over to where he stood waiting.

"I'm really busy, Bobby," Tony said as he approached him. "I don't really have time to talk."

"It's about Emily," Bobby said, looking around him as if making certain he wouldn't be overheard. "I . . . I saw something."

Tony frowned at him. "She's missing. What did you see?"

"I was out for a walk. I saw a man at Emily's house. He put her in the trunk of his car and drove away. I tried to stop him, but he drove past me."

Tony felt the blood drain from his face. "How long ago? Did you see where he went? What direction? Can you describe his car? What about the license plate? Could you . . ."

Bobby held up his hand. "You need to listen to me. I know where he took her."

Tony grabbed the skinny man's shoulders. "How could you know? What did you see?"

"It only took me a minute to run to my place and get my SUV. I guess whoever was driving the car didn't want to draw attention to himself by driving too fast, because I found him turning onto the road outside of town. I followed him." He started shaking his head. "Don't worry. He didn't see me. It was still dark, and I kept my headlights off."

Tony couldn't keep the frustration out of his voice. "You should have called the police. Maybe they could have pulled the car over before they got too far away."

Bobby looked away from Tony, his eyes darting back and forth. Obviously the guy was nervous. Tony didn't have time to feel sorry for him. He had to save Kate. If Bobby couldn't help him, Tony needed to move on.

Finally Bobby looked up and met Tony's gaze. "I'm sorry. I . . . I don't have a cell phone. There wasn't any way I could call anyone. They've only been gone about thirty minutes. I came back to find you because I know where they are."

"Where? Tell me."

"The car drove up Wilderness Road—into the mountains," Bobby said.

Shelter Cove was nestled at the bottom of the Ouachita Mountains. Although a lot of the range was spotted with resorts, homes, and tourist areas, much of it was still wild. But why would Gerard go into the mountains? As soon as he asked himself the question, he knew the answer. He wanted to be alone with Kate. To be isolated. The mountains were the perfect place to hide.

"I think we should go after her, Tony," Bobby said, his lisp even more pronounced than normal.

Tony hesitated a moment. "We need to give this information to the police. They can mount a search."

Bobby grabbed Tony's arm. "But what if they don't find her in time? I know those roads. I've been up there a lot. I have a good idea where he took her." He hopped from foot to foot anxiously. "If you wait too long, they'll be gone."

"What are you saying?" Tony asked.

"I'm saying we need to leave now." He pointed toward the vehicles from the police and sheriff's department. "By the time they get . . . organized, Emily could be dead."

Tony's law enforcement training told him to stay where he was—to wait for backup—but his feelings for Kate took over. Although he didn't trust Bobby completely, Tony realized he could be right. By the time a search was organized it might be too late. He thought about telling someone where he was going, but he was pretty sure they'd tell him to stay put, and he had no intention of letting Gerard get away with Kate. "Okay," he said finally. "We have to go back to my cabin first. I need ammo."

"You better make it fast," Bobby said, looking up at the stormy sky. "If it starts raining, it will be tough to make it up those roads. By the time these people are ready to look for Emily, the roads could be washed out. We're the only ones who can get up the mountain before that happens." He pointed to an old, beat-up SUV parked a few yards away. "We need to take my car. Yours won't make it. I have four-wheel drive."

"Are you sure it won't conk out on us?"

Bobby nodded. "It looks bad, but it drives great. New motor. We'll be fine."

Tony took one last look at the LEOs gathering at the café. Batterson had told him that if he went against his training one more time, he'd be in trouble. But Kate needed him now. He'd call the sheriff's department as soon as they were gone and leave Killian a message. Let him know where he was and why he'd left. After that, it was up to local law enforcement and the U.S. Marshals to decide what to do.

Tony nodded at Bobby. "Okay, let's go."

They got into Bobby's old SUV and drove to the resort. After Tony grabbed more ammunition and an additional weapon, they took off for the mountains.

Kate woke up in a small, dark, cramped space. Where was she? She tried to open her eyes, but she couldn't. She attempted to touch her face and find out why she couldn't see, but her hands were bound in front of her. Finally, she raised them together and touched her eyes. Her fingers came away wet and sticky. Even though she couldn't see anything, she could tell it was blood. Was she injured? Pain from the top of her head told her she'd probably been struck while she was sitting in bed. She remembered talking to Tony, and then she'd put down her phone. After that, she couldn't remember anything. She felt to see what she was wearing. The sweatpants and T-shirt she'd worn to bed. Her feet were bare.

At least she was conscious so it couldn't be too bad. Where was she? Had she been buried alive? As panic set in, she realized she was moving. She was in the trunk of a car. The carpet beneath her was scratchy and uncomfortable. She could smell oil and rubber. Her stomach rolled from fear and nausea. She struggled to ignore her physical discomfort. She had to come up with a way out of this situation.

Suddenly the car slowed. Were they turning? Now the road became rough and Kate was tossed around like a ragdoll.

Her fingers explored the trunk, hoping to locate a release switch, but with her limited ability to move, it was almost impossible to find anything.

The car lurched and bumped again. Where were they? Paved roads wouldn't feel like this. Were they going up into the mountains? She broke out into a cold sweat as fear began to overtake her, causing her to breathe too quickly. As she began to get light-headed, Kate realized she had to calm down. If she was going to stay alive, she had to keep her wits about her. She began to slow her breathing. She had to get out of this trunk. That was the most important thing right now. She wriggled around as much as possible, trying to touch everything she could.

Finally, she found a piece of metal. Part of the car's interior. It was sharp and she accidentally cut her finger. She wiggled up closer to it and began to rub the tape around her wrists against the ragged edge. It took several minutes, but she finally weakened the tape enough that she could rip it. Once her hands were free, she pulled the tape completely off. Then she began once again to look for a trunk release. Hadn't she read that cars built after 2002 were supposed to have inside releases? It was one of those odd facts that she'd picked up. Usually they only helped during games of Trivial Pursuit, but today, maybe one of them would save her life.

CHAPTER
FOURTEEN

"Just pass the message along," Tony said gruffly. He closed his cell phone and put it in his jacket pocket. The dispatcher at the sheriff's department had transferred Tony to a deputy who insisted Killian would want to take the message directly. Although Tony could have tried to wait until the deputy sheriff was available, he wasn't sure what kind of cell phone service he'd have once they started going deeper into the mountains. He had to let someone know where he was. He knew he should call Batterson, but he was also aware what his boss's response would be. Since Tony had no intention of changing his mind, he couldn't see any reason to listen to Batterson rant and rave at him. He made the deputy write down his message verbatim and read it back. Once he had it right, Tony hung up.

"Where are you going?" he asked Bobby, who seemed to be transfixed by the road ahead.

"This is the main road," Bobby said. "In a few miles, other roads begin to split off. Most of them lead to areas with cabins or homes. Not places anyone would go who didn't want to be seen. Up higher, there are roads that lead to a few cabins, some small resorts. Only one goes almost nowhere. It's secluded. The place you'd go if you didn't want to be found. I'm not an expert on this kind of stuff, but if I were trying to kidnap someone, it's where I'd take them. If this guy knows anything about our area, it's where he's headed."

"You can't be certain which direction he'll take," Tony said, trying to keep frustration out of his voice. He hoped this guy wasn't leading him on a wild goose chase. Why had he trusted him? Had he made a serious error in judgment that had led him farther away from Kate?

Bobby turned to look at Tony, uncertainty on his face. "I . . . I just think it makes sense. I mean, why go up into the mountains? I assume he's trying to get somewhere . . . private. Am I looking at this wrong?"

Tony remembered the book Bobby was reading when he checked in.

"Do you read a lot of crime fiction?" Tony asked.

Bobby flushed. "I . . . I know that doesn't make me an expert on this kind of stuff. If you think we should look somewhere else . . ."

"No, actually it's a good thing. Your instincts are probably right."

"Could the guy that took Emily be an ex-husband or boyfriend?" Bobby asked. "I don't really know much about her."

Tony turned over his options in his head. Even though he wasn't completely sure Bobby was going to help him find Kate, he couldn't figure out any way Bobby could possibly be a threat. Besides, right now Bobby was all he had. He decided to take a chance on the man. Kate's life was on the line and he needed all the help he could get. Bobby cared about Kate. If he knew how serious the situation was, Tony was certain he'd do his very best to locate her.

"A few years ago, Emily was a witness against a man charged with murdering her twin sister. The killer was put away, but because some of the evidence used in the trial has been thrown out, he's been released. I'm pretty sure that's who has her. My fear is that he plans on finishing the job he started. You see, he didn't know Emily was a twin. Not until the night of the attack. I believe he wants her dead, too. Just like her sister."

Bobby took his eyes off the road and gave Tony a perplexed look. "Are you talking about the Alan Gerard case?"

Bobby was sharper than Tony had given him credit for. "Yes, I am."

"You think Alan Gerard has Emily?" Bobby's eyes were large with alarm. "But that wasn't the name of the victim— or her twin sister. What was it? I saw it on TV, but I can't remember."

"Kate. Kate O'Brien."

"Oh yeah. That's right." Bobby glanced quickly at Tony. "Are you really Emily . . . Kate's cousin?"

"No, I'm with the U.S. Marshals, and I came here to escort her back to St. Louis. To testify against Gerard . . . again."

"Wow. A real U.S. Marshal. That's awesome. I'd love to help you," Bobby said. "It's an honor."

"Thanks, Bobby. I appreciate it."

"I . . . I heard on the news this morning that the authorities decided someone else was the Blue-Eyed Killer. That Gerard didn't do it. Is that true?"

Tony sighed. As Batterson had said, the story was out. It

had even reached Shelter Cove. "Yeah, that's the prevailing theory now. Has to do with a body recently discovered. DNA—fingerprints seem to point to someone else. Some people involved in the case think Kate's identification was wrong."

"Emily . . . I mean Kate, doesn't seem like the kind of person to make a mistake like that."

Tony nodded at him. "You and I agree on that. I think that's why Gerard may have taken her. He disappeared from St. Louis yesterday. Somehow I'm afraid he found out she's here."

"So maybe Gerard attacked Kate and her sister? And this Bodine guy killed the other victims?"

"That's what I'm thinking."

Bobby frowned. "So this is personal for Gerard? Nothing to do with B.E.K.?"

"That's just the thing. I don't know. I'm still not even sure that the man you saw was Gerard. But if it is him, my guess is that he really wants to be the next B.E.K. Now that he's out of prison, he's free to pursue the B.E.K. legacy." Tony shook his head and sighed. "Understand that I'm in the minority here. Most people believe Bodine attacked Kate and Kelly. They think Gerard is innocent."

"But Bodine is dead, right?"

"Yeah. That's why I think either Gerard or one of his insane fans took Kate."

At that moment, a curve in the road led to a fork. Bobby slowed the car. "We're going farther up into the mountains. The way I mentioned. Is that okay with you?"

"If you feel it's the best thing to do, let's try it. But if we don't find some sign of Kate soon, we'll have to go back to Shelter Cove. Our best bet is to coordinate with local law enforcement."

A crack of thunder drowned out Bobby's response, but Tony wasn't planning to argue about it anyway. The only reason he'd left with Bobby was because he thought they might be able to catch up to Kate quickly. If they couldn't, they'd have to turn back. Tony wanted to do whatever was best for Kate. He prayed he could find her quickly. The longer it took, the less likely they were to find her alive.

After moving things around inside the trunk and finding a blanket she could use to wipe her face, Kate began once again to look for a trunk release latch. There was some kind of box next to her. When she finally pushed it a few inches away, she saw something that glowed. She wiggled around a bit until she could reach it. It was a small handle emblazoned with a picture of a car, its trunk open. There was also an arrow pointing down.

"Thank You, God," Kate whispered into the dark. "Thank You."

Now she knew she could escape. But when? She had no idea where she was. Right now the car was going too fast, but when it slowed down again she'd make her move. If the driver of this car was Alan Gerard, she had to find a way to run. If she didn't, she wouldn't live to see another sunrise.

"What do you mean Tony took off?" Batterson asked Mark.

"When the Marshals got to Shelter Cove they were told Tony left with some local man. Said he might know where Kate O'Brien had been taken and that there wasn't time to wait for backup. Left his apologies to you with someone at the sheriff's department. That's where I got this information."

"Left me his apologies?" Batterson could feel his blood pressure rising, something his doctor had warned him about. "What was he thinking?"

"He was probably thinking that if he waited, Kate would die," Mark said. "I understand his decision."

"You know better than that," Batterson snapped. "We wait for backup. We're not cowboys, taking off on our own." He pointed at his phone. "If Tony thought he was right about this, he'd have called me and told me himself. We need the information he has, and now we're probably going to have to rescue him, too. What a knuckle-headed thing to do."

Mark handed him a piece of paper. "Here's what Tony dictated to the person he spoke to at the sheriff's office. It was supposed to go to a certain deputy sheriff, but he seems to have disappeared, too. One more weird piece of this insane puzzle. Supposedly Tony left you all the information you need. Where they went. Why they went. And who Tony is with. Hopefully, this will help, Chief." Mark hesitated a moment before saying, "With all due respect, Tony's a smart, well-trained deputy. If he felt he had no choice but to go after our witness . . . I trust him."

Batterson started to disparage Mark's comment but then thought better of it. Mark had a point. Still, protocol had to be respected. Without it there was anarchy.

He waved Mark away. After the door closed behind him, Batterson picked up the sheet of paper and began to read.

CHAPTER
FIFTEEN

Although Bobby was obviously trying to keep his vehicle steady, the paved roads were beginning to deteriorate. Potholes and uneven asphalt created a bumpy ride. Tony held on to the hand grip over his window while keeping his other hand on the dashboard.

Tony suddenly realized they were chasing a car he hadn't seen. "Describe the car you saw, Bobby. We need to be watching for it."

"Oh, sure. Dark green Toyota Camry. Four-door. Newer model."

That sounded like the car Tony had seen across the street from the cabin yesterday. He studied Bobby for a moment. "You know your Camrys?"

Bobby smiled his gassy-baby smile. "I like cars. Can't afford a new one, but I like to look at them."

"Is there anything else you remember?"

"The man who was driving." Bobby frowned. "He looked . . . familiar. But I don't remember where I saw him." He shook his head, his jowls wiggling a little. "Sorry."

"Did you ever see a picture of Alan Gerard?"

"Yeah, but it was a long time ago. It's hard to remember what he looks like after so many years."

Tony pulled his phone out of his pocket and attempted to bring up the internet, planning to find a photo of Gerard. Unfortunately, he couldn't pull up anything. His phone didn't seem to be getting reception. Must be the mountains. He sighed and stuck it back in his jacket pocket. "Great," he said. "Describe the guy to me."

"He wore a ball cap, had a beard . . . not a long one, you know. Just short. Blond hair? Oh, and he wore glasses."

Gerard had dark hair, no beard the last time Tony saw him, and he didn't wear glasses. Of course, it could very easily be a disguise. He was just about to mention that when Bobby slowed the car and pulled over to the side of the road.

"This is the way I told you about," he said, pointing to a dirt road that disappeared up into the trees. "If the man who has Kate wants to hide from the police, this is the road he would take."

"Stay here," Tony said. He got out of the car and walked over to the turnoff. There were car tracks in the dirt, and they looked fresh. Since he hadn't seen another car for a while, he took that as a sign Gerard actually might have headed this way. He took his phone out of his pocket and checked it again. Still no signal. He was getting ready to disappear into the Ouachita Mountains with a man he didn't really know—chasing after a serial killer who *might* have taken this route and *might* have Kate. And no one had his back. All his years of training screamed at him. This was stupid. One of the dumbest things he'd ever done.

He walked back to the SUV and got in.

"Let's go," he said to Bobby.

The car bounced and jolted so much Kate felt bruises forming on her hips and back. She tried to steady herself with her arms, but it was nearly impossible. She prayed that God would tell her when to make her escape. Would Gerard hear the trunk open? Would he see her? Would he chase her? The thoughts in her head bounced around just like the car that jerked her body unmercifully.

Suddenly, Kate heard a large clap of thunder and the loud din of rain. Not just light rain, a deluge. The car slowed in an attempt to deal with the sudden change in the weather, and Kate grabbed the trunk opener. Somewhere inside her head she heard *Now!* She pulled the lever, and the trunk popped open. The rain poured down on her, making the trunk slippery. She twisted around and pushed herself out, falling onto the soaked ground. Rather than stand up, she scrambled across the mud on all fours and headed for the nearby tree line. She wanted to look back, to see if Gerard was behind her, but fear made her keep going, her eyes focused only on what was ahead.

He was so intent on the road in front of him it took a while for him to notice the trunk was open. He cursed loudly and slammed on the brakes, causing the car to slide sideways. He jammed the car into park and twisted the key, almost breaking it. The rain made everything so much harder. Why was it raining now? His original plan had been perfect. Grab Kate, drive into the mountains, and take her to a secluded spot where they wouldn't be interrupted. Killing her in town was too risky. Especially now, with Tony DeLuca hanging around. Tony was supposed to be dead, but somehow he'd survived. Now plans had to change again. Was God fighting him? He quickly dismissed the thought. If there really was a supreme being, He would have stopped him by now. Would have struck him with lightning or something. If God could read people's minds, He knew his plans for Kate O'Brien. And a lot of other women whose lives now had an expiration date. He had to bring back the legend of the Blue-Eyed Killer. It was his destiny. He'd panicked and messed up with Kelly O'Brien. He'd had no idea there were two of them. He'd left Kate for dead, not realizing she was still breathing. He should have checked. Should have finished her off and moved the bodies. He'd never make that mistake again.

He got out of the car, a gun strapped to his chest and a large knife in his jacket pocket. He slammed the car door as hard as he could. His stomach was a hard knot of anger. He'd planned to take Kate somewhere special for their time together, but now she'd betrayed him. He should just kill her wherever he found her. Of course, if he did that, the other part of the plan would fail. He couldn't have that. Kate O'Brien was a thorn in his side. Somehow he had to get back to his original strategy. He'd make Kate suffer for interfering. Teach her that nothing could stop him. Especially someone chosen as a victim of the Blue-Eyed Killer.

He looked up at the sky, the rain running down his face like tears. Once the deed was done, he'd slip off the mountain unseen and start a new life. He was grateful to the man who'd helped him get out of prison and had planted Ann Barton's necklace. He'd even called the police in Garden City and directed them toward Malcolm. Poor Malcolm. Too bad he had to die. He'd wanted out. Wanted to walk away from the legend of the Blue-Eyed Killer. Of course, that could never be allowed. What if some day he'd told the truth? He had to be eliminated. All in all, it was for the best. If the Blue-Eyed Killer was going to rise again, it wouldn't happen through a weak, frightened man like Malcolm. He'd lost the thrill of the hunt. The thirst for blood. Malcolm had paid the ultimate price for his betrayal. Actually, he'd enjoyed slitting Malcolm's throat. Now he was in first place. Not an apprentice any longer. He was the master.

But right now, he had to concentrate on Kate. He looked around him, trying to see through the heavy rain. She was out there somewhere and he would find her. Then he'd set the record straight.

He cursed her name, squared his shoulders, and took off into the trees.

CHAPTER
SIXTEEN

"How far do we drive on this road?" Tony asked, holding on to the dashboard, trying not to bounce out of his seat.

Before Bobby could respond, the skies opened up and rain started coming down in torrents. "We've got to get up this mountain as soon as we can!" he yelled at Tony, trying to be heard over the sound of rain hitting the roof of the SUV. "When it rains this hard, it runs down the mountain like a flood. It's dangerous."

Tony didn't answer, just prayed silently. The tires slipped and skidded beneath them, but Bobby kept going. He had more guts and determination than Tony had given him credit for.

Both men were quiet as Bobby fought to keep the SUV on the road. Then Tony remembered Bobby saying something about having to walk after the road ran out. That would be suicide. Any confidence he'd had in Bobby's plan slipped away.

He was just getting ready to question Bobby when he noticed something ahead. Although it was almost impossible to see through the downpour, there was definitely a large object on the side of the road. He squinted through the rain. It was green, but it wasn't a tree.

"Stop!" he yelled at Bobby.

Bobby applied the brakes tentatively. Tony could tell he was trying to keep them from spinning out. Thankfully, he brought the vehicle to a stop without incident. Tony pushed open his door and got out, running through the mud, his gun in his hand. The green thing was a car, pulled off the road. Someone had tried to park it behind the trees so it wouldn't be seen, but it looked as if the sliding mud had moved it out a few feet, making it visible. It was a Camry. Tony stayed low as he approached the car. Was Gerard inside? And Kate?

He crept up next to the driver's-side door and waited a few seconds before standing upright, his gun pointed at the window. With the windows wet and foggy, it was impossible to see inside. He grabbed the door handle. It was unlocked. He yanked it open and braced himself, but no one was in the car.

Tony looked carefully through the front and back seats. Nothing. Then he pulled the trunk release. Praying he wouldn't find Kate's body, he walked around to the back of the car. Thankfully, the trunk was empty. Tony saw some shredded gray duct tape lying on the floor next to several spots of blood.

"She was here," Tony said to himself. "But where is she now?" He shivered, but he wasn't sure if it was because he'd left his jacket in the SUV or because he was anxious about what might be happening to Kate. He looked carefully through the trunk one more time. Something shiny caught his eye. Stuffed into the corner was a little piece of silver.

Tony tugged at it and pulled out a bracelet. Kate's bracelet. Not only was she alive, she'd left him a message. Now he needed to find her before it was too late.

"Anyone else hear from Tony?" Batterson asked Mark. "I can't get him to pick up."

The deputy shook his head. "Not that I know of. I've tried and tried to reach him. I don't think he's getting our calls."

"Or he's ignoring us."

"Tony wouldn't do that, Chief. He's a professional. You know that."

Batterson emitted a sound that reminded Mark of a growl. It made him uneasy. He'd seen Batterson upset, but this was something new.

"A professional who ignores protocol? No. When I get my hands on him, he'll be sorry."

Mark didn't say anything. Batterson loved his people. He loved Tony. Frankly, right now he was certain Batterson was more worried about Tony's safety than his commitment to procedure. But he would never admit to that.

"Wanna see the note he left me?" Batterson asked. "Obviously he was afraid to talk to me directly. His cowardly way of letting me and local law enforcement know where he'd gone." He shook his head. "I contacted the authorities near Shelter Cove. Officials are planning to go after them. They've got people who know that area like the back of their hands. They'll bring them out. I'm sure of it."

"Are you going out there?"

"Not yet. It's not my jurisdiction. I don't want to step on any toes . . . unless I have to."

Before Mark could respond, the phone rang. Batterson held up one finger, a sign for Mark to stay put. As Batterson listened to whoever was on the other side, his face began to turn red, a sure sign of trouble. Then he stood up.

Mark wished he could just leave. When Batterson got angry, usually whoever was close to him at the time paid the price.

When Batterson finally said something, the words shot out of his mouth like shotgun blasts. "What kind of law enforcement officers can't pursue a criminal because they might get a little wet? You people better get off your rear ends and find my witness and my agent, or I'm coming down there—and you won't like it. You understand me?" With that, he slammed down the phone with so much force Mark was pretty sure he heard the casing crack.

Trying to keep a straight face, Mark said, "Problem, Chief?"

After a stream of curse words that could curl a sailor's hair, Batterson plopped back down in his chair. He took a deep breath, as if trying to cleanse himself from the anger that had seemingly overtaken him. "It's raining in Arkansas so I guess the pansies out there can't go up the mountain to look for O'Brien and DeLuca."

Mark cleared his throat, carefully forming his next words. "I have a friend who lives in the area. He says when it rains hard it causes flash flooding and the mountain roads can become treacherous. Maybe that's why they're waiting."

Batterson's eyebrows shot up. "I've chased bad guys through sewers. A little rain? Really? Is that the kind of people we have to count on now?" He clapped his hands together. "Maybe I *will* drive down there and show them what law enforcement *should* be."

Since it wasn't really their case, Mark was pretty sure how Batterson would be received, but he kept his mouth shut. With everything going on in St. Louis, he knew Batterson couldn't afford to be away right now. He took his responsibilities very seriously. He'd stay put no matter how much he wanted to rush down there, straighten everyone out, and make sure Tony was safe.

"So now what, Chief?" he asked.

"I don't know. I guess we wait. For now." He shoved the piece of paper he'd been toying with toward Mark. "Read that. Tell me what you think."

Another land mine. Mark tentatively picked up the note and read it.

Chief,

I'm with the owner of the resort in Shelter Cove. He saw Gerard and Kate head into the mountains. He knows the roads up there. I know I'm supposed to wait for backup, but I'm afraid if I do that, Kate will be lost. I'm going after her. I'll leave my phone on in case you want to call and yell at me. If you can't get me, it's because the service out here is so bad. I'll contact you when I can.

If you decide I'm done, I can accept that. I just couldn't stand by and watch Kate die if I thought I could save her.

Serving under you has been one of the greatest honors of my life.

Tony

Mark took a deep breath and put the letter down on Batterson's desk. "Is he right? Is he done?"

Batterson grabbed the piece of paper and slammed it down in front of himself. "Of course not, and he knows it. Unless this whole thing goes south. Then I might not have much choice."

"All you can do is the best you can do," Mark said with a half smile. "You've told us that many times."

"And I was right. If he saves her, it would certainly help his case. Let's hope things work out for him."

"And for Kate O'Brien," Mark said.

Batterson took a deep breath and let it out slowly. "Amen," he said. "Amen."

Kate ran as fast as she could in her bare feet, but the wet ground caused her to slip time and time again. Her feet were cut and bruised, but she had to keep going. Besides the terrible conditions outside, she couldn't seem to control her body. Not only was it almost numb with fear, it shook violently, as if it were operating outside of her own impulses and will. The last time she'd fallen, she cut her lip on a broken tree trunk sticking out of the ground. Although she could feel the warm blood oozing from her wound, she didn't have time to worry about it. She had to get away from Alan Gerard. At least she assumed it was him. She hadn't seen his face yet. Not in Shelter Cove and not when she'd jumped out of the back of the car.

Even though the rain made progress difficult, Kate was thankful for it. The downpour helped to hide her and wash away her footprints. For now, she just ran blindly, trying to put distance between herself and Gerard. She had no cell phone, no way to reach anyone. All she could do was pray that someone would find her and get her to safety.

It seemed as if she'd run for miles, but there was no way to know for sure. She had no idea how far away she was from Gerard, but her strength finally gave out. She found a massive tree with a large trunk and decided to rest under it for a little while. She needed to come up with some kind of plan. Right now, she was just running blindly. And that wasn't smart.

Ever since she'd awakened in that trunk, images of Gerard and Kelly on the day Kelly died kept running through her head. The worst one was of the look of betrayal on Kelly's face. She'd survived a terrible car crash, and now some psychopath was going to rip her future away? Her wedding? Her children? Her career? Kate shook her head as tears flowed down her face, mixing with the rain. It wasn't fair. Where was God? Why hadn't He saved them?

She covered her face with her hands and sobbed. When she was done, she actually felt a little better. As she tried to peer through the rain, she couldn't stop thinking about Tony. Was he out there somewhere trying to find her? She knew she had to trust God, but ever since the attack, it had been hard. If God wasn't there when she and Kelly needed Him, how could she believe He'd be with her now?

"I'm sorry, God," she whispered. "Tony said I needed to face the truth. And the truth is, my faith has been shaken. That's why I . . . why I almost ended everything. If I can't trust You, who can I trust?"

She didn't really expect to hear a voice speak to her, but the lack of any kind of response only confirmed her feeling of being alone. Abandoned. She put her hands out in front of her and stared at her wrists. Tony's voice drifted through her mind. Almost as if he was right there with her. *"I would be injured, Kate. If anything happened to you, I would be injured."*

She took a deep breath, stepped away from the tree trunk, and started moving again. She wasn't alone. Even if no one else cared about her, Tony did.

Kate looked around her, trying to decide which way to go. She wouldn't give up yet. She decided to head into the thickest part of the woods. It would be hard for Gerard to find her there. She gathered her courage and took off.

CHAPTER
SEVENTEEN

"We need to pull over for a while." Bobby glanced over at Tony. "If we don't, we won't make it."

"Then let me out. I'm not giving up."

Just then, the SUV began to slip backward on the wet road. Tony held on tight as Bobby fought to bring it under control. Although it stayed on the road, the back tires became mired in thick mud. Bobby turned off the engine, and both men got out. This time Tony remembered to grab his jacket. It definitely helped against the chilly rain. As they assessed the area, Tony wondered how in the world he'd gotten into this mess. He needed help. A search team. A helicopter that could see what they couldn't. He had no idea what was going on back in Shelter Cove. Was anyone coming to assist them?

The SUV was stuck, and stuck good. With just Bobby's help, it would be impossible to get it out. Tony was a few feet from the back bumper when he heard a shout. He sloshed through the mud until he found Bobby hanging over the side of a steep drop-off, holding on to an exposed tree root for dear life. Tony plopped down on his stomach and reached down to grab Bobby's hand and pull him up. It took several attempts because Bobby had a hard time getting enough traction to push himself back onto the road. When Tony finally managed to get him back over the edge, Bobby lay in the mud for a few seconds, panting hard, letting the rain wash away the muck on his face.

"Sorry," he gasped out finally. "I don't know what happened. One minute I was standing, and the next I was hanging off the side of the road."

"Not your fault," Tony said. "The road has nearly washed away. We need to get back in the car and decide what to do."

Both men got to their feet, wet and covered with mud. They trekked back to the SUV. Although Tony tried to scrape off as much muck as he could, it was a lost cause. Then they climbed inside, dirtying up the interior of Bobby's SUV. Tony felt bad about it, but Bobby didn't even seem to notice.

"Look," Tony said, "I'm sorry I got you into this. Why don't you stay here while I look for Kate? This thing is stuck fast. You should be safe."

Bobby started to protest, but Tony held up his hand.

"This isn't your fight. You've done enough, Bobby, and I appreciate it."

"You don't understand," Bobby said. "There's a cabin not far from here. A place where we could get out of the rain. Without me, you'll never find it."

"I'm more interested in finding Kate than . . ."

"That's what I'm saying," Bobby interrupted. "It's the only property nearby. If she finds it, she might hole up there. Besides, if the police come looking for us, they could see the cabin from the air. Running around out here—they'll have a tough time locating us."

Tony turned Bobby's reasoning over in his mind. How would Kate know about the cabin? Stumbling across it seemed more like luck and less like reality.

"I don't know," he said.

"But she could be anywhere, Tony," Bobby insisted. "We can't search the entire mountain. What if we leave a note in the SUV? Tell her where we are? Then at least that would give her two different chances to find us."

"I . . . I guess we could. But what if Gerard discovers our note before Kate does?"

Bobby shrugged. "I guess it's a chance we have to take. You're armed, right? It's not like we're defenseless."

"Like Kate," Tony said quietly. Then he nodded. "Okay. Before we get out again, let me try my cell phone one more time. I'd really like to let the people on the ground know where we are."

Bobby waited while Tony reached inside his jacket pocket. Thankfully, his phone was in a protective case, so his excursion outside shouldn't have damaged it. But when Tony put his hand into the pocket where the phone was supposed to be, it wasn't there. Had he moved it?

"What's wrong?" Bobby asked.

"I . . . I thought I put my phone in this pocket, but it's gone." Tony began patting the jacket, looking in other pockets. He also checked his jeans. Nothing. Then he began to search the front seat. Maybe it had fallen out. Unfortunately, it wasn't there.

"When's the last time you used it?"

"I . . . I'm not sure. I think it was right before we took the last turnoff. I'm sure I put it in my inside jacket pocket. I wanted to keep it protected from the rain."

Bobby got an odd look on his face and nervously cleared his throat. "Maybe it fell out when you were helping me. When I slipped."

"I've got to see if I can find it," Tony said. "Stay here." He got out of the vehicle and sloshed through the mud once again, carefully watching the ground, hoping to see his phone. He searched everywhere he'd been, even looking over the edge of the drop-off, hoping it had gotten caught on something rather than ending up somewhere near the bottom of the mountain. Since Bobby didn't have a cell phone, they were completely out of luck. Suddenly, the cabin scenario began to make more sense. Maybe they'd find a phone there.

Tony stood in the rain for a moment, trying to assess his situation. As he counted all the ways he'd messed up, he came to one stunning conclusion: If he could go back and choose, he'd do the very same things all over again. Right now saving Kate was all that mattered.

Kate's entire body hurt. She needed to rest again, so she slumped down under another large tree, hoping it would help hide her. She didn't care that she was wallowing in mud, it was better than being inside that awful car. So far, there was no sign of Gerard. She was terrified, afraid that at any moment he'd come barreling through the trees. She could feel her heart pounding in her chest as if it were trying to escape her body. She had no idea what to do now. Should she try going down the mountain? It seemed to make sense. She needed help, and traveling farther up seemed silly. Except when she realized that Gerard would probably assume she'd head down to where she could find help and protection. Was he waiting out there? Counting on her to make that decision? Frankly, she had no idea where she was. Surrounded by trees, it was impossible to tell. If she could find a clearing, she might get a better sense of her location, but that could be dangerous. He might see her.

Kate's mind wandered toward Tony again. Where was he? Surely by now he knew she'd been taken. Her watch was back home on her nightstand so she had no idea what time it was, but she was certain someone had noticed she hadn't shown up at the café. Bella certainly would, and she'd be worried. Bella was protective when it came to Kate. A mother hen with a big heart and an iron will. She'd surely have gone to Kate's house to check on her, so people had to know something was wrong. She was certain Tony would do everything he could to find her—to make sure she was safe. If she could just stay away from Gerard long enough for help to come, she might make it out of this alive.

A crack of lightning made her jump. Which way should she go? If she stayed here, she was a sitting duck.

Finally, she decided to head down the mountain. If she could find her way back to a main road, it was possible she might see a car. Even though it was raining hard, surely someone would drive by. As she sat there, soaked to the skin and shivering, more than anything she wanted Gerard out of her life forever. He was like some kind of lingering illness that wouldn't let go. Kate wanted a life again, and as long as Gerard was alive, she wasn't sure that would ever happen.

She slowly struggled to her feet. As she looked around, she tried to figure out which direction to take. The ground was level here, so she couldn't be certain which way was up and which way was down. As she was deciding her next move, she heard something behind her. A rustling in the midst of the rain. The breaking of a tree limb. Had Gerard found her? She began to run but fell once again. As she tried to get back up on her feet, someone grabbed her from behind and she screamed. Although the knowledge that she was going to die should have been the only thing on her mind, for some reason all she could think about at that moment was Tony.

CHAPTER
EIGHTEEN

"You upset about something, Sarge?"

Kevin noticed Leon had been especially pensive ever since the feds hit town. They had Ann Barton's body, and Dorothy Fisher's grave had been covered up again. However, the area around the grave was still a crime scene and would be until they'd gone over everything with a fine-toothed comb. The FBI had no more need for the police, so as far as their department was concerned, everything was back to normal. Or was it? Leon leaned back in his cheap office chair, his feet resting on top of his old scarred desk. Kevin was surprised Leon had found an empty space. His desk was always covered with case files. Leon was a bulldog when it came to catching law-breakers. Minor crimes. Major crimes. Didn't make any difference. Each situation was a challenge he took seriously. But nothing bothered him more than the Blue-Eyed Killer case.

Leon sighed deeply and looked out the window next to him. "It just doesn't feel right," he said in a low voice.

"What do you mean?"

"First of all, burying a body in someone else's plot isn't easy. I mean, it can be done, but . . ."

"Well, the killer could have looked for a fresh grave. One that was easy to dig up."

Leon's right eyebrow shot up as he looked at Kevin. "So you're saying the Blue-Eyed Killer murdered Ann Barton and then carried her remains into a cemetery, dug up a grave, and dumped the body because it was so easy?"

Kevin felt his face flush. "Of course not, Sarge. Seems like someone would have seen him. But, well, he could have done it at night, right? If he worked in the dark, no one would notice."

"I suppose. Still, it was a pretty bold thing to do. I'm surprised no one noticed that the ground had been disturbed." Leon grunted. "And why not put Ann's necklace with her body? Why bury it in the dirt a few feet away?"

Kevin thought for a moment. "He probably meant to keep it. You know, as a keepsake or something. But he dropped it without realizing it."

Leon paused. "Maybe," he said finally. "I guess that makes some sense, although it's pretty careless, and B.E.K. has never been sloppy. But why reveal Ann's whereabouts now? Gerard's claiming he's not the Blue-Eyed Killer, and the Bodine guy is dead. So who called the station? Who put that song sheet on the grave? The whole thing is screwy."

"I guess the feds know what they're doing," Kevin said. "They'll figure it out."

"I hope so." Leon grabbed a telephone book out of his desk drawer and began turning the pages.

"What are you looking for, Sarge?" Kevin asked.

"Just wonderin' if Dorothy Fisher has any relatives still living in Garden City. I'd like to know why the killer chose her grave."

Kevin shook his head and went back to filling out reports. When something didn't sit right with Leon, he'd go after it with a vengeance. It was useless to try to talk him out of it. Kevin had learned a long time ago that it was best to just leave him and let him follow his gut.

"Kate! Kate, it's me!"

Tony tightened his grip around her, trying to calm her, but Kate seemed to be fighting for her life. Finally, he managed to turn her around so she could see it was him.

She was soaked to the skin, clad only in sweatpants and a T-shirt, her feet bare and bleeding. Her hair was plastered against her head and her face was cut and bruised, but to Tony, she was still beautiful beyond belief. He chided himself for allowing such an inappropriate thought to enter his mind. The only thing that mattered was that he'd found her alive.

"It's me, Kate," he said again. "It's Tony. You're okay. I've got you."

Slowly the panic drained from her face, and a spark of recognition appeared in her eyes. "Tony? Is it really you?"

"Yeah, it's really me." She wrapped her arms around him, and he held her tightly against his chest. He could feel her tremble. "You're fine. It's going to be all right."

As he released her, she began to cry. "I . . . I thought . . ."

"I know. You thought I was Gerard. I'm sorry I frightened

you. I didn't want to yell your name because I didn't want to give away our location."

Kate took a shuddering breath and stepped back. "I'm sure my screaming took care of that," she said, her voice breaking. "I'm sorry."

Tony smiled at her. "Not your fault. You've been through a lot. I doubt anyone can hear us over the rain, anyway."

Although he wanted to reassure her, Tony wasn't certain his assessment was correct. If Gerard was anywhere nearby, he certainly could have heard Kate's scream. They needed to move out of this area as quickly as possible. If Gerard had a gun and was hidden among the trees, Kate was vulnerable.

For the first time, Kate looked past Tony and noticed Bobby.

"Bobby, is that you?" she asked. "Why are you here?"

Bobby smiled shyly. "I offered to come. I know the roads and thought maybe I could help."

Kate seemed touched. "Thanks, Bobby. I really appreciate it. You're a good friend."

"Look, we can stand here in the rain bonding, or we can get moving and try to find some help," Tony said.

"You're here alone?" Kate asked, looking panicked. "Didn't anyone come with you and Bobby?"

"No. I was supposed to wait for backup, but Bobby saw the man who took you drive up this way, so we decided not to wait. I was afraid we wouldn't find you in time." He reached over and pushed a wet lock of hair off of her face. "Don't worry. I'm sure help is on its way. We'll be fine."

"But . . . don't you know where the police are? Can't you call them?"

"Uh, no. Bobby doesn't have a cell phone, and I lost mine. Sorry."

Kate just stared at him, and Tony realized he wasn't giving her a reason to have much confidence in his ability to rescue her.

"Look, I told people where we would be and they know that you were abducted. Someone will be here soon, Kate. I'm sure of it."

"I doubt anyone will venture up here until the rain ends," Kate said. "The roads are too dangerous. We've had people stranded in these mountains before during heavy rains. Help won't come until the roads are passable."

Tony glanced around the area. "I had no idea a little rain would cause this many problems." He looked at Bobby. "Can you find that cabin from here?"

Bobby nodded. "Yeah. If we can get back to the road, we can follow it part of the way. From there, we take a path through the woods."

Tony frowned at him. "I can't believe someone built a cabin they couldn't reach by car. Sounds pretty inconvenient."

Bobby shrugged. "The owner wanted something isolated— and he got it. Built it a couple of years ago but only comes once a year to stay there. Rich people. I don't get it. Coulda just stayed at my place and saved himself a lot of money."

"Well, right now I'm grateful to him. Hope he won't mind us breaking in."

Bobby grinned. "We don't have to. I help watch over the place and get it ready for his visits. I have the key."

Even though their situation was still desperate, Tony smiled. "Bobby, you're a blessing in disguise. Lead the way."

Tony was amused to see that Bobby looked embarrassed. He really was thankful for this strange man who had turned out to be a lifesaver. If not for Bobby, Tony never would have found Kate. And now, also because of him, they could get out of the rain and into a place where they could hunker down until help came. He felt a little guilty for being suspicious of him earlier. Tony's training had taught him not to take anyone at face value. It was a quality that could protect him—but sometimes, if he didn't rein it in, it made it difficult to trust anyone.

"Shouldn't we head back to town?" Kate asked, still shivering. "You drove here, right?"

Tony shook his head. "Car's stuck in the mud. I'm afraid we can't get it out until the rain stops and the ground dries some. Besides, if we tried, we'd be right out in the open—easy pickings. Visible if Gerard is looking for us. I think we need to get to the cabin. Look for a phone. Give ourselves a chance to regroup."

Kate seemed to hesitate. "Okay, it's just . . . I don't know. I think we need people. People who can get us safely off this mountain. Who can locate Gerard."

"Look, let's debate this later," Tony said. "Once we're dry and . . ." He turned to look at Bobby. "I don't suppose this guy has food in his cabin?"

"Yeah, there's some food," Bobby said. "Nothing fresh, but there's nonperishable stuff. Most of it's from last year, but it should be okay."

Tony led Kate over to an old tree stump and told her to sit down. He quickly removed his shoes and socks. "I'd give you my shoes, but they're much too big for you," he said.

"Put these socks on. They're wet, but they'll help to protect your feet."

"Thanks, Tony." She quickly pulled on the socks, then gingerly stood up.

"Lead the way, Bobby," Tony said after he put his shoes back on. "Let's get out of here."

Tony put his arm around Kate so she could lean against him, and the trio began to make their way through the woods, Tony praying they could get to safety before Gerard found them.

He stood behind a tree and watched as they headed toward the cabin. Even though he'd had to adjust to unfortunate circumstances, everything was falling perfectly into place. Soon he'd have Kate all to himself.

CHAPTER
NINETEEN

Kate's feet hurt so much she had to press her lips together to keep from crying out. She was determined not to slow them down. They had to find someplace safe. Why did it have to rain today? Arkansas in the spring was wet, but couldn't today have been a dry day? They could have driven off the mountain and back to Shelter Cove. Did Gerard plan this? Did he watch the weather reports, hoping he could get her up the mountain before the rains began? Although it was a stretch, in a way it made sense. He needed time to torture her. To kill her slowly. He liked to make his victims suffer. She already knew something about that.

She yelped when she stubbed her toe against a rock. Tony stopped walking and looked down at her.

"Are you okay?" he asked.

She nodded, trying to smile. "Sorry, wasn't watching where I was going, I guess. I'm fine."

Rather than start again, Tony appeared to study her. "You're in pain, aren't you?"

"I'm fine," she said again through gritted teeth.

Bobby had stopped and was also looking at her with concern. Kate realized that these two men had put themselves in danger to help her. Although she tried to fight it, her emotions spilled over and she started to cry. The past few hours had been so terrifying, and even though she was still in danger, she was incredibly grateful not to be alone.

"That's it," Tony said, his voice raspy. "I'll carry you the rest of the way."

"Don't be silly." Kate shook her head. "I'm not a child. I'll be fine." Although having him carry her sounded wonderful, Kate didn't want to be seen as weak. She took a deep breath and fought back her raging emotions. "I'm just reacting to . . . to everything. Being in Gerard's trunk . . . It was awful."

Tony frowned at her. "Did you actually see Gerard?" he asked.

Kate shook her head slowly. "No. Someone hit me over the head right after you called. I wasn't even out of bed yet. Then I woke up in the trunk of a car. Eventually I found the release latch and jumped out. I never saw him, but who else could it be?"

"Maybe it's one of his followers."

"I don't understand how anyone, including Gerard, could know I was here." Kate had been wondering about that ever since the kidnapping. Weren't the Marshals the only people who were aware of her location?

"Uh, maybe we could finish this conversation in the cabin?" Bobby said.

Kate and Tony looked at him. Bobby was not an attractive man when he was dry. But wet he looked like a drenched basset hound. Kate had to bite her bottom lip to keep from laughing. Since she'd just cried like a baby, giggling now seemed a little manic.

"You're right," Tony said. "Let's keep going." He peered closely at Kate. "Are you sure you can go on? You probably don't weigh one hundred pounds wet. I could easily carry you."

She forced a smile. "I'm fine. Let's get a move on. I'm forgetting what *dry* feels like."

Tony seemed reluctant to allow her to walk on her own, but Kate was determined to hold herself together. She'd survived this long. She had no intention of allowing Tony and Bobby to babysit her.

Once they started walking again, Kate literally had to bite her lip to keep from moaning.

"Thanks for seeing me, Mr. Fisher," Leon said.

The man who'd opened the door and let him inside his dilapidated house seemed too frail to be breathing. Now he sat in an old orange recliner with torn fabric, staring at Leon with large watery eyes, his face gray and his lips thin and pale.

"Before this week, ain't no one asked about Darrell for over twenty years. Had to find out what 'choo wanted." His eyes narrowed. "Do you know where he is?"

Leon shook his head. "I'm sorry, I don't. You said on the phone that you and your nephew are the only relatives Dorothy had who are still living?"

"Yep. Far as I know."

Leon was trying to ignore the stench in the house. It was almost overpowering. A combination of boiled cabbage, stale meat, and urine. That last smell seemed to be coming from the couch where Leon sat. Empty food cartons littered a rickety coffee table, and magazines were stacked up next to Fred Fisher's chair. The house looked as tired as its owner.

"You know we had to dig up your sister's gravesite?"

When Fisher nodded, it reminded Leon of a broken bobble-head doll.

"Yep. They called me before they did it. I told them it was okay. I mean, Dorothy's gone, right? Diggin' up her grave? I don't think she'd mind, so why would I?"

"Do you know what we found?"

"Sure, they told me all about it. Ann Barton. She was a sweet little thing. It's so sad."

"You knew Ann?"

"Sure. Everyone in town knew her. She worked over at the market. Darrell was really upset when she went missing. She was always nice to him when most people wasn't."

Leon nodded. "I've heard the same things about her. People seemed to like her."

"You didn't know her?"

Leon shook his head. "No, I didn't. I only met her family . . . after."

Fisher cocked his head to the side and stared at Leon, his eyebrows knit together in a frown. "Why are you here, Sergeant?"

"I just wanted to know more about Dorothy. I'm wondering why anyone would pick her grave as a resting place for Ann. Do you have any ideas about that?"

Fisher looked up at the ceiling for a few moments. Leon assumed it meant he was thinking, but he couldn't be sure. He resisted the urge to glance up. Finally, the elderly man lowered his gaze and met Leon's eyes.

"I truly have no idea. Dorothy seemed to draw trouble to herself, though. She was my sister, and I loved her, but she had her problems. When her boyfriend, Darrell's father, passed away, she started drinkin'. Runnin' around. Didn't spend much time with Darrell. He . . . he wasn't a happy child—or a happy teenager. When Dorothy died, I think he was . . . relieved."

"How did she die, Mr. Fisher?"

The old man waved his hand at Leon. "Fred. Just call me Fred."

"Okay, how did she die, Fred?"

The old man repositioned himself in his ratty recliner. He was not much more than skin and bones, and it was obvious he was in pain. "Got drunk and fell down the stairs. At least it was quick."

"And what happened to Darrell?"

"He and that friend of his took off right after the funeral. Never seen 'em since."

"His friend?"

Fred nodded. "Can't remember his name now. Sorry. Might be somewhere in Darrell's things."

"His things?"

Fred nodded. "After Dorothy died, I found a metal box full of stuff that belonged to Darrell. He hid it under loose boards in his closet. Dorothy would take stuff from the house and sell it for booze. I guess Darrell felt he had to hide his belongings. Nothing left in there worth anything, though. Even so, it's about all I have left of my sister and my nephew."

Leon took a deep breath. "Fred, would you let me see that box? I'll be careful with it."

Fred grunted. "Sure. Didn't tell that other policeman about the box. Something about him I didn't trust. But you can take the box if you want. That boy ain't comin' back. Not while I'm alive, anyway." Fred pointed toward the hallway. "It's up in the attic. Just pull on that rope and the ladder will come down."

"Wait a minute. Did you say there was another police officer who asked about Darrell?"

"Yeah, four or five days ago. After the feds asked me if they could dig up Dorothy's grave. This guy wanted me to tell him about Darrell and his friend. Told him just what I told you. That was about it."

Leon was aware that someone from the FBI had been by to see Fred about the gravesite, but was surprised he'd asked about Darrell. Maybe someone else was wondering about the connection just like he was.

Although Leon wasn't sure Darrell had left anything behind that would be helpful, he had to know why a serial killer would put his victim in Dorothy Fisher's grave. Leon couldn't let go of the notion that there was a reason behind it. Something that might be important. Linda had told him more than once that he was like a dog with a bone when it came to the Ann Barton case. She was right.

He got up and walked halfway down the hallway until he found the rope. He pulled it gently and, sure enough, an old wooden ladder slid down to the floor—along with several years of dust, making him cough.

"If you make a mess, you gotta clean it up," Fred called out.

Even though Fred's house was probably the definition of the word *mess*, Leon assured Fred he'd take care of it. He gingerly climbed up the old ladder until he could see into the attic. Thankfully, the metal box was only a couple of feet away. Leon leaned in and grabbed it, scooting it near him. Once he had hold of the handle, he carefully backed down the ladder. Then he pushed the ladder back up and the attic door closed. He walked down the hall to the kitchen. The smell of old cabbage was even stronger there, and he had to fight to keep from gagging. The source of the stink was easy to find. An old pot of boiled cabbage sat in the sink. Had probably been there for a week or more. He finally found some yellowed paper towels, turned on the water in the sink, and dampened them. After cleaning off the metal box, he wadded up several other towels so he could wipe up the dust on the old wooden floor in the hallway. Before he left the room, he opened the door to the refrigerator. Some old dried-up apples, a bowl of something that looked like lumpy oatmeal, and a bottle of mustard. That was it. Leon closed the door quietly. It was obvious the old man needed help.

After cleaning up the hallway the best he could, Leon took the box back into the living room.

"Put it there," Fred said, pointing at the coffee table full of trash.

Leon pushed some of the empty boxes and wrappers aside and set down the box. Then he unlatched it and opened the lid. Inside he found several items. Some assorted papers, baseball cards, a couple of pens, some Valentine's cards, two high-school yearbooks, and two small notebooks.

Fred leaned over and pointed at one of the yearbooks. "Wondered where that was. Darrell's in there," he said. "Don't got no other pictures of him. Used to, but I don't know what happened to 'em. Musta thrown 'em out, I guess."

Leon opened the book and thumbed through it. In the back, he found a list of students. Sure enough, Darrell R. Fisher was listed. Leon turned to the page and found him. An unremarkable young man with dead eyes stared back at him. Leon immediately felt compassion for the boy. For many kids, high school was like being thrown into a large pool of sharks. Children could be cruel, and it was easy for kids to believe that whatever happened in high school set the course for their lives. Of course, nothing could be further from the truth. Leon remembered running into the head cheerleader from his high school ten years after graduation. She was working at a fast-food joint while trying to raise two kids by herself after her football-hero boyfriend dumped her for someone younger. Her haughty attitude in high school had been replaced with eyes full of quiet desperation. Real life had trampled her high-school persona into dust.

On the other side of the coin, the high-school geek with the big glasses who carried a briefcase to school now owned a chain of real estate companies across the country. He lived in the nicest house in town and had married a beautiful woman.

High school wasn't all that important. A flash in the pan that meant nothing when it came to the rest of your real life.

If only young people could realize that, Leon was convinced it would greatly reduce the number of teenage suicides.

"That's Darrell," Fred said, pointing to the photo Leon stared at. Fred reached over and pulled out the other yearbook. Leon noticed for the first time that it was from a different school.

"Holcomb High School?" Leon asked. "Did Darrell attend Holcomb, too?"

Fred shook his head. "Nah, his good-for-nothin' friend went there. Those two boys were thick as thieves. Always gettin' into trouble. I think that kid talked Darrell into leavin' town."

"But you can't remember his name?" Leon asked.

"Nah, it's been too long. Besides, Darrell didn't call him by his name. Had some nickname for him. Just can't quite remember it."

Leon put the books back in the box. "You sure you don't mind if I borrow this for a while?"

Fred shrugged. "Like I said, you can keep it. I don't need it no more."

Leon stood up and stretched out his hand. Fred shook it. "Thanks, Fred. I really appreciate your help. If I find out anything, I'll let you know."

"You do that, Sergeant. Glad to have the company."

As Leon left, he wondered how many more days Fred Fisher had left on earth. At least he could make sure they were lived a little better. He and Linda would call their church and get some people to clean Fred's house and bring him some food. He knew Linda would probably cook up a storm. She had many talents, and cooking was certainly one of them.

Even though Fred seemed like a proud man, Leon was pretty sure he'd accept the help. He was obviously ill and needed assistance.

As Leon walked to his car, he wasn't certain he'd gotten any answers to his questions about Dorothy Fisher, but at least he'd become aware of Fred's situation.

For now, that would have to be enough.

CHAPTER
TWENTY

Warren's car sat lodged between two trees. It was impossible to keep a vehicle on the road when the rain poured down like sheets of glass. He pulled on his all-weather coat, flipped up his hood, and checked his gun. Thankfully, he had extra ammunition with him, so he put two more loaded magazines into his pocket. Thirty rounds might be overkill, but he had to be prepared. This had to end today, and Warren was determined to see it through.

He got out of his car and began to trudge through the rain and the mud, his loaded gun in its holster. Today was a day of reckoning. Warren was acting as judge and jury—and that was fine with him.

Tony was beginning to wonder if they'd ever reach the cabin. He prayed for the rain to stop. Once the LEOs at the bottom of the mountain knew it was safe, they would come. But could they find his small group in time? Or would Kate's abductor find them first?

As they walked, he began to think through everything that had happened. Someone was after Kate, and he couldn't be certain who it was. Kate believed it was Alan Gerard, and Tony tended to think the same way. But what if they were wrong? What if it was someone else connected to B.E.K.? Maybe Gerard really was a copycat trying to keep the Blue-Eyed Killer alive. Did that mean he was after Kate now? One thing that really bothered him was Gerard's knowledge of the song, something not released to the public until after he was arrested. How could he have found out about it? Could he have gotten inside information? If so, from whom? Gerard, a lowly janitor at the college, didn't seem like some kind of mastermind with followers in the police department. It was clear they were missing something, but Tony had no idea what it was. He hated being in the dark. It made it harder to keep Kate safe.

Realizing his mind had wandered, Tony forced himself to concentrate on his surroundings, sweeping the area with his gun every few minutes, making sure no one was following them.

After they got to the cabin, he would have to figure out their next move. Would they be easy targets once they were inside? Or were they more at risk out in the open—like they were now? It was impossible to be sure.

"There it is!" Bobby called out, pointing toward a rustic structure up ahead.

Tony started to chastise him for being so loud, but it was too late. He quickly scanned the area around them but didn't see anyone. As they neared the cabin, Tony stopped walking and quietly called Bobby's name. When he turned around, Tony motioned for him to come to where he and Kate stood.

"Let me check things out first," he said. "Wait here with Kate."

Bobby nodded and reached into the pocket of his jeans. "Here's the key."

Tony took it from him and noticed Kate staring at him. He could see the fear in her eyes. "I'll be right back," he said, trying to sound confident. "I just need to make sure no one's in there. We don't want any surprises." He took his extra gun out of his inside pocket and handed it to Bobby, who looked like Tony had just given him a rabid skunk.

"I . . . I don't know anything about guns," Bobby said, his voice higher than normal.

Tony quickly showed him how to take off the safety and fire the gun. "You probably won't have to use it," he said. "But it would help to know that we're both armed."

Bobby stood there holding the gun like he was afraid of catching a disease from it. Kate limped up next to him and reached out her hand.

"I'll take it, Bobby," she said softly.

Two pink spots appeared on Bobby's cheeks. "No, I can do this. I won't let you down."

Tony felt sorry for the guy. Taking the gun was obviously a big stretch for him. "You just pretend you're one of those guys in the books you like to read."

The tightness in Bobby's face relaxed a bit. "Okay. That actually helps a little." He frowned. "Where do I put it?"

"For now, keep it in your hand. Once we know everything's okay, just stick it in your waistband. Around the back. With the safety on, please. Just be aware of what's around you. Be safe. And Bobby . . ."

Bobby, who had been staring at the gun, looked up.

"If you have to fire your weapon, make it count. Do you understand what I mean?"

Some of the color drained from the man's face, but he nodded. "Yes. I understand."

As Bobby and Kate waited, Tony approached the cabin. Actually, it was rather nice. Looked well-made and sturdy despite being small. Tony slid the key into the lock on the thick wooden door, unlocking it. Then he put the key in his pocket, gripped his gun with both hands, and pushed the door open with his foot. When he stepped across the threshold, he swept the gun around the room. It was dark inside, but it didn't look like anyone was there. He reached behind him and flipped the light switch, praying the lights would come on. They didn't. The cabin probably had a generator, but either it was off or it had been removed.

He moved a little deeper into the interior. There was one big room that made up the living room and the kitchen. He opened three doors and found a bathroom and two small bedrooms. He cleared them and then checked the kitchen. No one hiding there, either.

Tony went back to the front door and motioned to Bobby and Kate to come in. Bobby checked his gun and then carefully put it in his waistband. Then he supported Kate as they made their way toward the cabin. Once they were inside, Tony closed and locked the door while Bobby helped Kate over to a nearby chair.

"There should be some battery-powered lamps in the

kitchen," Bobby said. "I didn't check the last time I was here, but I assume they're where he left them." He hurried over to the kitchen cabinets and opened one of the top doors, pulling out three lamps, which he turned on. Light blazed from them, dispelling the darkness caused by the clouds and rain that blocked the sun.

Now that he could see, Tony checked out their surroundings more closely. The small kitchen was at the front of the cabin, near the door. Although it was very basic, the wood cabinets were nice. Oak. Well made. There was a small fridge and a stove. Both newer models. A few feet away sat a kitchen table and four chairs. Again, made out of oak and with red pads on the chairs for comfort. The table seemed to separate the kitchen from the living room, which was decorated with furniture that looked new, as well. The patterned red and brown fabric of the couch matched two overstuffed chairs that sat across from it. A coffee table separated them. Over in the corner was a rocking chair and a smaller table near the window. The interior walls were painted a light beige. The cabin was attractive yet comfortable. Definitely furnished by a man. No touch of anything feminine.

"The lamps help," Tony said. "But where's the electricity?"

Bobby shrugged. "The guy who owns this place has a generator, but I didn't see it outside. He'll probably bring it when he comes next month."

"So how could there be a phone?" Tony could feel his frustration rising. Why had Bobby allowed him to think they might be able to call for help?

"I . . . I wasn't sure if the generator was here. Sometimes Mike comes up early and prepares the cabin. Brings the generator and other stuff he'll need. I do have another idea, though. Come here. I'll show you."

Bobby pointed to one of the back bedrooms. After checking on Kate, who was slowly peeling off Tony's socks, he followed Bobby to the rear of the cabin. In the bedroom, Bobby opened the closet and pulled out a ratty blanket covering something that sat on a small table. It was an old ham radio.

"Bobby, this is no use to us without electricity."

"I may not be very *technical*," Bobby said, "but I do know that much." He leaned down and opened the door to a cabinet under the radio. "Mike keeps a battery pack here. Should be strong enough to power the radio and get us some help."

Tony's irritation with Bobby melted away. If he could reach someone on the radio, they could notify law enforcement to send help.

Bobby handed the pack to Tony, who grabbed a nearby chair and sat down in front of the radio. He started to plug the radio into the pack, but then he remembered Kate. He pushed down his excitement. First things first.

"Let me check around outside; make sure we're secure. Then I want to make certain Kate's okay. After that we can fiddle with the radio. It might take a while." He nodded at Bobby. "Good job. You've saved the day in more ways than one."

Bobby gave Tony a small smile. "I . . . I'm just glad I could help. Not much happens in Shelter Cove. This is the biggest adventure of my life. I should be thanking you."

Tony patted Bobby on the shoulder and went back into the living room, where Kate still sat in the same chair Bobby had helped her to. She was staring at her feet. Tony's heart dropped when he saw them. They were a mess. He couldn't figure out how she'd been able to get as far as she had.

"There's an old ham radio in the back room," he told her. "Hopefully, I'll be able to call for help. I'm not sure how long it will take, so I wanted to check on you first."

"Getting someone here to rescue us is the only real way to help me," she said. "Except . . . maybe you could get some hot water for my feet?"

Tony stared at her. Water? Did they have any?

"Under the sink in the kitchen," Bobby said from behind him. "Mike had me bring water up here when the weather got warm enough."

Tony walked over to the kitchen and opened the doors under the sink. Sure enough, there were several gallons of water, as well as some individual bottles. Even though he didn't plan on being here long, he was grateful they had something to drink.

He found a large plastic bowl and filled it with the water from one of the jugs. Then he carried it over to Kate.

"Sorry, it's not hot, but it's not cold, either. Lukewarm." He set down the bowl in front of her, and she gingerly lowered her feet into the water. The look on her face made it clear the water felt good.

"Thank you so much," she said with a smile. "Never thought a bowl of water could be such a blessing." She waved one of her hands at him. "Now get on that radio and get us out of here. I want to go home."

He nodded at her and strode over to the window. He didn't see anything that concerned him. He looked out the other windows but saw nothing that indicated anyone was in the vicinity. After he tried the radio, he'd take his gun and do a perimeter check. Of course, someone could hide in the trees and remain unseen. But all he could do was the best he could do. Advice Batterson frequently doled out to his deputies. He checked the door to make sure it was locked.

Satisfied as much as he could be for now, he went back to the radio, where Bobby waited.

"I . . . I'm not sure how this works," he told Tony.

"I've got a pretty good idea. My grandfather had an old ham radio. He tried to teach me about it, but I wasn't that interested. Wish I'd paid more attention, but I think I know enough to get it started."

Tony put the battery pack near the radio, pulled out the plug, and stuck it into the radio. Then, after taking a deep breath and sending up a desperate, silent prayer, he turned it on. Immediately, the radio came to life.

"Hallelujah," he said under his breath. Leaving it on the channel it was set to, Tony pressed the button on the microphone. "Hello? Is anyone out there? This is Deputy U.S. Marshal Tony DeLuca. Can anyone hear me?"

He released the button and waited. Nothing. He pushed the button again, saying the same thing. This time a voice came over the radio.

"Hello? I hear you, Mr. DeLuca. Are you in need of assistance? Over."

Tony breathed a sigh of relief. "Yes, thank you. I'm up in the mountains, right outside of Shelter Cove, Arkansas. I need someone to contact my boss, Richard Batterson, in St. Louis. We . . ."

Without warning, the lights on the radio dimmed and

then went out. Tony shook his head and checked the connection. Nothing.

"What happened?" he asked Bobby.

"I don't know," Bobby said slowly. "But don't batteries need to be recharged? Mike always takes care of that. My guess is, the batteries are running low."

Tony stared at the silent radio for a moment. "Okay," he said finally, "let's see if we can find any other batteries." He slammed the microphone down on the small table that held the radio. "A lot of good that did us."

"You told someone who you were, and you told them to contact your boss," Bobby reminded him. "Isn't that a good thing?"

Tony grunted. "Sure. But Batterson's already aware that I'm on the mountain, and he knows he's my boss. He still doesn't know how to find us."

"I'm sorry. I'll start looking for more batteries. Maybe Mike has extras stored here somewhere."

Bobby started to leave, but Tony caught his arm and pulled him back. "Hey, Bobby. This isn't your fault. Forgive me, I'm just frustrated. Ignore my bad temper, okay?"

"Sure, Tony. I understand. It's all right. We're all under pressure."

While Bobby went back into the living room, Tony stared at the dead radio. Whoever kidnapped Kate was out there somewhere. He had no idea when the rain would end, and their car was still stuck in the mud. Should he stay here? Or leave and try to find help?

At that moment, neither option seemed desirable.

CHAPTER
TWENTY-ONE

"Thanks for coming in, Lieutenant Williams," Batterson said. "I know you were involved with the Gerard case, and I have some questions."

Tally Williams sat down in a chair in front of Batterson's desk. He was a large man, and the chair protested a bit under his weight, yet Williams appeared to be all muscle. Batterson respected him immensely, as did all the officers and deputies who'd worked with him.

"I know quite a bit about it. Before Kelly O'Brien's murder, there were three other local women who disappeared that were tied to B.E.K. I was even acquainted with the family of one of them. I've kept up on the case over the last several years."

"But the only bodies that have been found are Tammy Rice's and now Ann Barton's?"

"Yes, that's correct. There are at least fifteen other missing women who are considered victims of the Blue-Eyed Killer. The lyrics to that song were left behind after each abduction, and Alan Gerard admitted to killing them. He used to be a trucker and could have been in the area when each woman disappeared. Nothing was ever proven, though. The trucking company he worked for burned down years ago. All the records destroyed. Gerard would never tell us where the bodies were buried. Now it seems he didn't know because he had nothing to do with the murders."

"The killings have occurred only in Kansas and Missouri?"

Tally nodded. "Yes, that we know of. Tammy Rice was killed in Holcomb, Kansas. Ann Barton lived in Garden City. Other suspected victims have come from Kansas and Missouri, but to be honest, I think there are more than these fifteen. He certainly could have extended his reach beyond these states. There have been quite a few missing women in this area of the country since B.E.K. started killing. The FBI isn't sure they're connected to him, but they have reason to wonder if they're related." Tally shrugged. "No song sheets were found in the other cases, B.E.K.'s calling card. It's possible he doesn't use the song with every killing. At this point, we have no way of knowing."

"I find it interesting that this guy never left behind a clue— except for Tammy Rice—and then the Barton woman."

"We believe he grew more sophisticated as he escalated. That's why Tammy was found. He hadn't formulated his *modus operandi* yet. He's not stupid. In fact, even though he's clearly insane, he's cagey. He's learned how to keep a crime scene clean of evidence. We suspect he wears gloves, even the kind of booties we wear to crime scenes. I think he covers his clothes in some way, too. Very smart. Careful. To be honest, Alan Gerard didn't fit the profile we had of B.E.K.

Never seemed intelligent enough to pull off all these murders without tripping himself up. And he had a job in the public. We saw B.E.K. as someone who has trouble connecting with people. A loner. Gerard is much more social, although most people who knew him found him rather odd. He wasn't what you'd call a popular person."

Batterson pushed his glasses back off his nose and rubbed his temples. He had another headache that just wouldn't quit. "So we don't know exactly who this serial killer is. All we really know is that a man who called himself Malcolm Bodine murdered Tammy Rice and Ann Barton."

"And Kelly O'Brien?"

Batterson sighed. "I'm not sure. Tony DeLuca, one of my deputies, feels strongly that Alan Gerard really did kill Kelly. He has a lot of faith in her twin sister Kate's testimony. In fact, that's where he is now. With Kate. I can't tell you where. I'm sure you understand."

Tally nodded. "I do. Can I ask why he's with her?"

"Sure. We thought we were bringing her back to testify against Gerard since the DNA evidence was thrown out. O'Brien's testimony is the only thing that can put Gerard back in prison." He frowned at Tally. "Of course, at this point most people assume he's innocent. I'm not sure he'll be tried again."

"They'd have to find him to try him. As far as I know, he's still in the wind."

"That's another thing that bothers me. If he's innocent, why did he run?"

"I have no idea. His attorneys aren't too happy about it. Neither is the court. He has the right to do what he wants since there aren't any charges against him right now, but he was advised to stay in the area."

Batterson took a deep breath. "Between us, O'Brien's been abducted."

Tally's eyebrows shot up in surprise. "What? You think Gerard has her?"

"Well, he takes off and O'Brien is kidnapped. You can understand why I'd suspect him."

Tally was quiet for a moment. "This makes it look like he really did kill her sister. Maybe he wants to finish what he started?"

"That's just it. Maybe, maybe, maybe. This is one of the most confusing cases I've ever faced. And now my deputy is knee-deep in it."

"What do you mean?"

Batterson studied Tally for a few seconds before answering. Mark St. Laurent and Mercy Brennan trusted this man with their lives. And he trusted them. "Some guy in the town where Kate was relocated to told DeLuca he knew the direction her abductor took her. Instead of waiting for the FBI and local LEOs to organize a search, DeLuca took off with this guy. He was afraid she'd be long gone by the time the search personnel were ready."

"Sounds reasonable."

"But we lost contact with him and they've been hit with heavy rains on the mountain where they all are. Everyone's waiting for the weather to clear before launching their search. Seems too much rain can cause flash flooding there. Makes it incredibly risky for search crews."

"Well, as you know, most LEOs would march into hell

to assist someone who needs it—but if they don't survive, they're not helping anyone. The victim or their own families."

Batterson grunted. "I agree, but it's frustrating. I'm worried about O'Brien, and I'm also concerned about my deputy."

"I get that." Tally leaned forward in his chair. "Is there anything I can tell you that will help?"

Batterson sighed. "The FBI keeps their cases close to the vest, so I'm not sure you have any information I don't."

Tally smiled. "I have a good friend in the FBI. I may know more than you think. Ask away."

"What do you know about Malcolm Bodine? I mean, we've heard that he killed Rice and Barton—but just who was he?"

"Interesting question. Remember that we're only a little over a week into this investigation, so we're really at the beginning of this thing. But I can tell you that the real Malcolm Bodine died when he was ten years old. He lived in Oklahoma. There's no evidence our killer came from there. I think *our* Bodine acquired the name and Social Security number from some online database and carried on with his life. That takes some skills. The guy wasn't dumb. The FBI doesn't have a clue about his real identity. He didn't show up in CODIS, NDIS, or AFIS."

"So he'd never been fingerprinted or arrested? Great. How does someone who murders innocent people stay off the grid?"

"It's been done, but you've gotta be smart." His forehead furrowed. "And that's the odd thing. From what I've learned about Bodine, he wasn't the brightest pencil in the box. People who knew him described him as quiet, a little slow. His last job was as a busboy in a restaurant. Hardly sounds like a criminal mastermind. Just like Gerard, he didn't live up to our profile."

"Yet we've seen other serial killers with low-end jobs who didn't stand out in a crowd."

Tally nodded. "True."

"So we don't know where this guy came from? If he lived near Rice or Barton?"

"No idea. Obviously he was there, but there's no evidence he lived in the area. As I'm sure you know, not all serial killers stay in their hometowns. Sometimes they move to areas where they're not known to start their reign of terror. Since no one's been able to uncover Bodine's real identity, the trail's pretty cold. It's gonna take something unusual to figure out where he's from. Evidence we haven't found yet."

"His picture hasn't been released to the public, has it?"

"No, just to law enforcement. But the FBI will have to send it to the media soon. Hopefully, that will bring some information. Maybe we can track where he's been and figure out where he stashed his victims' bodies." He sighed. "Of course, going public will also bring out the kooks and everyone else who thinks they know B.E.K. It'll be a nightmare trying to weed out useless calls from any that might actually help."

"What about the woman whose grave Ann Barton's body was buried in?"

"FBI checked her out but couldn't find any connection at all. The woman died in an accident. It wasn't murder. They think her grave was used as a convenient body dump."

Batterson drummed his fingers on his desk. "You've got good instincts, Lieutenant. Do you think Gerard has O'Brien?"

Tally sighed deeply. "I honestly don't know. I wish I could

tell you. Your deputy thinks he killed Kelly O'Brien and he's back for her sister? If you trust his gut, I'd go with that."

"Well, I trusted him until he took off on his own. Left a note explaining himself with someone in the sheriff's department down there. Now a sheriff's deputy is missing, too. At this point, we have some fishing resort owner, my deputy, Kate O'Brien, and Deputy Warren Killian running around somewhere in the Ouachita Mountains."

Tally frowned at him. "Did you say . . . Warren Killian?"

Batterson nodded. "I think that's right." He shuffled some papers on his desk until he pulled out a copy of the note Tony had left with the sheriff's department. In the corner, Batterson had scribbled the name *Warren Killian*. "Yeah. That's the man DeLuca sent this message to originally. Is something wrong?"

"Tammy Rice's son's name is Warren Killian. She was married briefly, but when her husband took off, she went back to her maiden name. Killian's an unusual name. Hard to believe it's not the same guy. I don't suppose you have a picture or anything?"

"No, but I can contact the sheriff's department and request one. Shouldn't take long." Batterson pulled his keyboard over and began typing. Within seconds, he was requesting information from the sheriff's office in Shelter Cove. When he typed in the name Warren Killian, it took only a few seconds for a page with a picture to pop up on his screen. "Here he is," he said to Tally. He swung his screen around so Tally could see it.

"It's been a while, but I'm sure that's him." Tally pointed to a rather large spot near the deputy's ear. "I remember this mole." He frowned at Batterson. "You say this man works near your witness?"

Batterson nodded. "I believe he lives in the same town."

"When Tammy was killed, they suspected Warren at first, but after investigating, they discovered he had an airtight alibi. Then Ann Barton disappeared. The song sheet was left behind—just like it was with Tammy. That's when authorities started looking for a serial killer and quit paying attention to Warren."

"You think they were wrong? That Warren was involved?"

Tally shook his head. "No. His alibi was unshakable, but right now I have to ask myself what the son of one of the Blue-Eyed Killer's victims is doing on that mountain. Is he after Gerard? Or does he have another agenda?"

Batterson moved his computer screen back into place. "Maybe Bodine wasn't working alone."

Tally didn't respond, but Batterson was pretty sure they were both thinking the same thing. DeLuca and O'Brien could be in more danger than they realized, and there was no way to warn them.

CHAPTER
TWENTY-TWO

Kate, Bobby, and Tony took turns using the water from the jugs to wash their faces and hands. Bobby found some clothes in the bedroom, so the men decided to exchange their mud-soaked clothes for something drier and cleaner. Tony put on some jeans and a long-sleeved dark blue corduroy shirt that fit pretty well, but Bobby was so thin, almost everything hung on him. He donned a long-sleeved black turtleneck shirt fashioned to be snug. Even so it was still a couple of sizes too big for Bobby's slight frame. There was no way he could change his jeans. Mike's pants would have fallen down around his ankles.

Tony found some black spandex workout pants that fit Kate loosely but were too long. He used scissors to make them shorter. Bobby was worried about what the cabin's owner would say, but Tony assured him he'd replace the pants. The only clean shirt that could possibly fit Kate was a T-shirt with an eagle on the front. Kate didn't care and put it on immediately.

"I feel so much cleaner," she said. "And I love eagles."

Unfortunately, there weren't any shoes that fit her, but Tony found several thick pairs of socks and made her put them on. Then he slid a pair of boots on her feet over the socks. "I know this probably feels bulky, but can you walk in them?" he asked.

Kate slowly stood up and took a few steps. "I feel like I'm walking with my feet encased in concrete, but I have to admit that I don't hurt as much as I did. The fit may not be perfect, but I think this will work."

"Good. That's a relief."

Kate sat down again, and Tony checked out his leather jacket. It was ruined, but he didn't care. Clothing could be replaced, but people couldn't. He cleaned out the pockets and tossed the jacket in the corner of the bedroom.

"I found some food," Bobby said after rummaging around in the kitchen. He held up a can of tamales, some stew, and some corned beef hash.

"Sounds good, Bobby," Tony said, "but I don't know if we should eat them right out of the can."

"You might not have to. I think Mike's camping stove is around here somewhere. If we have propane, I can heat this stuff up."

Bobby held up another large can that was labeled *Peanuts* on the outside.

"Is there anything in that?" Kate asked.

Bobby shook the can. It sounded full.

"Thank goodness. I'm starving." She sat down at the small kitchen table, and Bobby pulled the lid off the can. Then he dumped some shelled peanuts into a bowl. Kate attacked them ravenously.

"What?" she said when she saw Tony watching her. "I missed breakfast, you know."

Tony checked his watch. One-thirty. No wonder they were hungry. They'd been on the mountain a little over six hours.

"You two should eat something, too," she said, looking miffed. "We all need our strength. Who knows when we'll get out of here?"

"She's right," Bobby agreed. "I'll get that stove and see if I can rustle up something hot."

"Good idea," Tony said. "I don't think there'll be enough peanuts left for you and me."

"You're very funny," Kate said, pushing the container toward him. Tony got a bowl out of the cabinet and joined her.

"I . . . I need to tell you something," he said once he'd downed a few handfuls. "Something happened concerning Alan Gerard. Something you don't know."

Kate sighed. "I know he's out, and I'm pretty sure he's on this mountain. What else could there possibly be?"

The last thing Tony wanted to do was add to Kate's stress, but he had to tell her the truth. If she found out later, and he hadn't been honest with her, she might never forgive him.

"You know there are several deaths attributed to the Blue-Eyed Killer."

"Sure."

"The only body recovered belonged to Tammy Rice, considered to be his first victim. There was DNA evidence left with the body, but it didn't lead investigators anywhere. After

Gerard confessed to the crime, they decided it was just accidental transfer."

Kate frowned at him. "Yeah, I know all of this. Why are you rehashing old information?"

"Just be patient a moment. Please, Kate." Tony took a deep breath and began again. "Even though Gerard would never give details about the other murders—or where he put the bodies—authorities believed him. I mean, he was caught after he attacked you and Kelly. And he left the song lyrics behind, a fact that had never been released to the public before his capture. Sure, it could have been leaked by a family member or someone working the case, but there's no proof that happened. Everyone wanted B.E.K. caught, so keeping that secret was important to authorities and victims' families alike."

Kate leaned back in her chair and crossed her arms. Tony knew she was growing more and more impatient, but he felt the need to lay the groundwork before simply springing the truth on her.

"A little over a week ago, Ann Barton's body was found. We believe she's the second victim. Her body was in Garden City, Kansas. Along with her necklace—something we thought had been taken as a souvenir."

"But . . . but that's great," Kate said. "If they can tie Gerard to Ann, it will mean my testimony isn't the only thing left that will nail him."

Tony took a deep breath and let it out slowly. "You're right, but unfortunately, that didn't happen. The necklace had a fingerprint, Kate. Even after all these years. It matched another man. A man named Malcolm Bodine. He was fingerprinted and his DNA collected six years ago when he was found dead in St. Louis. Before that, he wasn't in the system. The fingerprints were kept on file but not entered into any database until recently. Not sure why. Mistake, backlog—I don't know. When the fingerprint on the necklace matched Bodine, his DNA was compared to the DNA found with Tammy Rice." Tony reached over and took Kate's hand. "It matched too, Kate. Malcolm Bodine was tied to Tammy and to Ann. It means he was the actual Blue-Eyed Killer."

Kate just stared at him without saying anything.

"I'm afraid some people think it means Alan Gerard wasn't the man who assaulted you. That somehow you got confused and identified Gerard because you'd seen him around the school campus." He squeezed her hand. "That's the worst of it. Gerard may not be B.E.K., but I still believe he's guilty of killing Kelly and hurting you. The truth is, he may only be a copycat. That's why your attack was so different."

Kate blinked several times. "He's going to get away with it, isn't he?"

"No. We won't let that happen."

Even as he said the words, he realized he'd just made a promise he couldn't keep.

"I . . . I can't believe this." She frowned at him. "When did you find this out?"

"Yesterday. I was told to keep it from you, but I decided to tell you this morning. Then I went to find you . . . and you were gone."

Kate looked away from him, her face tight and her lips thin.

"I'm sorry if you're angry. My boss didn't want the information released to you yet—until we had more to go on. But now . . ."

"Now Gerard is after me, trying to kill me, so it seems I should be allowed to know what's really going on." Kate got to her feet and began to pace the room. "I don't like being lied to, Tony."

"I didn't lie to you. I just didn't tell you everything. Until now. It's only been a few hours since I found out. I'm sorry. I really am."

"Sounds like it was Tony's boss who decided you shouldn't know, Kate," Bobby said softly.

He'd been so quiet Tony had almost forgotten he was there. Bobby stood next to the table, his face twisted with concern.

"I . . . I know it's not my business. . . ."

"So you know who I am, Bobby?"

Tony held up his hand. "Yes, I told him. He's put his life on the line to help us. I thought it was the right thing to do. Sorry."

Kate leaned against the kitchen cabinets, shaking her head. "Don't apologize. I don't like being left out of the loop, but I guess I understand." She jabbed a finger at him. "But no more lies . . . or omissions, okay? I don't need to be *handled*."

"I know. You're right."

Bobby, who'd turned around and started fumbling around in the kitchen, held up an old camp stove. "I . . . I found the stove. And some propane. I can get it going and then we can heat up those cans of food."

Bobby's eyes kept jumping back and forth between Tony

and Kate. Tony could tell he was nervous, and he knew why. Bobby didn't like confrontation. Frankly, Tony agreed. He didn't like it, either. But it happened a lot in his profession.

"Bobby, where do you plan to fire that thing up?"

Bobby cleared his throat. "Well . . . I was thinking about putting it on the kitchen table with some tin foil underneath it. Do you think that would be safe?"

Tony nodded. "Should be okay, but be careful. We don't need to set the cabin on fire. Before you light it, I'm going to check things outside, make sure we're secure."

Tony didn't look at Kate because he didn't want to see the same guarded look in her eyes that she'd had when he first arrived in Shelter Cove. Her trust meant a lot to him, and she felt he'd let her down. "I'll be right back." He gestured to Bobby. "Lock the door behind me."

He walked over to the front door, drew his gun, and opened the door slowly. It was still raining. Would it ever stop? He stepped out onto the porch and let the door close behind him. He waited until he heard the click of the lock. Then he swept the area in front of the cabin. After that, he checked both sides and the back. No sign of anyone. Of course, the rain and the trees provided perfect cover. Gerard could be out there right now, watching them. Frankly, he'd rather face Gerard than Kate right now. He still had to tell her about Bella, and it was the last thing he wanted to do. He really thought it would be better if she didn't know until they were safe, but after what she'd just said, what choice did he have?

He took a deep breath and walked back up onto the porch, determined to make things right with Kate. He knocked on the door and waited for Bobby to open it. When he didn't,

Tony tried the door and discovered it wasn't locked. He turned the knob and stepped inside. But nothing could have prepared him for what awaited him there.

A man had his arm around Kate's neck, a gun pointed at her head. Bobby cowered in the corner, his face a mask of terror.

"Hello, Tony," the man said. "Glad you could join us. Now put the gun down and let's talk."

CHAPTER
TWENTY-THREE

"Don't scratch my table with that rusty old box," Linda said as she handed Leon a glass of milk.

"I put some papers under it. Don't worry." Linda was picky about her kitchen. In fact, she worked hard to keep every room of their small house neat and tidy. It was attractive—yet comfortable. Being inside Fred's house made him even more appreciative of Linda's efforts. He couldn't imagine living with that kind of mess. The memory made him shiver.

She tousled his hair. "Thanks. How about some cookies with that milk?"

"Your oatmeal cookies without raisins? You bet."

"You could just call them oatmeal cookies, you know. You don't need to always mention that they don't have raisins."

He winked at her. "I know, but I like to call them that because you take the time to make them the way I like them."

She shook her head. "Maybe I like them that way, too."

"No, you don't."

"You have a very high opinion of yourself, don't you?" she teased.

"You bet. By the way, did you get a chance to talk to someone at the church?"

Linda nodded. "We've got food going to Fred tonight. We'll assess his other needs once we get inside his house. Probably could use some paper products, toiletries. You said the place needs a good cleaning?"

"Big time. And maybe a new couch."

Linda giggled as she put some cookies on a plate and brought them to the table. She gestured toward the metal box sitting in front of her husband. "So that's the box you got from Fred?"

Leon nodded. "Probably nothing important here." He sighed deeply. "Something's bothering me about this case. It's like that old TV we used to have. Remember how fuzzy the picture got sometimes? I'd fiddle around with it until it got clearer. Well, this case is just like that. It's fuzzy. I'm trying to find a way to make it clearer so I can understand it."

Linda sat down across from him. "So what's fuzzy about it?"

"That's just it. I'm not completely sure, but for one thing, no one seems to think it's odd that Ann was buried on top of Dorothy Fisher."

"I'm sure they investigated that."

"You're right. They did. Couldn't find a connection."

Linda frowned thoughtfully. "But you think there is one?"

"I do."

"Can you tell me why?"

Leon stared at his wife. He started to respond to her question, but the words suddenly caught in his throat. They'd been married a long time, but to him, she grew more beautiful every day. Her strawberry-blond hair was streaked with gray, but it just softened her lovely features. Her smile could still make his heart skip a beat. They'd been through a lot over the years, but Linda was a rock. Her strength constantly inspired him. He cleared his throat, trying to regain his train of thought. "I'm not sure, but . . . why *that* grave? It was in the middle of the cemetery. I mean, if it was just a convenient body dump, why not pick a grave closer to the edge of the property? Where you wouldn't be seen? And why take a chance that someone would notice the site had been disturbed? That tells me the killer picked that spot for a reason. I just want to know why."

"And what does that have to do with Darrell Fisher?"

"I don't know, but I'm gonna go through his belongings and see if anything speaks to me." He grunted. "I might be wasting my time, but it's mine to waste, I guess."

"Speaking of time, have you told the department you're retiring?"

"Uh . . . not yet. I will. Quit badgering me."

Linda leaned over and caught his eye. "I'm not badgering you, and you know it. Retire. Don't retire. It's your choice. But make a decision and stick with it."

"I will, but right now I'd like to concentrate on this box, okay?"

"If this is evidence, should you have brought it home?"

"It isn't evidence yet. Not until I find something that will help solve this case." He smirked at her. "Is that okay with you, Chief?"

"Yes, dear. I'll leave you to it."

She got up to leave, but Leon grabbed her hand as she walked by. "I'll tell them. I will." He pulled her down and kissed her. "You're still my girl, right?"

She smiled and gazed into his eyes. "Always."

When she left the room, Leon thanked God one more time for putting him and Linda together. If he ever felt the need to question God's love for him, all he had to do was remind himself that God had given him Linda, a precious gift he would never take for granted.

He picked up a cookie and took a bite. Best cookies in the world. A few more bites and several swallows of ice-cold milk, and he was ready to dive into Darrell's box.

One by one, he lifted things out. First he put the two year-books to the side. Then he removed baseball cards, none of them valuable, some old pens, two small notebooks, and a couple of Valentine's Day cards. There were also some random papers. School assignments. They'd all earned high marks, but nothing on them meant anything to Leon.

He'd stacked everything in neat piles and was going to close the box when something rattled at the bottom. Leon put his hand in and pulled out an old cassette tape. It was black and hadn't shown up against the dark-colored bottom of the box. There was nothing written on it, no way to tell what was recorded on it. Leon put that in a different place. He and Linda used to have a tape player, but he hadn't seen it in a long time. Hopefully, they still had it and Linda knew where it was.

He opened the yearbook with Darrell's picture. After looking at it again, he glanced through the pictures of the other kids in his class. Nothing stood out. Then he checked out the inside covers of the book. When Leon was in high school, his friends would sign his yearbook and he would sign theirs. Darrell only had three comments. Apparently he wasn't a very popular kid. Someone named Janice had written *Have a great summer!* and a boy named Phil had scrawled *Be good, Dude.* Leon looked up the Janices and Phils in Darrell's class and wrote down their complete names. There were two Janices and three Phillips. The third comment was the most interesting. It read *Can't wait to get out of this crappy school and start having some fun. Our future awaits!* It was signed *Stinky.* Could this be Darrell's friend? He picked up the yearbook from Holcomb. This had more signatures. The owner was fairly popular, but it seemed his fans probably weren't first in their class. The spelling and grammar were atrocious. Many of the comments were directed to someone named *Barney*, but a few were written to *Stinky*.

Leon took a small notebook out of his pocket and picked up his cell phone. He looked up Fred Fisher's number. After quite a few rings, Fred picked up.

"Fred, this is Sergeant Leon Shook," he said. "I'm sorry to bother you, but could Darrell's friend's nickname be Stinky?"

After a moment of silence, Fred said, "Yeah, that was it. I remember now. But it wasn't because the boy smelled bad. He used to set off stink bombs in school. Darrell wouldn't do it because he didn't like gettin' attention from people. But he sure thought Stinky was cool for doin' that kinda stuff. Bad influence, like I said."

"Okay. Thanks for your help, Fred. I appreciate it."

"Look, Sergeant, can you tell me why you're so interested in my nephew?"

"Wouldn't do any good, Fred. I'm just shootin' at the sky, hopin' to hit something. You know, tryin' to figure out why Ann's body was buried with your sister. Might not mean anything at all. Might have just been a handy place to put her."

Fred was quiet so long Leon thought he'd hung up. "You still there, Fred?"

"Yeah. Look, Sarge, I don't know exactly what you're thinkin', but Darrell . . . Well, he was a cold-hearted kid. I mean, like somethin' wasn't plugged in all the way when it came to feelin' things for other people. Just thought you should know that."

"Thanks. I appreciate your honesty."

"Got a call from some local church. They're bringin' me some food and stuff later today. Was that your doin'?"

"Ah, I might have mentioned to my wife, Linda, that you might not be feelin' real good. Of course, she took it upon herself to start meddlin'. You know women. Sorry about that. I'd appreciate it if you'd just put up with her and not hurt her feelings. If you think you can, that is."

"I . . . I suppose I can allow it. Don't usually let people mess in my business, but I'll do it for you, Sarge."

"Well, thanks, Fred. I can't tell you how much that means to me. I love that woman. Even if she is a busybody."

Another silence. "I had a wife once. I understand. I'd do anything for her, too. Thanks, Sarge."

Leon grunted a good-bye and hung up.

Linda came back into the kitchen and put her arms around her husband. "So I'm a busybody, am I?"

"Yes, ma'am. The worst kind. I only keep you around because no one else should have to put up with you."

Linda kissed him on the top of the head. "Same to you, you old goat."

"By the way, do you have any idea where our old tape player is? You know, the one we used when we listened to those old Bible-teaching tapes?"

"Sure I do. Unlike you, I know where things are."

Leon grinned at her. "I don't need to know where things are. That's why I have you."

"Very funny. I'll get it."

While Linda was looking for the tape player, Leon scanned the Holcomb yearbook. The names of everyone mentioned in the book were listed in the back. He wondered if Tammy Rice's son was pictured, but he couldn't remember his name right off the bat. His last name was different from Tammy's. He found two Barneys. One taught shop and the other was a student. He turned to the page with the picture of Barney the student. Barney's last name was Clevenger. As he ran his finger down the row of pictures and settled on the right one, he got an odd feeling that he'd seen the kid before. Close-set eyes. Big ears. A mouth that seemed crooked somehow. No matter how hard he tried, though, he couldn't place him. Probably looked like some kid his son had gone to school with.

"Here it is," Linda said, coming back into the room. She dusted off the player, plugged it into a nearby outlet, and handed it to Leon.

"Thanks," he said. He popped the tape in and pressed the play button. When the song started, at first he didn't recognize it. Then it got to the chorus. *She has a heart as cold as ice. Frozen kisses that take my breath away. Blue-Eyed*

Angel who sees into my soul and somehow makes me whole.

Linda gasped and Leon turned back to the picture in the yearbook. Now he recalled that face. He'd seen a report about him at the office. Barney Clevenger was Malcolm Bodine. The Blue-Eyed Killer.

CHAPTER
TWENTY-FOUR

"What do you want?" Kate heard Tony ask the man holding a gun on them.

"You don't recognize me do you, Mr. DeLuca?" The man led her over to the couch and commanded her to sit down. He took off his cap and his glasses. Then he pulled off a fake mustache and some kind of soft, rubbery material he'd used to reshape his nose.

"No," Kate exclaimed softly. Somehow she'd known who it was from the moment he'd stepped inside the cabin. Everything started to come back, and she felt like she might faint. The blood, the screaming. Watching the light go out in Kelly's eyes. Gerard advancing on her, evil etched deeply into his expression. She felt her body begin to shake, and she couldn't control it.

Gerard touched his hair. "Yes, it's me. A little bleach on top and some hair on my chin. The rest isn't real."

"Kate, it's okay," Tony said. "Look at me."

She turned her head toward him. In his eyes she saw

something that gave her courage. Just as he'd done during the trial. If she kept her eyes on Tony, she knew she's be all right.

"He can't help you this time, Kate," Gerard said, his voice low and gravelly. "Put your gun on the ground and kick it over here, Mr. DeLuca."

Kate could tell the last thing Tony wanted to do was give up his weapon. He usually had an extra, but he'd given it to Bobby. She looked over at Bobby, but he seemed glued to the spot in the kitchen where he'd gone to fire up the camp stove. She doubted he'd be much help to them. Maybe Tony would remember the second gun and find a way to retrieve it.

"Please join Miss O'Brien on the couch," Gerard said, waving his gun at Tony. "And no tricks or I'll kill her."

Tony walked slowly toward her, but Kate could see in his face that he was considering a move toward Gerard. He was probably thinking the same thing she was. Gerard wouldn't just shoot her. That wasn't his way. He liked to take time with his victims. He enjoyed watching them suffer.

Even though she wanted Gerard dead, she didn't want Tony to do anything foolish. They needed time to come up with a plan. One that would work. If Tony died now, she and Bobby had no hope of making it out of this alive.

"I'm not an idiot, Mr. DeLuca," Gerard said. "I can see you're wondering if you could overpower me. Take my gun. But I assure you, it won't happen. You probably think I won't really shoot Miss O'Brien. That I have other plans for her." He swung his gun toward a terrified Bobby, who backed up several steps. "And you're right. But I wouldn't have any problem shooting your friend, whoever he is. If he's dispensable, then please, proceed with your strategy. However, if you don't want to watch him die before your eyes, then do what I asked and sit down."

Gerard's voice grew louder at the end of his diatribe, and Kate could tell he was serious. "Please, Tony," she said. "Do what he says . . . for now."

She prayed he would understand what she was trying to say. That this was not the moment.

As if he caught her hint, Tony put his gun on the floor, kicked it toward Gerard, and came over to the couch. He sat down next to Kate and took her hand.

Bobby closed his eyes, relief washing over his face. Kate felt sorry for him. Bobby had been brave enough to come looking for her. He certainly didn't need this. She was angry that he'd been dragged into Gerard's circle of evil.

"You," Gerard said, pointing at Bobby. "Come over here."

Bobby looked back and forth between Kate and Tony, obviously apprehensive.

"Do what he says, Bobby," Tony said, his voice strong and steady.

Bobby walked slowly toward Gerard, who opened a bag he had with him. He handed Bobby two long zip ties. "I have it on good authority these are used by the police. I think they will do for my use." He motioned toward Tony and Kate. "Put them on these two. And make sure they're tight."

Bobby took the ties and went over to Tony. Kate could see the fear in his eyes.

Tony stuck his hands out in front of him.

"No, Mr. DeLuca," Gerard said. "Turn around. I want your hands behind your back. That's what they did to me. It's good enough for you, as well."

Tony turned around and Bobby circled the tie around his wrists. Then he pulled the tab that stuck out of the locking mechanism. It was obvious he didn't pull as hard as he could.

Gerard walked over to him. "Do you want to die today, Bobby? Pull it tight."

"I . . . I'm sorry, Tony," Bobby said, his voice quivering.

"It's okay. Everything will be all right."

Bobby pulled the plastic tie until Gerard finally smiled. "That's good, Bobby. Now take care of the lady."

Bobby walked over to Kate. His eyes sought hers. "I'm sorry, Kate. I'm really sorry."

Gerard hit Bobby on the side of the head, causing him to cry out in pain. "Quit talking and do what I told you."

Kate stood up and then turned around. Bobby put the tie around Kate's wrists and pulled it tight. She felt the plastic cut into her skin but stayed calm so Bobby wouldn't know he'd hurt her. He obviously felt awful about what Gerard had forced him to do. She didn't want to add to his guilt.

"You can both turn around and sit down," Gerard said.

As Tony and Kate took their places back on the couch, Bobby turned around and stared at the killer. "Is there anything else you'd like me to do, Mr. Gerard?" he asked, his voice almost a whisper.

"That's it for now, Bobby," Gerard said. "Why don't you sit down in that chair?" He pointed toward a chair near the couch. Bobby sat down, a look of relief on his face. But before he had time to settle in, Gerard dashed toward him and hit him on the side of the head again, this time knocking him out.

Then Gerard turned toward Kate and Tony, his gun pointed right at them. "Now the fun begins."

Leon put down the phone. He'd told the entire story to some woman with the FBI. She'd been polite but not too interested. She'd promised to pass the information along to someone who'd worked on the Blue-Eyed Killer case. The feds probably went through the same stuff they'd endured here. Tips leading nowhere. But in spades.

He started looking through the rest of the box's contents. First he flipped through the small notebooks. Lots of strange drawings. Dead people. Blood. Guns. Bloody knives. None of it concerned him greatly. He knew firsthand that young boys liked to draw stuff like this. His son had done the same thing, and he was a great kid.

He picked up each item using a napkin. He'd bag it all for evidence. Maybe everything here had belonged to Darrell. But what if there was something from Barney? Could be important. Leon found himself smiling, even though there was nothing funny about a serial killer. But the "Blue-Eyed Killer" sounded a lot more ominous than . . . Barney.

The only thing he hadn't looked at were the valentines. He picked them up and opened each one. What he saw inside the cards made his skin crawl. One was written to *Tammy*. The other was written to *Ann*. The same thing was scribbled inside both of them. *I am your destiny.*

He gulped and called out to Linda.

"Look at this," he told her when she came into the room. "I can't believe I didn't check these out earlier. I just assumed they were cards from some old girlfriend. Got carried away with what was on that cassette tape, I guess."

"Oh, Leon. This is important evidence. You've got to get in touch with someone. Turn this over to whoever is in charge."

"I tried," he said. "But the FBI blew me off."

Linda frowned. "You've got to try again. Trust me, when they know what you've found, they'll be interested."

Leon thought for a moment. "I'll contact the police department in St. Louis. They were knee-deep in this thing when Gerard was tried. Maybe they'll be willing to listen to some rube policeman from the sticks."

"You're not a rube."

"Yes, I am."

"Well, you're a brilliant rube, then." She winked at him. "Even more important, you're my rube. Now make that call."

CHAPTER
TWENTY-FIVE

"Sir, you have a call on line four."

Batterson thanked his new administrative assistant and punched line four on his phone. "Batterson."

"This is Tally Williams. When I got back to the office, I discovered something I thought you might find interesting. A police officer in Garden City contacted the FBI with information, but they didn't take him seriously. He decided to call us and was referred to me."

"What kind of information?"

"Seems this guy was convinced there was a reason for Ann Barton's body being found with Dorothy Fisher. Investigating his suspicions led him to the real Malcolm Bodine. His name is Barney Clevenger. He went to school in Holcomb, Kansas. Left when he was eighteen. Took off with some other kid, a Darrell Fisher. Dorothy Fisher's son. Appears to be connected somehow to the whole Blue-Eyed Killer spree. Darrell left behind a cassette tape with the song 'Blue-Eyed Angel' on it. Not sure what happened to him. May have parted ways with Clevenger years ago."

"But it sounds like they started out together," Batterson said. "Well, I'm glad to have the name, but I'm not sure what good this will do us now. Bodine . . . or Clevenger is dead. He's not chasing my agent and my witness on that mountain."

"Just part of the puzzle, sir. One other thing. I checked, and Tammy Rice's son, Warren Killian, also went to school in Holcomb. Although he was a couple of years younger than Fisher and Clevenger, he would have known them. Now he seems to be chasing after your people for some reason. Of course, he might be looking for Gerard."

"You believe it's Gerard too, don't you?"

"Yes, sir. I do."

Batterson breathed heavily into the phone. "I think De-Luca was right all along. Gerard might not be B.E.K., but I think he killed Kelly O'Brien, and now he wants to make up for his failed attack on her sister. But why is Warren Killian in Shelter Cove? How in the world did he end up there? It can't be a coincidence."

Tally sighed. "I'm still trying to figure that out. I'm certain he's aware Gerard isn't B.E.K., so he can't want revenge for his mother's death. Gerard didn't kill her. Either he's trying to protect O'Brien and DeLuca, or . . ."

"Or what?"

"Or maybe he really did kill his mother and now he's hunting O'Brien. Maybe he and Clevenger were partners."

"But if he wanted to kill O'Brien, he could have done it any time over the past couple of years. Why would he go after her now?"

Tally was silent for a moment. "I just don't have an answer for you, sir. Feels like we're overlooking something."

"I would say that's a good bet. I got a call from the local Marshals in Shelter Cove a few minutes ago. They're getting ready to head out. Decided not to wait for the FBI to clear them. Some of the other LEOs are going with them." Batterson chuckled. "Sounds like a few of the feds are joining in, as well. Gutsy move."

"Will they be able to reach O'Brien and DeLuca? Safely, I mean?"

"I have no idea, but I believe they're thinking the same thing I am. Oh, and a civilian ham operator contacted our office. Got a call from my deputy, but it was cut off before it was completed. My deputy and my witness may not have much time left. If they're gonna be saved, they need help immediately. Gerard may already have them. There's no way to know."

"This is a mess, isn't it?"

Batterson grunted. "It's certainly unique. Usually I know exactly who the bad guys are, but this time I'm just not sure."

"Well, at least you know who B.E.K. really was."

"I . . . guess so."

"Something else bothering you?" Tally asked.

"Yeah. My gut. Like you said, it's telling me something's wrong, but I have no idea what it is." Batterson leaned back in his chair. "And I don't like it. I don't like it one little bit."

Leon picked up the phone. "Garden City Police Department. Sergeant Shook speaking."

"Sergeant, this is Lieutenant Tally Williams with the St. Louis P.D. I'm calling about the information you sent us in reference to Malcolm Bodine?"

"You mean Barney Clevenger?"

Tally chuckled. "Yes, sir. Good catch there. Great police work."

Leon could tell the policeman was sincere. After the run-around he'd gotten from the FBI, it was nice to hear from someone who didn't think he was mentally simple just because he came from a small town. "I appreciate that, Lieutenant."

"Tally."

"Then I'm Leon."

"Deal."

"Tally, I just went through the rest of the box that belonged to Darrell Fisher. This guy was definitely involved with Clevenger. There are a couple of Valentine's Day cards addressed inside to Tammy and Ann. I'm pretty sure they were meant for Tammy Rice and Ann Barton."

"Listen, Leon. Just keep that stuff safe. I'm going to contact the FBI and send them to you. They need to secure this box and its contents immediately. I heard they weren't too receptive when you tried to help them initially."

"Well, they certainly didn't roll out the red carpet. But hey, I'm not that sensitive."

"Good." Tally cleared his throat. "So, any opinions about this thing, Leon? We know that Clevenger was the Blue-Eyed Killer. Any idea how this Darrell kid fits in?"

Leon considered Tally's question before speaking. "I'd say he was involved. The two of them started out together, but somewhere along the way Darrell either dropped out or got out. I understand Clevenger died alone. Isn't that right?"

"Yeah. When we found his body, we traced him back to a sad little apartment in a bad part of town. Didn't seem to have any friends. Appears as if killing was his only hobby. We're sure he was B.E.K., but . . ."

Leon was quiet. It was clear that Tally was getting ready to tell him something he probably shouldn't.

"Between you and me, several things bother me about Clevenger. For one, we didn't find any trophies. Most serial killers keep them, you know. But there was nothing in that apartment to tie him to the murders. Nothing. And B.E.K. was the smartest serial killer I've ever encountered. No evidence left behind that could be traced. Except for Tammy and Ann, no bodies. Clevenger just doesn't seem that bright. Didn't fit the profile."

"I hear you," Leon said. "It doesn't sound right, does it?"

There was no response signaling that he and Tally were in agreement.

"Hey, if you don't mind a suggestion, I'd start checking cemeteries," Leon interjected. "You might find other bodies. Actually, it's a brilliant strategy. Who'd think to look for dead bodies in graveyards?"

Tally snorted, and Leon chuckled. "You know what I mean. Can't even use cadaver dogs. Wouldn't help. Especially if he wrapped all the bodies in several layers of heavy-duty plastic like he did Ann Barton."

"Seems risky, though. Wouldn't people notice an old grave that's been dug up?"

"Depends. Two reasons it could work. A new grave or an

old one. Lots of gravesites are abandoned because family members have passed away or moved. Might go unnoticed easier than you'd think."

"Yeah, that makes sense."

"I feel Clevenger had a reason to bury Ann in Dorothy's grave. Or at least his friend did. I have to wonder if Dorothy Fisher's death was really an accident."

"I see where you're going," Tally said. "Maybe she was the first victim. Sure would like to see a picture of her."

"I'll go back and talk to her brother. See what I can find out."

"And ask about Darrell. We need to locate him as soon as possible."

"He says he doesn't know where Darrell is, but I'll check again."

"Thanks, Leon. Would you do one other thing for me?"

"Sure."

"Before the feds pick up Darrell's things, will you send me a copy of the boys' pictures? Barney, Warren, and Darrell? Might not lead to anything, but I'd like to have them anyway. Just in case."

"Not a problem. I'll make copies and email them to you right away. Give me your email address." Leon wrote down Tally's address as he rattled it off. "Got it."

"Hey, Leon. Glad to get to know you. Hope Garden City, Kansas, knows what they've got in you."

Leon chuckled. "Hey, they put up with me. That might be all I can ask for."

The men said good-bye and Leon hung up the phone. He opened the yearbooks and took several pictures of each boy. Then he sent them to his own email address and forwarded them to Tally. He wasn't sure if the pictures would help, but at this point, they needed to follow every lead. Even if it felt like they were chasing the wind. Hopefully, the more pieces they found to the puzzle, the faster the picture would become clear. Before putting everything back in the box, Leon bowed his head and prayed for guidance.

CHAPTER
TWENTY-SIX

"You didn't have to do that." Tony felt his hands clench involuntarily behind him. He looked over at Kate. She hadn't said a word, but her eyes were wide and unfocused. She was probably in shock.

"I don't have to do anything," Gerard said with a smile that didn't reach his eyes. "But I'm in control now. Not you. There aren't any prison guards here to order me around. And you certainly won't." He gave an odd little laugh. "Even my mentor has given me carte blanche. I'm free from him, and I'm certainly free from you."

Tony caught the word *mentor*. "Are you talking about Malcolm Bodine? Was he your mentor?"

Gerard's expression turned stormy. "Don't be ridiculous. Bodine was a wimp. Wanted out. I killed him."

"He wanted out? What are you talking about? Seems like he was the successful one. You messed up your first kill. Ended up in jail." Tony wanted to keep Gerard talking. Keep him from thinking about Kate. It was the only strategy he could come up with for the moment.

Gerard stood up abruptly from his chair at the table, the legs scraping against the floor. He pointed his gun straight at Tony. Tony saw the barrel shake. Gerard's eyes were wild. "He lost his nerve. Wanted out. Our mentor decided he had to go. I took care of it, and now I'm taking his place."

"Wait a minute," Tony said. "Then why were you caught? What went wrong?"

Anger twisted Gerard's features. "I don't want to talk about it."

"You moved too fast, didn't you? Didn't wait for your *mentor* to approve your first kill. That's why everything went wrong. You didn't rely on his expertise. He would have known your target was a twin. That she wouldn't be alone when you broke in. And he wouldn't have allowed you to leave the bodies behind. He never does that."

"It wasn't my first kill," Gerard said, his voice growing louder. "I told you, I killed Malcolm."

"I'm sorry, you're right. I forgot."

Gerard seemed a little mollified by Tony's apology and sat down again. "Actually, you're correct. He was angry with me for a while. Said that my kill was *illegal*. But when I went to jail, he said it was a good thing. That I would be famous. Everyone would think I was the Blue-Eyed Killer. He was right, of course. Problem was, after a while, people forgot about me. And I didn't like prison. It was awful." He lowered his voice as if he thought only Tony could hear him. "The bathroom facilities are . . . out in the open." He shook his head. "Barbaric." He stared up at the ceiling, his eyes wide and unblinking.

At that moment Gerard seemed a million miles away. As

if he'd forgotten anyone else was in the room. If Tony could distract him, maybe he could get the gun. The type of plastic ties Gerard had used on him and Kate were easy to remove. Law enforcement had quit using this brand because just the right amount of force could break them. And Tony knew exactly how to do it. If he could get the gun, he could subdue Gerard and save Kate. No matter what, he was determined to keep Gerard away from her.

A low moan from Bobby told Tony he was coming to.

"So how did you get released?" Tony asked softly. "Was that your mentor's doing?"

Gerard nodded. "I told him that if he didn't get me out of there, I'd tell everyone about him. Tell the world who he was." Gerard smiled at no one. "So he told them where to find Ann Barton and proved I didn't kill her. Now I'm free."

"Where is this *mentor* now?"

Gerard gave him a blank look. "Wouldn't you like to know? Anyway, it doesn't matter. I've graduated. We parted ways."

Tony watched Gerard lower his gun a little. "I guess he has a lot of experience with . . . killing?"

Gerard laughed. "No, not really. He doesn't like to get his hands dirty so he recruited Malcolm. Then me. Likes to watch but doesn't like to do it." Gerard blinked several times, then his eyes seemed to focus on Tony. He waved his gun around. "That's enough. I'm not talking about him anymore. You want me to say something bad about him, and I won't do it. He helped me, and now he's letting me go. I'm not upset anymore. Everything's okay. From here on out, I'm on my own. The Blue-Eyed Killer will be famous again. And everyone will know it's me."

Gerard's insanity was in full bloom. Tony realized he was unpredictable and dangerous. Getting him under control was going to be tough. Tougher than he'd imagined.

He glanced over at Bobby, who was now conscious and looking at Gerard. Then he watched as Gerard's gaze swung toward Kate, who was still staring straight ahead. Her face was pale, and there was a sheen of sweat above her lip. She was in trouble, and Tony had to help her. He needed to get close to Gerard, and he had to do it soon.

Thankfully, Warren was able to follow the tracks in the mud. Even though it was still raining, it was finally coming down a little lighter. The tracks were fading but still clear enough for him to see. He slipped several times, almost washed over the side of an embankment once. It really was dangerous up here. He had to be careful. He couldn't risk injury or anything that would keep him from what he needed to do. He'd dedicated himself to a cause, and nothing would stop him. His mother had been the first. It was as if he could hear her whispering in his ear. His legs felt like rubber, so he found an old tree stump and sat down. For now he'd rest, but when he was at full strength, he would figure out a way to finally end this.

Once and for all.

U.S. Deputy Marshal Gil Bennett had made the decision to take his team up the mountain to rescue a witness under protection and one of their own, along with an innocent civilian. Although a few other law enforcement officers were going with them, there were others who had made it clear they felt his attempt was ill-advised.

"We've lost folks in those mountains," a local cop had told him. "The roads are more than just a little wet. We've got flash flooding up there. Getting yourself killed isn't going to help your witness or your fellow Marshal."

Gil was careful to thank him for his advice, but he still felt compelled to try. The people who'd been killed on the mountain were civilians, not law enforcement. He didn't plan to take any drastic measures. They'd go slowly and carefully, but standing around down here while people were in danger was something he just couldn't stomach.

He was waiting for the rest of his team to get geared up so they could take off when his phone rang. He was surprised to find himself talking to the Chief of the Eastern District of Missouri's U.S. Marshals' Office, Richard Batterson. He'd been in touch with Gil's boss about this operation, but why was he calling Gil personally?

"What can I do for you, sir?" he asked.

"I have some information I'd like you to pass along to my deputy when you find him," Batterson said. "So far, I haven't been able to reach him by phone. You probably know that a local deputy sheriff is missing. Warren Killian may be headed toward our people. I've discovered that he's the son of the so-called Blue-Eyed Killer's first victim. At the time she was murdered, her son was a person of interest. I'm not sure what this guy wants or why he's on the mountain, but I think you should all be very careful. I've written out everything that might be pertinent to this case. Please read through it as soon as you can." Batterson took a deep breath. "At this point, we're not sure who took our witness, but we suspect it is Alan Gerard. Consider him armed and extremely dangerous. Wish I could give you something more helpful, Deputy, but we just don't have all the facts yet. Just be careful, and watch out for Killian. Thanks for your dedication. It's appreciated."

Gil waited until he was certain Batterson had finished talking. He glanced at his phone and saw the message with attachments come through. "I have the information, sir. Thanks. We'll keep an eye out for Killian, and we'll deliver those people back safely, trust me. And we'll bring Gerard down dead or alive. He'll never hurt anyone else."

There was silence on the other end of the line for a moment, and Gil wondered if his bravado had offended Batterson.

"I like that, Deputy Bennett. Good man. Godspeed to you and your team."

"Thank you, sir."

The other line clicked off, and Gil pulled up the files Batterson had sent. He'd read through everything when he could and show them to Deputy DeLuca when he found him. If he was still alive.

On the way back to the station, Leon stopped by Fred Fisher's. Hopefully, the old man wouldn't get upset about another interruption. Especially since his home was going to be invaded in a couple hours by Linda and a few women from their church. It took a while for Fred to get to the door. When he opened it, he frowned when he saw who it was.

"You gonna move in here, Sarge? I can get a room ready for you if it would help."

Leon chuckled. "I'm sorry, Fred. I really am. My bosses tell me what to do, and I gotta do it. I'm sure you understand how it is."

"Sure, I guess so." He peered closely at Leon. "So now what?"

"Do you have a picture of Dorothy? One that I could borrow?"

Fred swung the door open and ushered Leon inside. "Yeah, I keep it hangin' on the wall in the bedroom. Follow me."

Fred's bedroom wasn't any cleaner than the rest of the house. The smell of urine was even stronger there, and Leon had to hold his breath. Fred walked slowly over to the wall and took down a cheaply framed picture. The glass was cloudy from not being cleaned for a long time, but when he put it in Leon's hands, a chill went through him. Dorothy Fisher had long brown hair and bright blue eyes.

Just like all the other victims.

CHAPTER
TWENTY-SEVEN

"Get over there next to your friends," Gerard told Bobby.

Bobby got up and moved over to the couch. Kate leaned against him for a moment, hoping to reassure him some. She could feel him tremble. It was as if she were trapped in the middle of a nightmare. Something that couldn't be real. Yet it was . . . wasn't it? She'd faced Gerard once. Why did she have to go through this again? Where was God? Had He abandoned her?

"I realize that your friends in law enforcement will get here at some point," Gerard said to Tony. "But it will be too late. I'll be gone."

"Why do you think that?" Tony asked. "You're stuck up here just like the rest of us."

Gerard's high-pitched laugh filled the small room. Kate had heard it before, and it chilled her to the bone. He'd laughed when he'd killed Kelly and when he thought he'd killed her. She felt as if she were back in that apartment. In that situation. Experiencing the same horrific moments that she'd been refusing to face. It was like some dark closet had burst open in her mind and everything was coming back. The pain, the rage, the terror. It was just like Tony had said. "*. . . deliverance isn't denial, Kate. And it isn't delusion. God wants to heal you, but you have to be honest with Him . . . and with yourself.*"

She felt as if she was coming apart. Bit by bit. Piece by piece. Again, she heard Tony's voice. "*. . . you'll go on like this until the day comes when your mind can't protect you any longer. And when that happens, it will be worse than you can imagine, and I'm afraid you won't have anywhere else to hide. You might not escape next time.*"

Was that what was happening? Would she lose her mind trapped in a small cabin on a mountain?

"Actually, you're wrong, Deputy DeLuca," Gerard said. "I have a way off the mountain. There is one, you know. Too bad you don't know about it."

"I don't need to. I'll be leaving this place alive. You won't."

"Big words for someone in your situation. You weren't supposed to be here, you know. That injection should have finished you. Can't figure out how you survived."

He turned his attention to Kate. "Could have drugged you, Kate, but I didn't want to risk having your senses dulled. I want you to experience every little moment I'm going to have with you." Gerard got up and walked over to where the three sat. "Stand up," he told Kate.

She looked at him, trying to comprehend what he was saying, but she couldn't. Gerard grabbed the front of her T-shirt and pulled her to her feet.

"Take your slimy hands off her," Tony said, trying to stand up.

Gerard slammed the side of his gun into Tony's head. Tony grunted and fell back.

"The next time I shoot him in the face," Gerard told Kate. "Is that what you want?"

"Please . . . please, Tony. Don't."

"Don't worry, Sir Knight," Gerard said, an evil smile twisting his features. "I'm not going to hurt the damsel . . . yet." He stared at Kate. "Turn around."

Kate didn't want to break her gaze away from Gerard. If she could keep her eyes on him, she felt safer. If she couldn't see him, it was like knowing the boogeyman was hiding in your room. Unseen monsters were always scarier in your head.

"I said, turn around!"

Kate jumped at the sound of his raised voice. She slowly turned around, praying for God's protection. She couldn't hold back the hot tears that streamed down her face. She looked at Tony and saw the anger in his expression. She kept her gaze locked on his. It was the only way she could stay on her feet.

She felt Gerard grab her bound hands. He seemed to be fiddling with the plastic ties. She cringed at his touch.

"Okay," he said finally. "Now turn around and look at me."

Kate did as he'd asked. As she looked into his wild eyes, she felt as if her mind would break. Her whole body shook, and she couldn't control it.

"Kate, it's going to be all right." Tony's voice broke through the fog, and she fought to hold on to it. "Don't give in to him. Don't give him the satisfaction."

Gerard laughed again, and then he got right up in her face. "I saw your wrists. How can you despise me for giving you

scars when you've given them to yourself? Makes you a hypo-
crite, doesn't it?"

Kate didn't say anything. She couldn't get the words out.
Was Gerard right? He'd tried to destroy her, but she'd tried
to destroy herself, as well. The feeling she'd had when she'd
cut her wrists was back. She just wanted it to be over. She
wanted peace. She wanted to sleep at night without hearing
Gerard's voice, hearing his laughter, hearing Kelly's screams.
Perhaps letting him kill her would finally make the pain stop.
Maybe it was an answer to prayer.

"Kate, don't listen to him."

Tony's voice broke through the fog. "You're stronger than
he is. You're more valuable. He's just a sick, twisted coward
hiding behind a gun. Without a weapon in his hand, he's
useless. Impotent."

Kate knew instantly that Tony was trying to divert Gerard's attention from her. Gerard pushed her down on the
couch and took a step toward Tony, his gun pointed at Tony's
head. She had to do something.

"But . . . but I chose to live," she squeaked out. "I changed
my mind. The scars I caused are healing. Your scars are
bleeding all over you and everything you touch. You can't
control yourself, and I can. I'm getting better. You're still
a loser."

Her last sentence seemed to draw his attention, and he
turned back toward Kate.

"Big talk for someone who has very little time to live. I'm
glad you think you're better than me. Maybe you are . . . for
now. But I'm going to walk away from this, and you aren't.
So who's the loser, Kate? Not me."

"Actually, you've lost already. I changed your plans when I got out of your car. You didn't count on that, did you?"

Gerard glared at her. "It was a rental car. I had no idea there was a release inside the trunk. But regardless, here we are, huh? In the end it didn't do you any good."

"But it proves your plan isn't working perfectly. That you're not ensured of success. Maybe there are other things you've forgotten. Other things that will go wrong. Just like with Kelly and me. That didn't go according to plan, either, did it?"

Kate couldn't believe the words coming out of her mouth. It was as if someone else were talking through her and she was just listening. But somehow, little by little, challenging Gerard was making her feel stronger.

At first Gerard looked furious, but suddenly he smiled. "You're right, sometimes things don't go as planned. Like when I went to your little café. You weren't there, but your cook was."

Kate felt as if Gerard had just struck her in the face. "What . . . what are you talking about?"

Gerard rocked back on his heels with glee. "Oh, I see your *friends* haven't told you. Wow. Great friends. Can't trust them to tell you the truth."

"Gerard . . ." Tony said, his voice a warning.

"What's he talking about, Tony?" Kate said. "Tell me."

"I'm talking about your cook," Gerard said. "I went to the restaurant looking for you before I went to your home. Unfortunately, your cook was in the kitchen, singing at the top of her lungs. She's tone deaf, by the way."

Gerard got closer to Kate's face. She could smell his sour breath.

"She didn't hear me. Not until the last second. Right before I plunged my knife into her chest."

Kate felt her brief bravado turn to mush. She whirled toward Tony. "Is he telling the truth? Did he kill Bella?"

A tear ran down Tony's cheek. "I'm so sorry, Kate. I was going to tell you once we were rescued. I . . . I just didn't want you to have to deal with it until you felt safe again."

Kate turned back to Gerard. He'd taken Kelly. And now he'd taken Bella. Something rose up inside of her. Something she'd never felt before.

Alan Gerard was done stealing from her. She was going to see him dead if it was the last thing she ever did.

CHAPTER
TWENTY-EIGHT

Tally stared at the picture of Darrell Fisher's mother and shook his head. She'd died in an accident, hadn't she? Why did she look like the other victims? Was it coincidence, or was it something more?

While waiting for the pictures from Leon, he'd done an online search for Darrell R. Fisher. Unfortunately, he'd found a death certificate. Seemed Fisher had died not long after leaving Garden City. A little further research revealed he'd died in a motorcycle accident. Obviously, Darrell's uncle had no idea his nephew had been dead all these years. Leon had told him the uncle was dying. For now, Tally decided to keep this information to himself. As a law enforcement officer, Leon would feel obligated to tell Fred his nephew was dead, and Tally couldn't help but wonder if the old man's death would be a little more peaceful without knowing the truth about Darrell.

Tally had all kinds of notes scattered across his desk, along with the B.E.K. file. Interesting, but there was no way to make sense of it all. He grabbed some index cards and began to write on them. Each fact as it came to him. Then he began to put the cards in order. What happened first? What had caused the emergence of a serial killer?

He put the card with Dorothy Fisher's name on it at the top of his desk. Under that, he put a card with Tammy Rice's name. Then Ann Barton's. He stared at them for a while. This seemed to be the order in which they'd died. He picked up the first card and wrote *Darrell Fisher* on it. Then he wrote *Warren Killian* on Tammy Rice's card. After staring at it for a few seconds, he added *Barney Clevenger*. Were these boys murderers? Had they really killed together? He picked up the card with Ann Barton's name on it. He wrote *Barney Clevenger* on that. He put all three cards together and studied them. First of all, it was entirely possible that Dorothy Fisher had simply died in an accident. The police had investigated, and from what Tally could tell, they'd done a thorough job. Darrell was never suspected of hurting his mother. However, Darrell had been Barney's friend, and authorities knew Barney was involved in killing Ann Barton and Tammy Rice. So Tally couldn't rule out the notion that Dorothy's death was something else. Part of this murderous arrangement. And what about Warren? He and Barney went to the same school. Barney knew Darrell; therefore it made sense to conclude that Warren probably knew Barney, too. A little research had uncovered some of Barney's history. His mother had died of cancer when he was young. She'd hardly had time to twist him into a serial killer. And why was Ann buried in Dorothy's grave? What was the significance? Why would Barney care about Dorothy Fisher? Unless he'd killed her, too. Maybe he and Darrell killed her together. That made the most sense.

So . . . Darrell and Barney kill Dorothy Fisher. Then they kill Ann? And what about Warren? Could all three of them be involved? Maybe B.E.K. had started out as a three-man team. But now Barney Clevenger was dead, so was Darrell, and Warren was living in Shelter Cove, Arkansas, where the only survivor of the Blue-Eyed Killer lived.

Tally picked up the card with Warren's name on it. He was the only person still in play. Could there be more to him than met the eye?

Tally scribbled one more name on a card. *Alan Gerard.* He put the card next to the others. No matter what, Alan didn't seem to belong. He picked up a file with information about Gerard. Gerard was born in Lincoln, Nebraska. He barely graduated high school, then moved to St. Louis when he was twenty-five. He'd spent almost fifteen years as a truck driver. A year before the attack on the O'Brien girls, he'd secured the job at the college. Tally couldn't find any connection between him and Clevenger or Killian . . . at first. Then, on a hunch, he went back through some notes he'd made a long time ago. It only took him a few minutes to find what he was looking for. Three hours after fleeing the scene of Kelly O'Brien's murder, Gerard was arrested and hauled down to the St. Louis P.D. There, on the list of arresting officers, was the name . . . Officer Warren Killian.

Gerard ordered Bobby to secure Kate and Tony's plastic bonds together as a way to keep them in one place. Easier to control. Once he'd completed the task, Bobby stepped back and stared at the crazed serial killer. "I . . . I did it," he said.

"Good. Now step outside," Gerard hissed.

"What are you doing?" Tony asked. "He stays with us."

"You're not in charge, Mr. DeLuca." Rather than being reassuring, Gerard's smile made Tony's stomach turn over.

"Tony . . ." Bobby looked petrified.

"He was only doing what I told him to do," Tony said. He wanted to rush Gerard, but now that he was attached to Kate, he couldn't risk putting her in the line of fire. "If you want to punish someone, punish me. Bobby's innocent."

Gerard laughed. His high-pitched voice was manic. He wasn't in a place where reasoning with him could make a difference.

"Please, Gerard. Alan. Please . . ."

Gerard ignored Tony. Instead, he grabbed Bobby and shoved him outside. He followed after him, slamming the door behind him.

"Tony, we have to do something," Kate cried.

"I know." Tony gritted his teeth and began to pull on the plastic ties. But before he could break them, he heard the sound of a gunshot. And then silence.

"What have you done?" Tony asked when Gerard came back into the cabin. "Is he . . ."

"Let's just say your friend Bobby won't be a hindrance anymore."

Kate gasped, and a surge of anger flowed through Tony. "I'm going to kill you, Gerard," Tony said. "You have my word on that."

Gerard closed the door behind him and grinned. "I don't

think you will, Mr. DeLuca. You're not in charge here. I am. But let me tell you what you *will* do. You will watch as I complete my assignment with Miss Kate. This time it will end the way it should have the first time."

"I'll never let you touch her, you piece of human garbage," Tony growled, his voice shaking with rage. "It won't happen."

"Oh, but it will. You see, even if I want you to watch, in the end, if you don't, it's not a big deal." He turned his attention to Kate, who was strangely silent. "Your choice, Kate. Either you cooperate or I'll kill him. What's your choice?"

"Don't hurt him," Kate said quietly. "Please. Just don't hurt him."

Tony turned to look at her. "Kate, don't be stupid. We'll get out of this. Help is on its way. Don't give up."

She gazed into his eyes. "I'm not giving up, but I won't allow you to die. Not if I can stop it from happening." She took a deep breath, and a tear ran down her cheek. "I love you, Tony. You don't need to say anything. I just wanted you to know."

Tony felt as if his heart had crawled up into his throat. She was probably speaking out of fear and would regret her words once they were off the mountain, but he was touched and deeply moved.

"We'll be okay," he said. "We're going to make it through this."

"Well, that was sweet," Gerard said. "Really. But you won't *make it through this*. I can guarantee it." He put down his gun and took a large knife out of a pocket of his jacket. He ran it down his own cheek. "You have an appointment, Kate, and it's time to keep it."

Gerard ordered them to stand up. Although it was difficult with the zip ties holding them together, they managed to get to their feet.

"Now turn around."

Gerard walked over to them as they faced the other way. Tony felt the muzzle of the gun against his head. Then Gerard cut the zip ties with his knife and separated them.

"You sit back down on the couch, Mr. DeLuca," Gerard said. "You come with me, Kate."

"No." Tony wasn't about to stand by and watch Kate be murdered by this madman. He had to find a way to stop this. Even if it was the last thing he'd ever do.

He swung around, intending to knock Gerard to the ground, but before he got the chance, he heard Gerard say, "You're not supposed to be here."

As he dove toward Gerard, Tony heard a shot ring out.

Leon followed Linda into Fred Fisher's house. Although he felt like nothing more than a pack mule carrying supplies, he was happy to know that Fred would soon be living in better conditions.

"I'm going to need some time in your kitchen," Linda told Fred, who seemed overwhelmed by the people invading his home.

Leon was happy to see that Fred had changed out of his bathrobe and underwear into slacks and a shirt. He'd even run a comb through his hair.

"Best if we get out of the way, Fred," Leon said as he followed Linda to the kitchen. She began moving things off of

Fred's kitchen table and instructed Leon to put everything down.

"I need to clean the refrigerator before I put food in there," she whispered to her husband. Then she stepped out into the hallway and waved three other women from the church into the kitchen. Leon was pleased to see that none of the women appeared to be repelled by the mess and the smell. In fact, one woman, Dawn Reed, was talking to Fred as if they were old friends. The smile on Fred's face made Leon think this intervention was going to work. Dawn was the kind of person who could make an angry mountain lion lie down and purr like a kitten. She was a godsend in this situation.

"Fred, we need to get out of here for a while," Leon said as Dawn passed him in the hallway. She winked at him, and he smiled at her. Thank God for Christians who took the commandment to love your neighbors seriously.

For just a second, a look of uncertainty flashed across Fred's face. But Dawn's laughter coming from the kitchen seemed to wash away his apprehension.

"Let's sit outside," Leon said. "It's going to be a nice evening."

Fred nodded. "Okay."

As Fred headed for the front door of the small house, Leon noticed he seemed to have trouble walking. Leon stepped in front of him and opened the door. He wanted to ask Fred if he needed help, but he knew the old man's pride would probably keep him from accepting it. Fred held on to the doorframe and then grabbed the arm of one of the lawn chairs on his front porch. Leon breathed a sigh of relief when he finally sat down. Leon pulled up the other lawn chair and sat down next to him.

It was late afternoon, and a light breeze wafted past them. Leon loved Kansas in the spring, and he breathed in the fresh air. A real treat after being inside the smelly house.

"So did you hit anything when you shot at the sky?" Fred asked suddenly.

It took Leon a moment to figure out what he was talking about. "I'm not sure, Fred," he answered slowly. "Ever since we found Ann Barton's body, something's been bothering me. I just can't put my finger on it."

"What's that, Sarge?"

Leon took a deep breath and blew it out. "I've been trying to figure out why Ann was buried with Dorothy. What's the connection?"

Fred grunted. "Not sure there is one, Sarge. You might be looking too hard."

"Just seems . . . odd somehow." He shook his head. "We have three boys with dead mothers. One of the boys is dead. One is missing, and the other is . . . well, I'm afraid he might be going after the only woman who ever survived an attack by the Blue-Eyed Killer."

Fred raised his eyebrows. "Who are you talkin' about?"

"Warren. Warren Killian. Tammy Rice's son."

Fred snapped his fingers. "That's it. That's the guy who came by here and asked about Darrell. I didn't make the connection."

"Warren Killian was here?"

Fred nodded. "Yep, a few days ago. As I said, there was somethin' about him I didn't trust. That's why I didn't tell him about Darrell's box. I'll bet a part of me recognized him. I just couldn't remember him well enough to realize who he was."

"And he was asking about Darrell?"

"Yeah. He wanted to know if I knew where Darrell was. I told him I didn't. Hadn't seen him for years. Ever since he left town." Fred shook his head. "He didn't seem to believe me."

"Did he ask about Barney Clevenger?"

"Yeah, but I didn't recognize the name. Like I told you, I only knew him by his nickname. Stinky."

"And Warren didn't know the nickname? Even though he went to school with him?"

"Didn't seem to. They were a couple of years apart, you know. Darrell and Stinky left town before they graduated. Makes sense that Warren didn't know too much about them."

Leon turned this information over in his head. "So the only thing he learned from you is that you didn't know where Darrell was?"

"Yeah. He asked some questions about Dorothy's death, but I told him I didn't want to talk to him about that."

"Fred, is there any possibility Darrell killed his mother?"

"Nah. No possibility whatsoever."

Leon studied Fred for a moment. "But you said Darrell was cold-hearted. And that Dorothy was a bad mother. You don't think he could have had something to do with her death?"

Fred shook his head and looked up at the sky. "Look at those clouds. Never have seen clouds like Kansas clouds. So white and fluffy."

Leon didn't know whether to push Fred a little bit or let it go. Maybe it didn't matter after all these years. Darrell was gone. Might even be dead. "Yeah, they're great. Sometimes I like to sit outside and just watch the clouds. Relaxes me."

"Yeah, me too." Fred turned his head and looked at Leon. "Darrell didn't kill Dorothy, Sarge. I'm sure of it."

"How can you be certain?"

"Because I did it. I killed my sister."

CHAPTER
TWENTY-NINE

At first, Tony thought he'd been shot, but there wasn't any pain or blood. He could hear Kate weeping softly. Then he noticed Gerard lying on the floor, his eyes open and sightless. Tony looked over toward the door and saw Bobby standing there, a gun in his hand. His eyes were wild, and the gun shook uncontrollably. If Tony didn't get it away from him, he was going to accidentally shoot him or Kate. Tony put his wrists together and then yanked suddenly on the zip ties. As he knew they would, they broke immediately. Tony shook them off and left them on the floor. Then he got up and walked carefully toward Bobby. Bobby pointed the gun at Tony, his whole body trembling.

"Bobby, it's me," Tony said. "It's Tony. Give me the gun. Everything's okay now. We're safe."

Slowly, recognition dawned on Bobby's face. He held out the gun. "Is he . . . is he dead?"

Tony gently took the gun from his hand and breathed a

sigh of relief. "Yes, he's dead, Bobby. You saved us. We're safe because of you. Kate's safe because of you."

Bobby nodded. "I didn't want to shoot him. I just didn't know what else to do."

Tony put the gun on the kitchen table. He noticed Bobby sway a little. "Here, sit down, okay?" He helped him over to a chair. Once Bobby was settled, Tony went over to Kate, who was still crying. "It's okay, Kate. Gerard is dead. He can't hurt you anymore. Do you understand?"

She looked up at him, her eyes full of tears. "I . . . I thought he'd shot you. I was so afraid."

"I'm fine. Thanks to Bobby, we're okay. I need to get those ties off your wrists, okay?" He went over to the kitchen and got a knife. Within seconds, he'd cut the ties off and freed Kate, who couldn't seem to take her eyes off Gerard.

"Are you sure he's . . . dead?" she asked. "Could you check?"

"Yeah, I'll check." Tony knelt down next to Gerard and put his finger on his throat even though he knew the man was gone. After a few seconds, he nodded. "No pulse, Kate. He's dead. He'll never hurt anyone else."

He was surprised to see her smile. "Good." She swung her gaze up to his. "Can you move him outside? Please?"

"I can't do that, I'm sorry. It would compromise evidence we need to protect."

"Evidence?" Bobby said. "What do you mean? Am I in trouble?"

Tony stood up. "No, Bobby. Absolutely not. Gerard had a gun to my head, and he was threatening Kate's life. Trust me. You'll be hailed a hero. Even so, this scene will be processed. It's just procedure, as in any unnatural death."

Bobby nodded slowly, looking relieved.

"What happened outside?" Tony asked. "We thought you were dead."

"I thought I was too at first. But Gerard told me to get out of here. He fired his gun in the air. I guess he thought I was a coward, and I'd run away."

"I don't think that's it. He knew it would take hours for you to get down the mountain and find help. And he wanted someone to let the world know he's the Blue-Eyed Killer. With Kate and me dead, no one could be sure it was him. You were his witness." He smiled at Bobby. "But you weren't the coward he thought you were."

"He . . . he said you weren't supposed to be here," Kate added. "He was sure you'd left us." She walked over to Bobby, leaned over, and hugged him. "You saved my life. I'll never be able to thank you enough."

When she straightened up, Bobby smiled at her. "You don't have to thank me. I'm grateful I could help." He looked over at Tony. "And glad you made me take that gun, Tony. If you hadn't . . ."

Tony held up one hand. "Let's not think about that now, okay? We're alive and Gerard is dead." He got a paper towel and picked up Gerard's gun. Then he carried it into the kitchen. After finding a new plastic storage bag, he gently lowered the gun into the bag and put it on the table. "Not that you planned on grabbing this any time soon, but please don't touch it." Although he didn't want to contaminate the crime scene, he went searching for a clean sheet. Usually, if bodies were covered at all, law enforcement used special paper blankets that wouldn't add transfer. A clean sheet, washed several times, was the next best thing. CSIs might not appreciate his actions, but he was willing to take the heat. Tony didn't want Kate to have to look at Gerard any longer. Besides, it wasn't like they needed to preserve evidence so they could identify the shooter. They knew exactly what had happened. He found what he was looking for in a linen closet and carried it into the living room. He was about to cover Gerard's body when Kate stopped him.

"Wait a minute," she said. She walked over to Gerard's lifeless body and stared down at it. "You lose," she said. Her voice held a note of triumph. "I'm still here, and I'm gonna make it." She turned around and smiled at Tony. "Cover this creep up. He's out of my life now, and I don't want to see his ugly face ever again."

Tony nodded and carefully positioned the sheet over Gerard's body, his knife still clutched in his hand. Kate's reaction surprised him. "Are . . . are you sure you're okay?" he asked her after he was done.

Kate walked over and put her hand on his arm. "I'm fine. I guess I'm facing my demons, and I've decided I'm going to win this battle."

Tony felt his heart swell with pride. He was proud of her strength, but he was even prouder of her willingness to stand up to the things that had held her in bondage for so long. She still had a long road of healing ahead of her, but she'd make it. "Good for you," he said. "It's perfectly understandable. He's spent enough time taking up room in your head. I don't want to look at him, either."

"So now what, Tony?" Bobby asked. "What do we do?"

Tony walked over to the front door and looked out. The

rain had turned to a fine mist. "It's looking better. I guess we wait it out for a while longer, and then we can try to get back to the car. Or . . ." He looked back at the sheet covering Gerard.

"No," Kate said. "Oh no."

"It's just a car, Kate. If we can get down the mountain, we need to do that. Gerard pulled his car over. It's much closer, and it's not stuck in the mud like Bobby's SUV. It might be our only chance." He looked at Bobby. "What was Gerard talking about? Some road that could get him off the mountain safely?"

Bobby shook his head. "I have no idea. There are a lot of roads up here, but nothing anyone would call safe after a heavy rain. They're all dangerous. He had really bad information."

"I wonder who gave it to him," Kate commented. "Could someone be working with him?"

Tony shrugged. "He could have simply overheard something. Seems to me he headed up here because he thought he'd have you all to himself. He didn't count on the rain, and the only reason he found the cabin is because we led him to it. Doesn't sound like someone who was getting help."

"I hope you're right," she said. "I'd hate to think he has another partner."

"Well, he said he was free from his mentor," Bobby added. "Doesn't sound like anyone else was involved."

"Regardless, we need to get out of here." Tony took a deep breath and went back over to the sheet. He lifted it and put his hand into Gerard's jacket pocket. His hand closed over a set of car keys along with a piece of paper. Tony was grateful he'd found the keys, since he didn't relish going through Gerard's other pockets. After pulling out the car keys, he put them on the floor next to the body. Then he grabbed a paper towel, carefully pulled out the piece of folded paper, and opened it. He wasn't surprised to find the lyrics to "Blue-Eyed Angel." Thankfully, Gerard had never gotten the chance to use them. Being careful not to touch it directly, Tony refolded the paper and put it back in the pocket where he'd found it. Then he checked the other jacket pocket. His fingers closed around a phone. Once again, he lifted it out with a paper towel. After turning it on, he was disappointed to find it wasn't getting a signal.

Tony carried it over to the kitchen table and put the phone in a plastic bag. "We should leave this here, but we've got to be able to call for help as soon as we can. I'm taking it with me." He stuck it in his pocket. Then he held up the keys. "This creep might actually help us get to safety. That would be justice, wouldn't it?"

Bobby stood up, a little steadier now. "I really would like to get off this mountain." He looked over at Kate. "But what about your feet?" he asked her. "Do you think you can make it to the car?"

Kate smiled. "I feel like I can do anything now. Besides, these shoes are really helping. I'll be fine."

"Good," Tony said. He looked over at Bobby. "Let's heat up that food and get something in our stomachs. Then if help hasn't arrived, we'll try to make it to Gerard's car, okay?"

"Sure." Bobby went back into the kitchen. Within a few minutes, the propane stove was going. Bobby opened the cans, plopped the contents into a couple of metal pans, and began heating everything up. When the food was hot, they all sat down at the kitchen table and ate. Tony couldn't believe how hungry he was now that the danger was past. They finished off the tamales and the corned beef hash.

Bobby had just taken the stew off the little stove when Tony held up his hand. "Okay, I've had all I can eat. This might be cheap food, but I can't remember the last time anything ever tasted this good."

Kate laughed. "I agree."

"You're both delusional, but I'm glad you're satisfied," Bobby said with a smile. He plopped the stew into a large serving bowl and put a ladle in it. He grabbed a couple of bowls from a nearby cabinet. "I'm still hungry even if you're not."

Tony shook his head and grinned at the skinny man who could eat more than he could. "You go on and eat," he said. "You deserve it."

"You're eating free at the diner from now on," Kate said. "I'm sure . . ." She stopped talking, and her face fell. "I . . . I forgot. Bella won't be there, will she?" She looked away. "I'll just close it. Without her, I don't want to mess with it anymore."

Tony reached over and put his hand on hers. "Don't make a decision like that now. This isn't the time."

She didn't respond but nodded as if she understood.

Tony stood up and opened the front door. The rain had finally stopped. "Thank God. Everyone finish eating, and then get ready to leave. Boy, I love the mountains, but I don't think I'll be doing any hiking for a while. It will feel good to get back to civilization. Give me level ground . . . at least for a while."

"I agree," Bobby said. "I'll get this cleaned up and be ready to go in a minute." He rinsed out their dishes, turned off the stove, and quickly cleaned up. "I'll come back before Mike arrives and get everything in order. Uh, after they get Gerard out of here, that is. But right now, I just want to get far away from this cabin."

Kate stood up. "I agree. Let's go."

Tony found a trash bag and put their dirty clothes in it. "Can you get this when you come back here, Bobby? I don't want to carry it all the way to the car."

"No problem. Just put it in the corner."

A few minutes later, they were ready to go. Bobby was turning off the battery-powered lamps when Tony cocked his head toward the door. "Ready?"

Kate and Bobby nodded and they headed outside. Bobby made sure to lock the door behind him, and they all stepped out into the clearing.

Tony was reaching into his pocket to check the phone again when someone stepped out of the tree line, pointing a gun at them.

"Deputy Killian," Tony said, surprised to see the lawman standing there with his weapon drawn. "What are you doing? Put the gun down."

Killian shook his head. "No way. This is going to stop. Today."

Tony was trying to decide if he should reach for his own gun when another man ran out of the trees a few yards away from Killian. Dressed in plain clothes, with the words *U.S. Marshal* stamped on his windbreaker, he had his gun pointed right at Warren Killian.

"You heard the man," the deputy said. "Put the gun down now. I won't ask a second time."

"I can't," Killian said. "You don't understand."

Killian didn't have the chance to get another word out. The deputy fired and Killian collapsed.

CHAPTER
THIRTY

Leon and Fred sat silently, watching two butterflies flit around a tree in the center of Fred's small yard.

Finally, Leon said, "Just what did you mean, Fred? About killing your sister?"

The old man cleared his throat. "I meant exactly what I said, Sarge." He leaned back in his chair. "That woman terrorized Darrell. Beat him. Locked him in the closet. Burned him with cigarettes. I know I said there was something wrong with him. And there was. But my sister made him that way. She was sick in her head and in her soul."

"I read the report of her death. Coroner ruled it accidental."

"Yup. He did. Mr. A. W. Simpson. He was the coroner for this part of the country for many, many years. Used to be Dorothy's neighbor. Knew how troubled she was."

Leon straightened in his chair and leaned forward, staring at Fred. "Are you trying to tell me Dr. Simpson falsified his report?"

Fred shook his head. "Nope. Wouldn't do that. He was a fine man with a good reputation. I'd never say or do nothing to put a damper on that."

"So he didn't write the report to protect you?"

Fred was quiet for a while, his eyes following the carefree butterflies. Finally, he said, "You know, Sarge, sometimes we're faced with a situation. You gotta make a quick decision. Let's say you were standing on the stairs with . . . Hitler. Hitler stumbles. You can reach out and grab him. Save him. Or you can give him a little push the other way. What would you do?"

Leon snorted. "Dorothy wasn't Hitler, Fred. She was your sister."

"You didn't answer my question."

"I'm sworn to uphold the law. To protect life."

"So you think saving him would protect life?"

Leon stared down at the ground for a moment. "Honestly, Fred? No. I wouldn't save him. I'd probably push him."

"Then that's my answer to your question. I knew what was happening to that boy, and I had to do somethin'. I'd hoped it would save him, but in the end, I guess it didn't really make any difference. Some people are too badly damaged. They just can't be saved."

"Now, I can't agree with you there, Fred. God can save anyone. Heal anything. Turn the worst person around."

"Can He give them a new heart?"

Leon grinned at him. "As a matter of fact, He can. That's what He's best at."

Fred was quiet for a moment. Then he said, "Will you do me a favor, Sarge?"

"If I can."

"The doctors give me about a month. Prostate cancer. Too far gone to fight. Before you leave, talk to me again about this God of yours. I think I'd like to know more."

"I will. You have my word."

Leon could hear the women chattering inside the house. The home's unkempt condition sure didn't seem to be getting them down. Of course, they loved to help people. Made them feel needed.

"What are you gonna do, Sarge?" Fred said.

"About what?"

"You know about what. About Dorothy. About the way she died."

Leon took a deep breath and blew it out. "Well, seems to me Doc Simpson already took care of the situation. Deemed it an accidental death. It's not like he's around so anyone can contest his findings. Best if we just let sleeping dogs lie."

"Thanks, Sarge." Fred sighed. "Sure wish Darrell woulda turned out different. Woulda done anything to see that."

"Maybe he did, Fred. You don't know where he is or who he is now. Could be he turned his life around."

"I tell myself that all the time. But in my heart, I know it's not true."

Leon shrugged. "Maybe your heart's wrong. Better to keep a positive attitude. It'll make it easier to sleep at night."

"I wonder sometimes if I'd left things alone and Dorothy woulda killed him . . ."

"Hey. Nothing can be gained by thinking that way." Leon turned toward Fred. "You're a good man, Fred. You made a decision based on your concern for your nephew. Right or wrong, you were trying to protect him."

"Wish I could get it out of my mind. It haunts me. Every day."

"Time to let it go."

Fred ran his hand over his stubbly chin. "Do you think God will forgive me?"

"I can guarantee it."

"But will I ever be able to forgive myself?"

"That will be up to you. But it seems kinda silly to hold something against yourself if God has forgiven you, doesn't it?"

"I . . . I guess you're right, Sarge. Sounds right to me, anyway."

The front door swung open and Linda stood there with two small plates. "Thought you two might like some of my brownies."

"Why yes, ma'am," Fred said. "That sounds wonderful."

"Wait 'til you taste 'em, Fred," Leon said, smiling at his wife. "You're in for a treat."

"Why, just for that, I'll get you guys something to drink. Coffee? Milk?"

Fred frowned at her as he reached for his plate. "Ain't got no milk, lady. And my coffee's pretty old."

"Nothing to worry about, Fred. We brought both."

Linda went back into the house, and the door closed behind her. Fred took a bite of his brownie. "Good," he said once he'd swallowed. "Can't remember ever havin' a better brownie." He turned to look at Leon. "You're a lucky man, Sarge. A really lucky man."

Leon nodded. "Don't I know it."

As they sat and enjoyed Linda's brownies, Leon turned over his conversation with Fred in his mind. This was one bit of information he wouldn't be passing along. It wouldn't change anything. It was time to walk away. His part in the drama of the Blue-Eyed Killer was at an end. Tomorrow he'd put in for retirement.

But now it was time to save a man's soul.

Tony could hardly believe they were finally on their way down the mountain. Thankfully, the LEOs who had come to rescue them had four-wheel drive with more power than Bobby's old SUV. The rain had finally stopped. The roads were wet, but the flooding seemed under control.

Tony sat in a vehicle driven by the deputy Marshal who shot Killian. He'd introduced himself as Gil Bennett. Killian was being transported to the hospital by two other deputy Marshals. Kate was in the back seat with Bobby, and Tony was up front with Gil.

The FBI had claimed the crime scene. Of course, local officers had a problem with that and had voiced their bid for territorial rights. It didn't matter to Tony or Gil. Marshals weren't investigators, so the crime scene didn't matter much to them now. The FBI would transport the body. The most important thing was that Kate was finally free from Gerard. No testifying.

Tony wondered what she'd do now. Would she stay in Shelter Cove or go somewhere else? Would she consider going back to St. Louis? He doubted she'd be in a hurry to return to the city where she'd faced such horror. He also wondered about Gerard's fans. Now that they knew he wasn't B.E.K., they would probably fade away.

He glanced up at the rear view mirror. Kate was looking out the window, her expression pensive. Tony had noticed a change in her. As if she'd found herself again. He prayed she would finally be able to put the past behind her.

"So tell me more about Killian," Tony said. "You say he was in league with Gerard?"

Gil shrugged. "I don't know all the details. Just what your boss sent me. Killian knew a kid named . . . Barney something. Barney is Malcolm Bodine's real name. I guess they started out together, until Bodine was killed." He turned to look at Tony. "I've got a file from Batterson on my phone. Pictures, too. Anything yet?"

Tony tried Gil's phone again. "Not yet. I guess we're still too far up the mountain."

"Might not work well until we get down. It's real spotty out here."

"Yeah, believe me, we found that out. You know, Gerard kept going on and on about some *mentor*," Tony said. "Must have been Killian."

"Maybe."

"Why was Killian in Shelter Cove? That can't be a co-incidence."

"I can't believe Warren had anything to do with Gerard," Kate said. "I know Warren Killian. He's not anything like him. I doubt he even knows who I really am."

"Well, unfortunately he does," Tony said, turning around to look at her. "He told me he saw TV coverage of the trial and recognized you. Said he was trying to protect you."

"So why did he show up with a gun? And why didn't he put it down when I ordered him to?" Gil asked. "Your boss told me to watch out for you. He was right."

Tony nodded. "He usually is. It is odd that Killian refused to drop his weapon. He knew he was in danger."

"Probably didn't want to go to jail," Gil said.

"Maybe."

Kate turned to Bobby. "You know Warren. Do you think he'd have anything to do with Alan Gerard? That he's someone who wanted to hurt me?"

Bobby shook his head. "No, I don't. He doesn't seem like that type of person at all."

"Do you agree with the EMTs, Deputy Bennett? Will he recover?" Kate asked.

"Please call me Gil. Yeah, he should be fine. I just wounded him enough to get him to put down the gun. I don't like killing people I don't know much about."

"I'd like to talk to him," Tony said.

"We'll have to check when we get back to Shelter Cove. He needs to be transported to the hospital. Maybe after that you can visit him. 'Course, the feds are gonna be all over that. You might not get the chance to see him."

"Yeah, that's true." Tony agreed with Gil's assessment, but he was determined to get to Killian somehow. Although he wanted to believe the situation had been resolved, Tony still had questions. Why was Warren in Shelter Cove? Why did he come after them? To kill Kate? Why wait until she's kidnapped and being chased by someone in law enforcement? Didn't make sense. Besides, if Killian was in on Kate's abduction, why not let Gerard just carry out his plan?

And what did he mean about not being able to put down the gun?

There was one other huge concern. If Killian wasn't Gerard's mentor, it meant someone was still out there. Someone who could still be a threat.

Tony rubbed his forehead. He wanted to feel relieved. They'd been rescued. Kate was safe. But something inside him was still churning. As if he was still missing something. Something really important.

CHAPTER
THIRTY-ONE

Batterson hung up his phone. "Well, they're on their way down," he told Mark, who sat in a chair across from him. It was late, but neither man had been willing to leave until they knew their deputy and their witness were safe.

"And Gerard is dead?"

Batterson nodded. "Seems like that local guy who helped Tony find O'Brien shot Gerard before he could hurt her. Thank God."

"Wow. Good thing he was with them. But you haven't heard from Tony yet?"

"No. The vehicle with Killian in it got down the mountain first. They've called for an ambulance to transport him to the hospital. DeLuca's vehicle shouldn't be too far behind. Should be getting a call from him soon."

The phone rang and Batterson picked it up. "Batterson." He nodded at Mark and smiled. "About time, DeLuca. I was about ready to come down there and pull you off that mountain myself."

"Sorry about losing touch, Chief. No reception during the storm, and then I lost my phone. It's on the mountain somewhere. I'm using Deputy Bennett's phone."

"Listen, get back to town, clean up, get some rest, and call me tomorrow with the details. And we need to talk about O'Brien. Gerard's dead, so obviously she doesn't need to show up in court. She has some decisions to make."

"Yeah, she does. Thanks, Chief. To be honest, I'm beat. Can't wait to get something to eat and crash. Thanks for getting us help."

"A lot of those LEOs went against orders to go up there and rescue you. They're the ones to thank. Not me."

"Okay, Chief. Talk to you tomorrow."

"Good-bye." Batterson started to hang up but suddenly pulled the phone back up to his mouth. "Tony? Are you still there?" But Tony had already hung up.

"Something else you wanted to say to him?" Mark asked.

"Yeah, just wanted to make sure he got the information I sent to Deputy Bennett, but I guess that can wait until tomorrow. He needs to know the truth about Killian."

"You believe he wanted to hurt O'Brien."

Batterson nodded. "I assume that was it. Can't think of any other reason. Like I said, Gerard didn't kill his mother."

"But it isn't sitting well with you, is it?"

"No, but I'm tired and hungry. Maybe that's the only message my gut's sending me."

Mark chuckled. "That could be. Why don't you and I head to Bailey's Range for cheeseburgers and fried pickles?"

Batterson sighed deeply. "Sounds perfect. Let's do it." He

raised an eyebrow at Mark. "But what about your fiancée? Won't she mind?"

Mark laughed. "No. She wouldn't mind anyway, but tonight Mercy and her mother are going to their recovery group. I'm free as a bird."

"Good." Batterson turned off the computer, grabbed his jacket, and headed for the door. Before he left, he looked around the room. Another day's work done. The darkness beaten back a little more. His mother would be proud. He hesitated for a moment, his hand on the door. So why was there still a knot in his stomach? Although he usually followed his instincts, he couldn't find a reason to question the results they'd gotten today. He took a deep breath, closed the door, and walked away.

After Tony talked to Batterson, it took another twenty minutes for them to finally turn down the road toward Shelter Cove. Kate couldn't help but look back at the mountain as they drove away from it. So many things had happened there. She'd faced her greatest fear and survived. She'd confessed her love for Tony, and she'd confronted her anger at God.

Something else had happened on that mountain. When Kate stood face-to-face with her greatest fear, it began to grow weaker and the knowledge that God loved her got stronger. It was as if fear had blocked her ability to connect to Him. She still had no idea why Kelly had died and she'd lived, but she knew God hadn't abandoned her. No matter what happened in life, God's love and grace were constant. The one thing that would never waver. Never change. For the first time in years, Kate felt peace.

She had no idea what would happen next, but she was ready for something new. Without the specter of Gerard hovering over her. She needed time to think. Time to plan. She'd spent six years living a life centered around Gerard's actions. Now he was gone, and she was free. But who was she now? What did she want?

She glanced over at Bobby, who'd fallen asleep. He'd given up so much to protect her. She felt a rush of affection for him. How could she ever repay him? She knew Tony had wanted to take Gerard down himself. Frankly, she'd wanted to do it, too. To avenge Kelly and Bella. But it would have added to her scars. Given Gerard one more part of her soul. It seemed Bobby had accepted the new scars. No matter what happened next, she would never allow her friendship with him to suffer. It was all she could give him, but she knew somehow that it would be enough for Bobby.

She turned and watched the trees go by on the road back to Shelter Cove. Although she felt great peace, she still couldn't accept that Warren was some kind of mentor to a serial killer. Maybe it was true. She'd been wrong about people before. Still, she'd always felt that Warren was someone she could trust. Someone who watched over her. How could she have been so wrong?

When they drove into Shelter Cove, Tony looked for the SUV that had carried Deputy Killian to town. He wanted a chance to talk to him before the ambulance arrived. When they pulled up near the café where all the LEOs' cars were parked, Tony turned to look at Bobby, who had dozed off during the ride. He was blinking and looking around, as if trying to get his bearings.

"I have something to do. Bobby, will you walk Kate over to her house? I'll meet you there, Kate, after I'm done."

"Sure, Tony," Bobby said, obviously trying to suppress a yawn.

"You can go home after she's inside," Tony said, smiling. "She'll be fine."

"I don't understand why anyone needs to 'walk me,'" Kate said. "I'm not a dog."

"I know, I know," Tony said. "I'm probably being overprotective, but there's still something about Killian that doesn't sit right with me. I want to talk to him before I feel you're completely safe." He noticed the look on Kate's face. "Don't worry," he said, smiling. "Always a Marshal. Always a protector."

"It comes with the territory," Gil confirmed. "It's in our DNA." He nodded at Tony. "I can walk her home, Bobby."

"No, I'll do it," Bobby said. "I want to."

"Thanks anyway," Kate said to Gil. "But I feel safe with Bobby, and I'm sure you need to check in with your team."

"Yeah. It's been a long day, and we still have to inform our chief about the results of our . . . insurgence."

"You won't get into trouble, will you?" she asked.

Gil shook his head. "No. We got results. It's hard to argue with that. Besides, our chief was secretly cheering us on, I'm sure."

"As was mine," Tony said. "Don't worry about us, Kate. Let's just get you home. I'm sure you'd like a shower."

Kate laughed. "Are you saying I'm dirty?"

Tony and Bobby laughed, too, looking down at themselves.

"Yeah," Tony said. "I'm saying we're all filthy. I don't think I've been this dirty since I was a kid and my brother pushed me into a mud hole. Boy, was my mom mad."

"Well, no one's mad at you tonight," Kate said softly.

Kate gazed around the vehicle, taking in all three of the men who'd saved her life. "Thank you. There aren't enough words in the English language to thank all of you enough. If it wasn't for you . . ." Her words trailed off because of the lump in her throat. All she could do was nod as tears slipped down her face.

Bobby reached over and awkwardly patted her on the shoulder. "Don't cry, Kate. We're just all glad you're okay. And like I told Tony, this was the adventure of my life. My boring existence has been shattered forever."

Kate laughed through her tears. "I'm glad we're friends, Bobby."

Bobby smiled. "I guess everyone has a destiny. I was just where I was supposed to be."

Kate leaned over and hugged him. "I think you're right."

Tony got out of the SUV and then leaned back in and nodded at Kate. "I'll see you in a little bit."

Kate said good-bye and took off her seat belt. Then she opened the door and climbed out. It was a beautiful evening in Shelter Cove. The rain clouds were gone, and the stars twinkled brilliantly in the sky. She breathed in the night air and thanked God for getting her home.

Once Bobby got out, Gil said good-bye and drove over to where the rest of his team waited.

"Ready to go home?" Bobby asked.

"More than ready. Let's go."

She and Bobby walked away from all the flashing lights and emergency vehicles. All Kate really wanted now was a nice long bath and a hot cup of tea.

CHAPTER
THIRTY-TWO

Tony made his way over to the SUV that had transported Killian. Two of Bennett's team stood guard. "How is he?" Tony asked.

"Alive," the young female deputy said. "He'll recover. We cleaned him up and dressed his wound the best we could. When the ambulance gets here, the paramedics will treat him and transport him to the hospital. After that, he'll have plenty of time to think about what he's done."

Tony frowned at them. "And what is it you think he's done?"

The other deputy, an older man, stepped forward. "We heard he partnered with Alan Gerard. That he may have helped kill all those women. But . . ." He turned to look at the female deputy. "We don't draw conclusions. 'Innocent until proven guilty' means something in this country. And to the U.S. Marshals." He looked at Tony. "She's new."

The girl colored. "He pointed a gun at you," she said to Tony. "Kinda blows away his innocence, don'tcha think?"

"I don't know," Tony responded. "But I want to." He addressed the older deputy Marshal. "I'd like to talk to him. Just for a couple of minutes."

"You're not gonna shoot him, are you?" the deputy asked.

"No, not planning to."

The deputy smiled at his own joke. "Okay, but make it fast. The ambulance should be here any moment."

"Okay. No problem. I just have a couple of quick questions."

"Go for it." The deputy pointed his car door remote at the SUV and it beeped, signaling the doors were unlocked.

Tony thanked him and opened the door. Killian was leaning against the other end of the back seat, his eyes closed. Tony got in and shut the door behind him.

"Are you awake, Killian?" he asked.

The deputy grunted and opened his eyes. When he saw Tony, he struggled to sit up. "I need to talk to you," he said. "I need to explain. . . ."

"That's why I'm here. Kate doesn't believe you were working with Gerard. She seems to think there's something else going on. I'm not sure she's right, but I have to admit this whole thing isn't sitting well with me somehow. I talked to you before I left town. Your concern for her sounded real."

Killian nodded, wincing from the pain of the gunshot wound in his shoulder. "It was." He glanced out the car window. "They'll be coming for me soon. You've got to listen to me. It's important."

Tony nodded. "Okay. Go for it."

Killian twisted a bit but moaned from the pain.

"I can hear you just fine. Stay still. You don't want to start bleeding again."

Killian waved his hand at Tony. "Okay, okay. Let me talk and don't interrupt. I don't know how much time I've got."

"I'm listening."

Killian took a deep breath. "My mother was Tammy Rice, B.E.K.'s first victim. When she was killed, the police thought I'd done it. But after an investigation, they realized I didn't have anything to do with it. I wasn't even home when she was murdered. Not long after her death, another woman went missing. Ann Barton. She lived in Garden City, which isn't far from Holcomb, where my mother and I lived. The killer left behind lyrics from the song 'Blue-Eyed Angel' in Ann's bedroom. He also left them with my mom's body. The authorities finally realized they had a serial killer on their hands and completely lost interest in me." He winced in pain, took another breath, and started again. "There were these two boys. Troublemakers. One from Garden City. One from Holcomb. I'd caught them hanging around outside my house more than once. Ogling my mother. She was beautiful. Long, dark hair and lovely light blue eyes. I understood it, but I didn't like it."

"Who were these boys?" Tony asked.

"Barney Clevenger and Darrell Fisher."

"I don't know the names."

"You wouldn't. But I think they had something to do with my mom's murder. I always have. When I found out that Alan Gerard wasn't really the Blue-Eyed Killer, I went back to Garden City and talked to Darrell's uncle. Barney's family moved away long ago, and I have no idea where they are. Darrell's uncle didn't know where Darrell was. He and Barney disappeared not long after Ann's death. Seems suspicious to me."

"I don't get what this has to do with anything," Tony said, growing impatient. "I'd like to know what you're doing here. In Shelter Cove. Near Kate."

"I was a police officer in Kansas City when women started going missing from St. Louis. I transferred to St. Louis because I wanted to help catch the killer. I was actually involved in capturing Alan Gerard. The trial was on TV and, just like everyone else in the country, I followed it. I felt really close to Kate because we'd both lost loved ones to B.E.K. Two years ago, a buddy of mine came back from a fishing trip and told me he thought he'd seen Kate O'Brien in a little town in Arkansas. I didn't believe him at first, but I decided to check it out. Came here and saw Kate. That was when I joined the sheriff's department here."

"So you gave up your life to be near her? Even if you felt some connection that doesn't make sense," Tony said.

Killian sighed. "I don't know if you can understand this, but since I never really believed Gerard was B.E.K., I was afraid the real killer would come after her. I moved here so I could protect her. It meant something. Maybe it's because I couldn't save my mom. I don't know. All I can tell you is that it just felt right."

Tony could hear a siren getting closer. His time with Killian was coming to a close.

"Okay. Now tell me what you were doing on that mountain."

It was obvious Killian knew they didn't have much time.

The muscles in his face tightened. "Listen, Tony. When I got back from Garden City, I couldn't let go of the idea that the police had missed something. Then Kate disappeared. I needed her to know that there was someone else." His last sentence was mumbled, his words thick. Tony noticed he'd grown extremely pale.

The sound of a vehicle door slamming got Killian's attention. Voices outside made it clear someone was approaching. The back door of the SUV swung open, and a paramedic looked in.

"I'm sorry, sir," he said to Tony, "but I need you to step out. We've got to get this man to the hospital."

"Wait," Killian said weakly. "There's more . . . ." With that, he lost consciousness.

"Sir, I need you to step out now," the paramedic said with more emphasis. "He's bleeding. If we don't get it stopped right away, we could lose him."

"Okay, I'm gone." Tony jumped out of the SUV and strode away. He intended to check out what Killian had told him, but at this point, he figured the man was just trying to find a way out of his situation. Nothing he'd said explained why he'd pulled a gun on them. Malcolm Bodine was dead. The Blue-Eyed Killer was dead. The ravings of Warren Killian didn't change that.

As Tony started walking through the city park that sat in the middle of town, someone called out his name. He turned around to see Gil Bennett waving him down.

"Hey, DeLuca. I need to give you something your boss wanted you to see."

Tony waited for him to catch up.

"It's that file from Batterson. Can I send it to your email?"

Tony shook his head. "Wouldn't do any good. Lost my phone up on the mountain."

Gil frowned. "Just use mine. After you go through this, bring it back to me. I'll be here for a while."

"I can just get it later," Tony said.

"He acted like it was important. I get the feeling Richard Batterson doesn't like it when people don't follow his instructions."

Tony laughed. "You're right about that. Okay. Let me see it. I'll bring the phone back in a bit. Right now I want to check on Kate."

Gil handed him the phone. "Sounds good. See you later."

Tony clicked on the file Gil had pulled up. Then he sat down on a nearby bench and began to read.

Batterson's notes detailed the information that Killian had just given him. It certainly seemed that Batterson suspected the deputy of collusion in the B.E.K. murders. Still, Killian seemed genuinely convinced that someone else was involved. But how could that be? There wasn't anyone else. Was there?

Tony started to turn off Gil's phone, but then he noticed an attachment. He clicked on it and some pictures came up. All teenage boys. One looked like a young Killian. Another one reminded Tony of Malcolm Bodine. Tony briefly looked at the third picture. A boy he'd never seen before. Tony closed the file and put Gil's phone in his pocket. He'd gotten up and started toward Kate's when something struck him about one of the pictures. He pulled the phone out of his pocket and brought up the photos again. He stared at the phone for a few seconds as a horrible realization flowed through him. He quickly jammed it in his pocket and began to run for Kate's house, praying he wasn't already too late.

CHAPTER
THIRTY-THREE

When Tony reached Kate's house, he didn't bother to knock. The front door was unlocked and he ran inside, calling her name. A quick look made it clear she wasn't there, and neither was Bobby. Realizing he needed backup, he pulled out Gil's phone and called Batterson since he didn't have numbers for the LEOs onsite. No one answered, so he dialed 911. After he identified himself, the operator connected him to the local U.S. Marshals' office. They put him through to one of the deputies on the scene in Shelter Cove.

Deputy Dan Harper responded to Tony's call.

"This is Deputy Marshal Tony DeLuca," Tony said. "I need to speak to Deputy Bennett right away. It's an emergency."

A few seconds later, Gil's voice came through the phone. "What's up, Tony?" he asked.

Tony quickly brought Gil up to speed.

"Are . . . are you sure about this?" Gil asked.

"Yes. I'm positive. I need you to ask around. See if anyone

has seen Kate in the last few minutes. See if they have any idea where she might be. She's in extreme danger."

"I'll do it right away. And what are you going to do?"

"I'm going over to the resort. I'll check in with you after I get there. If you don't hear from me in the next fifteen minutes, send someone over there."

"Will do."

Tony ran out Kate's door and back to the other side of the park. His car was still next to the café, so he got in and drove quickly over to the resort. He pulled up next to the office, got out, and ran inside.

"Kate!" he yelled. "Kate, are you here?"

He looked around the front office, but no one was there. He pushed open the door behind the front desk and let himself into Bobby's apartment. Although Bobby had made Tony think he had no technical expertise, the computers and equipment in the apartment said otherwise. He ran back out into the office and was about to leave when he saw something on the front counter. It was a laptop sitting open with *Play Me* scrolling across the screen. He clicked on it and a picture came up. It was the same picture he'd seen on Gil's phone. A boy with dark hair and dead eyes. Tony moved the mouse to the face and right-clicked. It opened a video. A man appeared and began to talk. This was a man Tony didn't know. He looked like Bobby, but Bobby's innocence wasn't there. His clumsiness had vanished. The lisp was gone. This was an educated man, smooth and sure of himself. The antithesis of Bobby.

"I'm sure by now you know the truth, Tony," the man said. "Sorry to lead you astray. I know you liked Bobby.

I do, too, but alas, I'm not Bobby. My name, as you may know by now, is Darrell R. Fisher. The R is for Robert." He smiled, a cold, soulless smile. "I know, I shouldn't have given in to vanity, but one likes to keep at least a part of their identity if they can." Darrell shook his head sadly. "Hope you've located Kate by now. No worries. She's still in Shelter Cove."

"Tony?"

Tony turned around to see Kate standing in the doorway. He paused the video.

"Thank God you're okay. What are you doing out by yourself?"

"Bobby went home, and I wanted to see you. Before you get mad, I took my car so I wasn't in any danger. When I couldn't find you, I thought maybe you'd come here. Is everything okay?"

Tony walked away from the laptop and put his arms around her. "No. I was so worried about you." He pulled his head back and gazed into her eyes. "I came very close to losing you today, Kate. It made me realize how important you are to me. I'm determined to keep you safe."

She looked confused. "I don't understand. Has something happened?"

He let go of her. "I think you need to see this," he said, gesturing toward the laptop.

"What is it?"

Tony started the video over. Kate's eyes grew large and her mouth dropped open as the part Tony had already watched played.

Tony paused the video again. "I think we're about to finally get the answers we've been looking for." He pushed the play button and the video began again.

"Let me start from the beginning," Darrell said. "I grew up in Garden City, Kansas. My father killed himself when I was nine years old. My mother blamed me. Told me my father would be alive if I'd never been born. That could be true, I don't know. Mother started running around with men. Drinking, taking drugs. She hated herself. She hated me more. The abuse was constant. She would lock me in the closet for days. When she finally let me out, she'd punish me for soiling myself by making me clean up the mess before I could eat or drink. Many times, I actually passed out in that closet. She also liked to burn me with cigarettes. Eventually I learned how to endure pain without flinching. After a while I stopped feeling anything at all. Until one day when my uncle was at the house. He knew what was going on, but he'd never lifted a finger to help me. My mother was standing at the top of the stairs that led to the basement, yelling at him, demanding he give her money so she could support me. Of course, any money he gave her was used to buy liquor and drugs. As she railed and carried on, she lost her balance. She reached out to him, expecting him to catch her. But he didn't. He looked at me and then gave her a push. She fell down the stairs and broke her neck. It was the only time any human being had ever tried to help me."

A slow smile spread across his face. "It was the best day of my life."

"What are you watching, Tony?"

Tony turned around to find Gil and a couple other deputy Marshals standing behind them.

"It's a video left by the man you know as Bobby Wade. His real name is Darrell Robert Fisher. I'm guessing he's been the man pulling the strings of the Blue-Eyed Killer for years."

Gil looked at him as if he couldn't understand what he was saying. "That mild-mannered man? I don't believe it."

"Keep watching," Tony said. He pushed the button that started the video again.

"As I watched my mother die, I realized I wanted to kill her myself. She needed to be punished. My uncle had taken that privilege away from me." Darrell shrugged. "Even though he was trying to help me."

Darrell looked away, as if he'd heard something. It was the sound of a siren. Probably the ambulance that had picked up Warren. The video shut off. Then it came back on again.

"So, Tony, you're talking to Warren. I guess he's telling you who I am. Great minds think alike, I guess." Darrell laughed as if he'd said something really clever. "I'll have to speed this up a bit. You'll be here soon, won't you?" Darrell took a deep breath and began again. "So there I was. A boy without a mother to kill. I'd always had the desire, but to be honest, I couldn't seem to do the deed myself. Couldn't bring myself to end her life. I don't know why. But the urge kept growing. Wouldn't go away. So I enlisted help. My best friend, Stinky . . ." Darrell shook his head. "Sorry, you know him as Malcolm Bodine. He offered to do the killing if I helped him. Mentored him, so to speak. Our first kill was Tammy Rice." Darrell sighed. "It was messy and amateurish. We realized afterwards that we had to find a better way. I'd always been an avid reader. I added the topic of forensics to my impressive pile of books. I learned how to kill efficiently. How to keep the crime scene clean of trace evidence. I began to teach Barney—" He put his hand over his mouth as if he'd said something he shouldn't. "I mean I taught Malcolm how to kill without getting caught. Our next victim, Ann Barton, was done perfectly. No one could find her body. In fact, no one ever found any of my bodies." Darrell pointed a finger at the camera and shook it. "Don't be impatient. I'm going to tell you where they all are once I'm done here." He inhaled deeply. "Now let's see. Where was I? Oh yes. I taught Barney how to kill. And we were good. We killed my mother over and over and over. . . . Well, you get the idea." Suddenly he snapped his fingers. "Oh, the song. My mother's favorite. She used to sing it constantly." He grinned. "She sang worse than Bella, Kate. I assume you're watching, too." He paused for a moment, and for the first time, something that looked like regret showed on his face. "I'm sorry about Bella. Truly. Alan did that. It wasn't my idea at all. He went looking for you and found her. Just one of his many mistakes."

"Tony," Gil said.

Tony paused the video again.

"Don't you think we need to be looking for this guy before he gets too far?"

Tony shrugged. "I'd bet every penny I have you won't find him. He's smart, and he's already figured out how to get away without being caught. But it's up to you."

"You two go ahead and watch the rest. I'm going to talk to the feds and the local LEOs. We need to locate this man. I'll be back."

Tony waited until they'd left, then started the video again.

"Well, to make a long story short, things were great until Barney grew tired of killing. I don't know why. I thought serial killers grew more thirsty for blood as time went on, but for some reason, the opposite happened with Barney—or Malcolm. Whatever you want to call him is fine. Then I met Alan Gerard. He was malleable, easy to train, and he had a real thirst for blood. In fact, he took care of Barney for me." Darrell's eyebrows shot up. "What? You wonder how I could have my best friend killed?" Darrell shrugged. "Wasn't hard. Maybe it should have been, but after twenty years, things change. He became a liability. If we hadn't gotten rid of him, he would have gotten careless. Been caught. And I couldn't take that risk." Darrell frowned and looked up for a moment. "Let's see, where was I? Oh yes. Alan. Well, my first impression of him was correct, but he had a fatal flaw. He couldn't seem to understand the rules. *I* pick the targets. *I* decide destiny. Instead of waiting for my instructions, he went after Kelly O'Brien, not realizing she had a twin sister. And he made a mess of it. Got caught." Darrell peered into the camera. "I'm sorry about that, Kate," he said. "I really am. That wasn't your destiny. It wasn't Kelly's, either. Alan broke the rules, and I had to get rid of him. When he got caught, I convinced him it was the best thing that had ever happened to him. Even though he was going to jail, he would be known all around the world as the Blue-Eyed Killer. And that was enough for him. For a while." He stopped talking and looked behind him. "Hey, gotta go. No more time. But there's more to tell. You'll hear from me soon." With that, Darrell stopped recording.

"Excuse me, sir?"

Tony turned around to find one of the FBI agents staring at him—and at the laptop.

"What can I do for you?" Tony asked.

"I'm Agent Phillips. I'm going to have to secure that laptop. It's evidence in our investigation."

Tony raised his hands in mock surrender. "No problem." He and Kate both backed up while Phillips and another agent took the laptop. They were careful to put it into a plastic bag using gloves so fingerprints and other trace evidence wouldn't be destroyed.

Although it was procedure, Tony found the whole scene rather ironic. He could tell them right now what they'd find. Tony's fingerprints. And that was it. There would be no trace of Darrell Fisher's prints—or anything else linking him to the video. He was a ghost.

And just like a ghost, he'd disappeared.

CHAPTER
THIRTY-FOUR

Phillips and another agent had just left when Gil returned. "Sorry about all this," he said.

"Nothing you could have done," Tony replied. "Besides, we heard the entire video. Unfortunately, Fisher ran out of time. We still don't know why he was here, and why Gerard came to Shelter Cove." He looked at Kate. "Wish we both knew more."

"We've got a BOLO out for Fisher," Gil said. "Maybe we'll nab him and get some answers. There are a lot of unanswered questions."

"You won't find him," Tony said.

"I have a feeling you're right, but maybe we'll get lucky." He frowned. "By the way, his truck is still here. Have any idea how he got out of town?"

Tony shook his head. "Not a clue. Sorry."

"Thank you for everything you've done, Gil," Kate said. "I don't know what we would have done without you."

Gil nodded. "I was happy to do what I could to help. I'm

sorry you've had to go through so much. Hope things turn out right for you." He glanced at Tony. "Do we need to get protection for Miss O'Brien?"

"I don't think so," Tony replied. "I seriously doubt she's in any danger, but let me get back to you on that." He looked at Kate. "Let's go to your house. I'm tired and hungry. I'm sure you feel the same way."

"I do," Kate agreed. "And I'd really like to soak my feet."

Gil looked at his watch. "Wow, it's getting late. We'll probably be here another hour or so. Just call me. . . ."

"Whoops," Tony said. He reached into his pocket, then handed Gil his cell phone.

"You can use my phone until you get a new one," Kate said.

"Okay. And thanks again, Gil." Tony shook Gil's hand.

"Oh, wait a minute," Gil said. "Almost forgot. Agent Phillips gave me his card and asked me to give it to you."

Tony took the card from his hand. "Couldn't be bothered to hand it over himself, huh?"

Gil grinned. "Hey, he's with the FBI. We're all supposed to be impressed."

Tony laughed. "I know I am."

"Me too," Gil said, rolling his eyes. He nodded at them and left.

Tony looked at Kate. "Your house?"

She nodded, and they left the office. They were on their way to Tony's car when someone called out to them.

Tony turned to see the fisherman who had helped him after he'd been drugged.

"Sorry to bother you," the man said as he approached, "but I'm wondering what's going on. I went to the office earlier to check out and Bobby wasn't there. I noticed the police presence in the middle of town. . . . Is there something I should be concerned about?"

"It's . . . Steven, isn't it?" Tony said.

The man smiled. "Yes. I'm surprised you remember. You were pretty out of it when we met."

"Yes, I was. Thanks again for helping me." Tony turned to Kate. "This is my friend, Kate O'Brien."

Steven put his hand out and Kate took it. Tony hadn't been able to get a good look at the man the first time they'd met. He was younger than Tony had originally thought, and he was quite good-looking. Dark hair and blue eyes. Good strong build.

"Nice to meet you, Kate."

"Look, Steven," Tony said, "there's been some trouble, but everything's okay now. The authorities will be leaving soon. Nothing for you to be concerned about. We're looking for . . . Bobby, though. Do you have any idea where he might be?"

Steven shook his head. "Sorry, don't really know the guy. Just rented a room from him. Besides, I've been out on the lake all day since it stopped raining. Just got back a little while ago."

"Why don't you stop by the park before you leave and let the officers there know you stayed at the resort? Just in case they have questions for you."

"Sure. I can do that. Not much I can tell them, though." Steven looked puzzled. "Did Bobby do something wrong?"

"Yeah, he did, but it has nothing to do with you."

"Not sure how to pay him for my stay."

Tony grinned. "I would say this visit's on him. Don't worry about it."

"Thanks. Guess I'll get going." Steven smiled at Kate. "Again, it was nice to meet you. I'm glad you're okay, Deputy."

Steven started to leave but then stopped suddenly. Tony was reaching for his gun but he wasn't fast enough. Steven turned and pointed a gun right at Tony's chest.

He sighed dramatically. "Almost made it, didn't I? I wasn't supposed to know you're a U.S. Marshal, was I? No one would have told me, especially if I was out most of the day." He used his other hand to gesture toward Tony's holster. "Lift it out slowly and put it on the ground. Now, or I'll shoot her."

"Darrell wouldn't like that, would he?" Tony asked. "His last little psycho ended up dead when he crossed his *mentor*."

Steven shrugged. "Hey, doesn't matter to me. I'm just starting out. I can plead ignorance. Put your gun on the ground. *Now!*"

Tony could tell Steven wasn't playing around. Reluctantly, he put his gun down and kicked it a few feet away.

"I don't understand what's happening, Tony," Kate said softly.

"This is Darrell's new protégé," Tony said. "Right, Steven? The new Blue-Eyed Killer."

"Yeah, that's right, and this time the title actually fits. Now, let's all get in the car like we're good friends, just in case someone's watching." He waved the gun toward Kate's car. Not knowing what else to do at that moment, Tony took Kate's hand.

"Let's go," he said to her. "You stay close to me. I won't let anything happen to you, I promise."

"Well, how sweet is that?" Steven said, making a face. "But I'll decide what happens to both of you. Let's go."

Tony and Kate walked in front of him to the car.

"You drive," Steven said to Tony. "I'll sit in the back seat with Kate."

As they got into the car, Tony looked around, but all the LEOs were over near the park. No one was anywhere near them.

Tony was quiet as he drove to Kate's, trying to come up with a way out of their situation. He thought he understood Darrell Fisher, but he didn't know this guy. Steven was a wild card. Darrell believed in destiny, and he was convinced it wasn't Kate's destiny to die. Did Steven have the same beliefs? Or was he more independent than Barney Clevenger had been? He had to come up with a plan.

He looked in the rear view mirror, worried about her. Was this the final straw? Would it be too much for her to bear? But the expression on her face wasn't the one he'd expected to see. She looked angry. And determined. If they weren't in so much trouble, Tony would have welcomed her new attitude. Unfortunately, Kate's triumph over fear wasn't enough to save them. They needed God's wisdom. Tony prayed silently, asking God to show him what to do. How to play this.

When they got to Kate's, Steven ordered them out of the car and into the house. Tony obeyed his instructions, but he watched carefully for a mistake. A chance to overpower him and get his gun.

After they got inside, Steven told them to sit on the couch in Kate's living room.

"When Darrell finds out what you've done, he's gonna be

mad," Tony said. "He never ordered anyone to kill Kate—or her sister. If you hurt her now, he'll kick you to the curb. Just like Alan. You'll never become the Blue-Eyed Killer."

Steven laughed. "But don't you see? The only thing that can really stop me is you. You know who I am. You have to die."

"But what about Darrell?" Tony asked. He realized that Steven's reasoning was a death sentence. He had to find a way to change his mind.

"He told me my destiny was to become the Blue-Eyed Killer. That means I can't allow anything to stop me. It makes perfect sense."

Tony could see the madness in his eyes. It was clear there wasn't any way to talk him down. Tony had to do something and he had to do it quickly, or he and Kate would die.

"How will you explain our deaths?" Tony asked.

"B.E.K. lives," he said softly, echoing B.E.K.'s website. He reached into his pocket and pulled out a piece of paper. He slowly unfolded it and showed it to Tony and Kate. A song sheet. For "Blue-Eyed Angel." "You'll both be dead. Usually B.E.K. doesn't kill men, but hey. Something new isn't always bad."

"You're not wearing gloves," Tony said. "Crime scene techs will find your fingerprints. Hard telling how many things you've touched since you walked in here."

Steven grinned at him. "My mentor has a lot of rules to protect us, but I don't have to worry about fingerprints." He held up one hand and turned it palm out. His fingertips were red and scarred. He put the song sheet and the gun in that hand and held up his other hand. The same scarring. "See, no fingerprints, and before you ask, my DNA isn't in any database. That's something Darrell insists on. I've been a good boy. Up until now, that is."

Still holding the gun, he reached into his jacket pocket and brought out a knife. Just like the knife used in previous B.E.K. killings.

Tony looked at Kate. For the first time since Steven grabbed them, she looked afraid. She turned to stare at him, and suddenly that same determination he'd noticed earlier washed over her features.

"So how are you going to do this?" she asked Steven. "I mean, if you try to hurt me, Tony will happily kill you. And if you attack him, I'll tear your heart out. You see, I'm a little tired of being ambushed and pushed around by crazy people."

Steven seemed surprised by her reaction. "I'll shoot him, and then I'll take a little more time with you."

"But the Blue-Eyed Killer doesn't shoot people. Plus, you'll leave behind at least one bullet. And that can be traced back to your gun. Unless that gun is unregistered. Is it?"

For the first time, Steven looked unsure of himself. Finally, he smiled again. "I'll dig out the bullet and take it with me."

Tony shook his head. "Bullets don't always go just where you want them to. Besides, you can't get out of town without being stopped and checked. If you're soaked in blood, I think someone will notice."

Steven sighed as if Tony's attempts at reasoning bored him. "I'll cover myself with plastic bags. Then I'll toss them inside a clean plastic trash bag. When I'm away from here, I'll throw the bags away. Believe it or not, no one checks plastic trash bags for evidence. They assume it's just trash."

So that was how B.E.K. was able to walk away without

attracting attention, Tony realized. It had worked before, and it would work again. Smart.

"I find this confusing," Tony said. "Your boss tells you it's your destiny to be the Blue-Eyed Killer, but he tells Kate it's her destiny to live. How can they both be right? Doesn't make sense."

"You'd better call him, Steven," Kate said, picking up on Tony's strategy. "Something's wrong, and you need to find out what it is."

"No, I don't. I know who I am."

"I don't care who you are," a voice said from behind Steven. "Now put the gun down. I won't tell you twice."

Steven turned around and found Gil Bennett pointing a gun at him. He hesitated for a moment but then lowered his own gun. Gil took it from him, and Tony grabbed him from behind, putting Steven's hands behind his back. Gil handed Tony a pair of handcuffs, and he secured the would-be serial killer.

"How did you know to come here?" Kate asked, getting up from the sofa.

"I noticed Tony's car at the resort. Wondered why it was still there. Imagine my surprise when I found his gun lying on the ground and he was nowhere to be found. Came here to see what was going on. Looked through the window and saw this guy holding a gun on you. What the heck is going on?"

Tony nodded toward Steven. "Meet Darrell's new protégé. He was supposed to be the next Blue-Eyed Killer. We were going to be his first victims."

Gil grinned at Steven, who obviously didn't find the situation humorous. "Guess you'll have to find another job. You're going to be busy for a while. Pointing a gun at people and threatening to kill them is a no-no. Guess your friend Darrell will have to move on and find someone else to fill your position."

Gil got behind Steven and pushed him toward the front door. Tony and Kate followed them outside. Gil had just turned around to say something to Tony when a shot rang out. Tony grabbed Kate and threw her to the ground. Gil dropped down behind his car and pulled Steven along with him. But it was too late for Darrell's protégé. He'd been shot through the forehead. He was dead.

CHAPTER
THIRTY-FIVE

Tony got to his feet slowly and let his gaze sweep the area. He couldn't see anyone. It was deathly quiet. Gil raised up and looked around, but there weren't any other gunshots.

"Get Kate inside," Gil said. "I'm calling for backup."

Tony grabbed Kate, covered her with his body, and guided her back into the house. He closed the door. "Stay down until we're sure you're safe."

She sat down in front of the couch with her legs crossed. "What in the world, Tony?" she said. "Was someone trying to shoot us? Did they miss and get Steven by mistake?"

Tony sat down next to her, keeping an eye on the front door. "I don't believe so. I think the shooter got the person he was aiming for. It was a great shot. Just like the shot Darrell took when he killed Gerard."

Kate gasped. "You think the shot came from Darrell? How could that be?"

"I can't be sure, but he believes in this destiny stuff. Steven threatened to kill you. Change your destiny. I think Darrell took him out."

"But I thought Darrell said he didn't like killing."

"No," Tony said grimly. "He said he didn't like the idea of *killing his mother.* I guess that means he doesn't have a problem with murdering people who don't remind him of her."

"He's really sick, isn't he?"

"I think *sick* is the mildest thing you could call him."

Kate put her hands over her face for several seconds, then said, "Is this ever going to end?"

"I can understand why you feel that way. I mean, you've been abducted. Twice. Held at gunpoint three times. You've jumped out of a moving car, fought your way through a flash flood. I've been drugged, stuck in the mud, held at gunpoint. Rescued you and one of the madmen . . . not knowing he was a madman, mind you. . . . Not that I'm complaining, but I think this has been an unusually busy day. We could both use a break."

Kate pressed her lips together in an obvious attempt not to laugh, but she lost the battle. "Really not funny. I'm just so tired I'm goofy."

At that moment, Gil came through the front door. Tony automatically tensed even though he was certain Gil could be trusted. The way things had been going, he was almost ready for Gil to point a gun at them and confess to being part of the Blue-Eyed Killer fan club. He realized immediately how ridiculous that was. Getting back to normal after what he and Kate had been through was going to take some time.

"Backup is on its way," Gil said. "Stay put and we'll try to get out of your hair as soon as possible."

"Thanks." Tony watched as Gil strode back outside. The sound of sirens made it clear help was on its way.

Kate got to her feet. "I don't know about you, but all this excitement's made me hungry. Peanuts and tamales just didn't do it for me."

"Any of that manicotti left?" Tony asked. "I'll make garlic bread if you'll heat it up."

"Deal." Kate sighed. "Wish Darrell could have told us more."

"He said he would. I believe him. Somehow he'll give us the rest of the story. I'd like to know what the plan was on that mountain. Obviously there was one."

"You're right. I can't even guess about that, but whatever it was, things clearly didn't turn out the way Gerard thought they would." She took the manicotti out of the fridge and put it in the microwave. Tony found some Italian bread and smeared butter and garlic powder on it. His mother made garlic bread with olive oil, spices, and minced garlic, but at home Tony went for fast and easy. It was still good. A little while later they were sitting next to each other at the kitchen table.

"Why don't you pray?" Kate said.

Tony bowed his head and thanked God for the food. "And thank You for Your protection," he said. "It's a miracle we got down that mountain in one piece. And God, we still have questions. Would love to have the answers, if at all possible. But whatever happens, we'll trust You. Amen."

"Amen," Kate said softly.

Tony scooped up a big bite of manicotti. "Boy," he said when he'd swallowed, "it tastes even better than it did last time."

Kate chuckled. "I know. I think it's because we're so hungry."

Tony put down his fork and stared at Kate. "So now what? You have some decisions to make."

She shook her head, a pensive look on her face. "Do I? As long as Darrell's alive, the Blue-Eyed Killer is out there. What if he changes his mind someday? What if he decides my destiny has changed?"

Tony picked up his fork again. "I really don't believe he will, Kate. Serial killers are a strange breed. They have their own moral code. Not that it makes sense, but I've seen it before. It's as if they console themselves and justify their actions as long as they never break that code. Darrell believes you weren't *called* to be a victim of the Blue-Eyed Killer. Hurting you would go against everything he believes. And as much as he can regret . . . anything . . . I believe he regrets Kelly's death. And Bella's."

"Bella." Kate shook her head solemnly. "I haven't had time to grieve for her. She was such a good friend. Knowing me ended up costing Bella her life."

"Don't go there, Kate. It wasn't your fault." Tony smiled and put his hand on hers. "One thing I'm sure of—she's singing those hymns right now in heaven. And she's finally on pitch."

Kate laughed and wiped tears from her eyes with her other hand. "I believe you're right."

Tony studied her for a moment. "Something happened to you out in the woods, didn't it?"

She nodded. "I'm not . . . whole yet, Tony. But I cried out to God. Admitted I needed help. Admitted that I hadn't dealt with the past. I was honest with Him, just like you told me to be. And it was funny, but just being real . . . started something. I guess when we're genuine with God, then He can be genuine with us. Give us *real* healing. Anyway, I know the process has begun." She put her other hand over his. "I won't shove my pain into that closet anymore. I intend to face my fears, my hurts, and let God deliver me. The right way."

"I'm glad."

Kate pulled her hands away and stared at him. "There's something else. I mean, since we're being honest. I need you to know that I meant what I said. About loving you, Tony. For a long time I thought it was a crush. I was young. You were my protector. I looked up to you. But I'm not a child now. I'm a woman." She shrugged. "Maybe you don't feel the same way, but I had to tell you. I don't want to hide my feelings anymore."

Tony looked into her startling blue eyes. For a few moments, he felt as if he were drowning in them. Finally he said, "I . . . I can't address this now, Kate. To be honest, I don't know what I feel. You're younger than me, and a witness under our protection. There are a lot of reasons this isn't a good idea. But . . ."

"First of all, you're only seven years older than me. There are a lot of couples with even larger age differences than that and they're very happy. And I'm not a witness anymore. I mean, there's no one to *witness* for, is there?"

"Not now. But what if Darrell is caught someday? We both may be called to testify."

"Different situation. I was a target for Gerard. Not for Darrell. Besides, the only person I *know* he killed was Gerard. Not sure about Steven. It's just conjecture."

Tony could see the wisdom in what she said, but he still wanted Darrell caught . . . or killed. Those were the only two options that would free Kate completely. What if Darrell found another apprentice? Steven had gone after her. Why not someone else? The idea made his stomach turn over. He couldn't voice his fear to Kate. She wanted her life back, and more than anything, he wanted that for her too. "So what are you going to do?" Tony asked. "Are you leaving the program?"

She nodded. "Definitely. But where I'll go from here is up in the air. I haven't made a final decision yet."

"Look," Tony said, "let's talk about this again . . . soon. But right now we both need to rest. And I can't walk away yet. Even if Darrell has no intention of hurting you, I can guarantee you he plans to hurt someone. I'd like to stop him before that happens. If at all possible."

"I understand. But we will talk, right? About us?"

Tony smiled. "Right." He hesitated a moment, wondering just what he should say—or shouldn't say. Finally, he decided that if Kate could be honest, he could, too. "I . . . I do have feelings for you, Kate. Maybe you already figured that out. I just need some time, okay?"

A smile spread slowly across her face. "Okay. That's all I need to know for now."

Tony could feel his heart pounding in his chest. He wanted to take Kate in his arms, tell her he loved her, but he couldn't. Not until he was sure it was right. He was still her protector, and he couldn't walk away from that role—even if he had to protect her from himself.

Tony and Kate finished their meal, and Kate cleaned up

the dishes. "So now what?" she said after loading the last dish in the dishwasher. "Frankly, I need a good, hot shower and a lot of sleep."

"Me too," Tony said, yawning. He suddenly realized that he might not be able to go back to the resort. "Can I use your phone?" he asked.

Kate picked it up from the kitchen counter and handed it to him. "Just keep it. I hardly ever use it. When you get another phone, you can give it back."

"Thanks. I appreciate that." He checked his pocket for the card Agent Phillips had given him. He dialed the number. When Phillips answered, Tony asked him about his room at the resort.

"Sorry. It's being processed. Fisher's apartment is locked down."

"I don't want to get in Fisher's apartment," Tony said. "I just want my room."

"Can't do it. Sorry."

Tony sighed. "Can I at least get my personal items out of there?"

There was a brief pause. "Meet me in ten minutes. I'll let you take out what you need."

"Thanks."

He hung up the phone and told Kate what Phillips had said. "So I'll have my clothes, but nowhere to sleep. I haven't seen a motel in town."

Kate shook her head. "No motel. Mrs. Ingersoll rents rooms, but she's usually full. That's it." Kate snapped her fingers. "What about Warren's house? He's not there."

Tony frowned. "Not without his permission. I doubt he's ready to talk about something like that yet."

Kate shrugged. "Then you'll stay here."

"Absolutely not. I can't do it."

"And why not? You'll sleep on the couch." She scowled at him. "For crying out loud, Tony. With everything we've been through today, worrying about what other people will think is just . . . stupid."

"I understand what you're saying, but . . ."

Kate stamped her foot, which probably hurt a bit since her feet were still sore. "That's it. I'm not putting up with some ridiculous fear of impropriety. Go get your clothes and come back here. My couch is quite comfortable. I've spent nights out here. By the time you get back, I'll have it all ready. Clean sheets. A nice soft comforter. Pillows. You'll be asleep before you know it."

Tony started to argue, but Kate held up her small hand like a traffic cop. "No. That's it. No arguing. Now go."

Although he still wasn't sure it was a smart idea, Tony was too exhausted to debate further. He'd figure out something else tomorrow. "Okay, okay. I gotta meet Phillips. I'll be back soon. Lock the door behind me."

"Okay, but I'll be fine."

"Boy, you can be pushy when you want to be," Tony said, grinning.

"You better know it. Now get going."

As Tony walked out Kate's front door, he looked up. The clouds had disappeared, and the night was covered with a blanket of bright stars. But at that moment, the love in his heart for Kate felt more intense than all the stars in the sky.

CHAPTER
THIRTY-SIX

Tony woke up to the smell of coffee and bacon. He sniffed the air a couple of times just to make sure he wasn't dreaming. He'd slept like a baby last night and awoken ravenous. What was it about food that made bad times seem better? He swung his legs off the couch and sat up. After running his hands through his hair, he got up. A hot shower last night had made him feel human again. He pulled his suitcase over near the couch, took out some jeans, and looked for a shirt. He'd had to quickly stuff everything into his suitcase last night, so most of his clothes were wrinkled. Thankfully, he found a blue sweater that wasn't too bad. He grabbed it and hurried into the bathroom to change. Even though his sweats were modest, he still felt undressed somehow. A few minutes later, he emerged fully dressed and feeling more presentable.

"Something smells good," he said, walking into the kitchen.

Kate smiled at him. She was wearing jeans and a green blouse that highlighted her red hair. She looked incredible.

"Here's your coffee," she said, pouring a large cup and putting it on the kitchen table. "Your breakfast will be ready in a few minutes."

"Thanks. Think I'll go out on the porch for a bit, if you don't mind. I'm getting addicted to country air, I'm afraid."

Kate laughed. "Go right ahead. There's plenty of time."

Tony walked over to the front door and pulled it open. But before he stepped out on the porch, he froze. There was a package in front of the door with his name and Kate's name on it. And under their names someone had drawn an angel . . . in blue.

"Thanks for calling us and not picking it up."

Tony stood with Agent Phillips and Kate, watching as a crime scene tech carefully put the package in a large plastic bag.

"Look," Tony said. "This is actually addressed to us. We want to see what's inside." He frowned at the FBI agent, who at first appeared to ignore him.

Finally, Phillips sighed. "Why don't you come with us to our command center? I can't allow you to touch it, but I don't see why you can't watch while we take a look at it."

"Thanks." He turned toward Kate. "Do you want to come?"

She shook her head. "I'm really tired, Tony. I need a break from . . . all this."

"I understand." Tony frowned at Phillips. "I would feel better if you'd post someone outside this house. Just in case."

Phillips nodded. "I'll ask someone to drive over and keep

an eye on the place." He walked out the front door and called someone on his cell phone.

Tony turned back to Kate. "Are you sure you don't want to come?"

She nodded. "I'd rather have you tell me what it says. I don't want Darrell's voice in my head again. Are you able to understand that?"

He nodded. "Absolutely. Can you keep breakfast warm? I'll be back as soon as I can."

"I'll do my best. And don't worry about me. I'll be fine."

He nodded and stepped outside. He and Phillips waited until the other agent pulled up. Although Tony felt better when the man had stationed himself outside Kate's house, he still sent up a quick prayer for Kate's protection.

Kate waited impatiently for Tony to return. It had been almost two hours. His breakfast was waiting in the oven. She'd covered his plate with tin foil and put the oven on low. Hopefully, the food would still be edible by the time he returned. She was thinking about calling him when she finally saw his car driving toward the house. She jumped up and grabbed the coffeepot. She'd just made a fresh pot, since the other coffee had been sitting for so long. She poured the coffee into a cup and set it on the table. Then she got two pot holders and removed Tony's plate from the oven. She'd just put that on the table when the front door opened and he came in.

"Took you long enough," she scolded.

"I know. Sorry. They were being really careful with the

package. It was a letter. A really long letter. I had to wait for them to process each page. I thought I'd be there forever."

Kate pointed at the table. "Sit down and eat your breakfast. I'm sure you're starving."

"I am. Thanks." He sat down and picked up his coffee cup. After taking several sips, he grabbed a fork and took several bites of eggs and bacon.

Kate waited as patiently as she could, but she really wanted to find out what Tony had learned. He seemed to understand that she was anxious.

"Okay," he said, "I'm going to try to remember everything. I wanted to take notes, but I was afraid of upsetting Agent Phillips. He didn't seem real happy to have me there in the first place. I'm surprised he let me come at all."

"He's not a bad man," Kate said. "He's just trying to do his job. I think he realizes you and I have the right to know what Darrell wrote to us."

"Yeah, I guess so." Tony picked up a piece of bacon and put the whole slice in his mouth. "This is delicious," he said once he'd chewed.

"Thanks. Now talk."

"Okay. Well, first of all, Darrell wasn't sure who I was when I first came to town. I had a file about you. He went into my room and found it. Realized I was the Marshal assigned to you during the trials."

"But he didn't hurt you."

"No. It seems he appreciated knowing I was here to protect you."

"Thank God for that. So tell me more about Gerard and his relationship with Darrell."

Tony nodded. "Well, as Gerard told us, it seems he didn't like prison as much as he thought he would. Once people quit paying so much attention to him, he decided to let Darrell know if he didn't get him out, he was going to tell people about him."

"Yeah. That's what Gerard told us in the cabin. Not a very smart thing to do."

"No, it wasn't," Tony agreed. "But Darrell got him out. He put Ann Barton's necklace in Dorothy's gravesite. He knew Barney's fingerprint was on it." Tony shook his head. "I have to wonder if the print would have shown up if it had really been in the ground that long. But no one questioned it. Anyway, after he planted the necklace, he called the police. You know the rest. Gerard was already out of prison because of the tainted blood evidence. This made it seem as if he'd never really been the Blue-Eyed Killer."

"So why did Gerard come here? And how did he know I was in Shelter Cove?" Kate asked.

"Darrell is a computer genius. Ran the B.E.K. Lives website without ever being tracked. Used it to control Barney. When a scripture verse was posted, it was a call for a new murder. However, toward the end of Barney's time as B.E.K., he lost the will to kill. That's why there were scriptures but no disappearances. That's also why Gerard murdered him."

"Back to how he found me?"

"Oh, sure. Sorry. Just trying to remember everything. Anyway, he hacked into the U.S. Marshals' private files and found out where you were. The government was aware of the hack but assumed it was random when nothing came of it."

"They didn't realize that Darrell was only after one bit of information."

"Right. Well, Darrell wasn't happy with Gerard. Hadn't been since he attacked you and killed Kelly. So he contacted Gerard and told him where you were. Gave him the chance to come to Shelter Cove and finish what he'd started."

"Wait a minute," Kate said, her eyes full of alarm. "I thought Darrell wanted me alive."

"He did. He only brought Gerard here so he could kill him. He told him how to find you and gave him directions to the cabin. Even lied to him about some kind of safe way down the mountain. It doesn't exist."

"So Darrell planned to kill Gerard all along?"

Tony grunted. "Yeah. Here's where it gets even crazier. Supposedly, the original plan was to allow Gerard to kidnap you. Darrell . . . as Bobby . . . was going to rescue you. He was going to shoot Gerard and make it look as if he was saving your life. But then the rains came, and I was here . . ."

"So Darrell decided to take you with him? Why?"

"Actually, Darrell told him he was going to kill me. Get me out of the way. Darrell injected me with a drug the night before Gerard planned to take you. But he only gave me enough to knock me out. After I came to, he called Gerard and told him I was alive. Since I hadn't died, Darrell told Gerard he had a new plan. He was going to get me to come up the mountain with him. He convinced Gerard that having me there would ensure Gerard was identified as the Blue-Eyed Killer. My testimony would be much more convincing than Darrell's. Gerard didn't like it, but somehow Darrell convinced him it was a good idea. Actually, it shows how clueless Gerard really was. Having a trained law enforcement officer on the scene made him more vulnerable. But Gerard didn't understand that, I guess. Or he put more stock in what Darrell told him than his own common sense."

Kate shook her head. "One thing that confuses me. Well, one of the many things that confuse me, I should say. Wasn't Darrell taking a chance that Gerard would kill me before you two got there?"

"Actually, Darrell mentioned that. He'd ordered Gerard to wait until he arrived. He believed Gerard would obey him."

"So Darrell was convinced he had time to get there and save me."

"As you can imagine, he was relieved when we found you. Ensured his plan was still in effect."

"But then Darrell betrayed Gerard. He came back and shot him."

Tony nodded. "That was always his intention. To murder Gerard. And I was there to tell the story. That Gerard was planning to kill you, and Darrell rescued us. That he was a hero."

"But what if law enforcement looked into Darrell's past? Couldn't they find out who he was?"

"With his computer skills?" Tony shook his head. "My guess is that they'd find exactly what Darrell wanted them to find. I'm certain there's a death certificate out there somewhere for Darrell R. Fisher. And a birth certificate and Social Security number for Robert Wade."

She was quiet a moment before saying, "But why did Darrell come to Shelter Cove in the first place, Tony? What did he want?"

"Believe it or not, he wanted to watch over you. Make sure you were okay. It was his way of . . . paying penance for his part in hurting you. He takes this destiny thing seriously and believes you were wronged by Gerard."

Kate shivered, but it wasn't because she was cold. To think someone like Darrell Fisher was watching over her was like being told you were being guarded by a cat—when you're a mouse. "So what happened when Gerard pushed him outside the cabin and there was a gunshot?"

"Prearranged. It was supposed to be Darrell's chance to go back to town. Tell everyone that B.E.K. had killed you. Gerard thought he had plenty of time to take care of you. Of course, Darrell just waited until he could come back and be our savior."

"Wow. This whole thing is so convoluted it almost hurts my brain."

Tony nodded. "But Gerard bought it. He played right into Darrell's hands."

"So Darrell had everything figured out—except for the rain."

"Yeah, and that almost ruined his entire plan in one way. Saved it in another."

Kate looked at him quizzically.

"You see, Gerard was supposed to take you straight to the cabin, but you got out of his car. If it hadn't been raining, you could have made it back to one of the main roads and flagged down help. But with the rain, no one was out there, and we had to head for shelter. Darrell led us right to the cabin, and the plan was on again."

"One thing I don't understand."

"Just one thing?"

Kate smiled. "What if you hadn't given Bobby your gun?"

Tony took a big bite of scrambled eggs and washed them down with coffee. "He had a gun strapped to his ankle. I don't know how he would have explained it, but he would have found a way."

"You didn't drop your phone, did you?"

"Nope. Bobby's slide down the embankment was planned. He'd already taken my phone out of my jacket when we found Gerard's car. Then he used his . . . accident to explain why my phone was missing. Couldn't take a chance that I'd call for help before his *mission* was complete. And he actually called it a mission. Crazy."

Kate noticed Tony staring longingly at the remainder of his breakfast. She laughed. "Finish up. I'll hold my questions until you're done."

"Sorry," he said, looking somewhat guilty. "This is delicious, and I'm starved."

Kate got up and began cleaning the kitchen. She turned over in her head everything Tony had said. At least some of it was making sense. But she realized that dealing with a crazy person meant any explanation would probably just leave her with more questions. The odd thing was, she found she actually missed Bobby. Felt as if he'd died. She'd cared about him and couldn't quite reconcile the knowledge that Bobby had never really existed. He still felt real to her.

"Could I have another cup of coffee?" Tony asked.

Kate brought the pot over and poured his coffee. His breakfast had disappeared. "Boy, you really were hungry."

"Yeah. Thanks. It was great."

Kate took the pot back over and set it on the coffeemaker. "Did Darrell know who Warren was?"

"Yeah. But Warren didn't know who Bobby was until right before you were kidnapped. When I took off with Darrell, Warren went after us. He was trying to save you."

"But Gil shot him before he could explain."

"That's right."

Kate sat down, her eyes wide. "If Warren had died, Darrell could have gone back to being Bobby and no one would have been the wiser."

"Actually, that's not true. First of all, *Bobby* made a mistake. One that I would have noticed eventually. He mentioned the name Bodine before the name was released to the public. He started planning to leave town right after he flubbed up. He knew I'd remember it at some point. And then there's the picture. That's what finally led me to the truth."

"What picture?"

"Batterson sent me some stuff about Killian. Attached to his email were some photos from a high-school yearbook. At first I didn't recognize him, but then I realized it was Bobby . . . Darrell. He was friends with Barney Clevenger, the man who would eventually call himself Malcolm Bodine."

"The real Blue-Eyed Killer."

Tony nodded. "That meant Bobby knew a lot more than he'd been saying. And if Warren wasn't Gerard's mentor . . ."

"Bobby was."

Tony stopped and took a sip of coffee. When he put down the cup, he leaned back in his chair and sighed. "I'm really not sure Darrell planned to hang around much longer anyway. I mean, if he intends to keep the Blue-Eyed Killer alive, I'm not sure Shelter Cove would work for him anymore. Not after everything that's happened. Even if he hadn't tripped up, I think he was planning to leave. He just wanted to make sure Gerard was dead and you were finally safe."

"Is that it?" Kate asked.

"Not quite. He told us that all the missing women are buried in graves with the name Dorothy." Tony sighed. "The FBI is going to be visiting a lot of graveyards. Hopefully, they'll recover some remains."

"That's . . . disturbing."

"Yeah, it is."

"Anything else?"

Tony picked up his cup, stared at it, and then put it back down, an odd look on his face.

"What's wrong?" she asked. "What else did he say?"

Tony sniffed, and Kate's stomach tightened. "You sniff when you're getting ready to lie."

"I wasn't going to lie."

"Maybe not, but you're thinking about how to soften the blow. Tell me. Remember, no secrets. Just honesty."

"I sniff?"

Kate smiled. "Yes. You did it during the trials. When you told me what you thought I wanted to hear, you sniffed first. I watched for it. Knew when you were being straight with me and when you were trying to protect me."

Tony sighed. "Well, great. Now I'll have to think about not sniffing when I talk to witnesses."

"It's not a bad thing. You cared. I knew that."

"Good. Well, I wasn't going to get into this, but Darrell

said he never had real feelings for anyone except his uncle—and us."

Kate felt her face grow hot. "You've got to be kidding."

"No, I'm not. And I think he meant it, Kate. In his own insane way, he cares about us."

"I don't want someone like Darrell Fisher *caring* about either one of us."

Tony shook his head. "Then you really won't like this."

Kate raised her eyebrows. "What?"

"He said that before he left Shelter Cove, Steven would be dead. He was going to be Darrell's next apprentice, but he found a *flaw* in him. Darrell's word, not mine. He didn't trust Steven, and he was determined to keep you out of danger. He said he was going back to the internet and would recruit his next protégé from there. He wanted you to know that when the next Blue-Eyed Killer emerges, he will never come anywhere near you. He promised that you will always be safe. He wrote a letter years ago and sent it to the police. I still remember it word for word. It said, 'Everyone has a destiny. Every step we take only brings us closer to the inevitable. There is no way to change what must happen. Kate O'Brien's course is ordained, and there is nothing anyone can do about it. Accepting this truth is the only thing that can free our souls.' At the time, that letter worried me. But now I realize he was saying you were destined to live. And he truly believes that."

Kate shuddered. Somehow Darrell's reassurance was even more frightening than if he'd threatened her life.

CHAPTER
THIRTY-SEVEN

Linda woke up and stared at the phone on her nightstand. It was Leon calling. He'd left early for the office, and she'd gone back to bed for a bit. She glanced at the clock. Nine-thirty. She hadn't meant to sleep for so long. She and her friends from church had worked hard to clean Fred's house yesterday, and her joints let her know they didn't appreciate it. When they left, Fred had hugged each one of them. He'd seemed so happy and appreciative of everything they'd done. Linda had gotten a ride home with one of her friends since Leon and Fred wanted to talk a while longer. Leon got home late, and she knew he was tired. She'd be glad when he retired so he could get some rest.

"Good morning," she said, her voice still full of sleep.

"Good morning," he said.

Immediately she could tell something was wrong. "Has something happened?"

"Yeah. Called to check on Fred this morning, but he didn't

answer his phone. I'm at his place now. He passed away last night sometime after we left."

"Oh, Leon. I'm so sorry to hear that."

"At least he was happy. And we talked about the Lord after you left. He prayed for salvation, Linda. I know he's in heaven."

"I'm so glad you were able to befriend him, honey. I don't think he had a lot of happy days. Thanks to you, he has an eternity of them ahead of him."

"Just grateful to God that He directed me to Fred." Leon sighed. "No one to take care of him now. Can you call the church? See if they can take up a collection to pay for his funeral costs?"

"Sure. I'll do that as soon as we hang up. Call me later. It'll be okay." Linda paused before saying good-bye. "I love you, Leon. And I'm proud of you."

She put down the phone and flopped back down on the bed. As sad as she was that Fred had left them, last night a wounded soul had found his way home. And that was cause for celebration.

Batterson hung up the phone after talking to Tony. He'd already spent three days in Shelter Cove after Gerard and the new apprentice had been killed. Now he was asking for even more time off. Although Batterson was happy to give it to him, especially since he had accrued several months' vacation, he was still concerned about Tony's feelings for Kate O'Brien. Being thrust together in the middle of danger could bind people together—but it didn't necessarily mean their feelings were real. Batterson couldn't warn him about being involved with a witness because things had changed. O'Brien's attacker was dead, and she'd left the program. The way was clear for Tony. Batterson had no plans to interfere. All he could do was hope Tony knew what he was doing. Frankly, Batterson was just happy his deputy and his witness had survived one of the strangest cases he'd faced since he'd joined the U.S. Marshals. He wanted to believe that the Blue-Eyed Killer case was over. But as long as Darrell Fisher was alive, they'd never be able to close the file.

Kate and Tony sat on Kate's front porch swing, enjoying the spring weather. A light breeze wafted past them, carrying the aroma of the honeysuckle that bloomed all over town. Most of the authorities had left, and Shelter Cove was returning to normal.

Warren was recovering in the hospital and had graciously allowed Tony to stay in his house. Since he didn't live far from Kate, it was working out really well.

"So what happens now?" Tony asked.

"Well, I was thinking it was time for me to go back to St. Louis."

Tony was surprised. "I thought you liked it here."

"I do. It's a safe place to hide. Or it was, anyway."

"What do you mean by that?"

Kate sighed. "I felt shielded from Alan Gerard. From the Blue-Eyed Killer. But I wasn't. Darrell was here, and Gerard was able to find me, too. I guess I've realized that real safety isn't a place you are. It's being held in God's arms. Protected by His love. And I can have that anywhere." She leaned her head back and closed her eyes for a moment. "Thank you for being honest with me. I know I fought you when you first came here. I couldn't deal with my anger and my pain, so I tried to ignore it. I really thought I was dealing with things the only way I could. But you taught me that running away and hiding wasn't the answer. It hurt to confront the darkness, but it was the only way to let God's light dispel it." She turned her head and gazed into his eyes. "I know it might take some time for me to become completely whole again, but at least I'm on my way."

"There's a therapist in St. Louis who might be able to help you," Tony said. "I hear she's pretty good. I could introduce you."

"I'd like that."

"You know that the authorities will never stop looking for Darrell Fisher, right? Eventually they'll catch him."

"I hope so, but I'm determined not to give him any more space in my life. He's stolen enough."

"I agree," Tony said. "So what happens to the café?"

"Remember the woman I told you about? The one who covered for me when you came over for dinner?"

Tony nodded.

"She wants to buy it. And she'll pay me enough money so I can get a place to live in St. Louis and not worry about money for a while."

Tony laughed. "So you're planning to be a lady of leisure?"

Kate chuckled. "No. I think I'd like to go back to school. When I first enrolled, I wanted to be a teacher because . . . well, because I couldn't think of anything else. But over the past few years, I've thought about it a lot. I think I'd really enjoy working with young people. People like Darrell . . . Maybe if he'd had stronger positive influences when he was a kid, he might have become something else. I know a lot of children have tough lives. I can't be their parent, but maybe I can be someone they could come to for help." She smiled at him. "You spend your life dealing with people who turned out badly. Maybe I could catch some of them before you do."

Tony smiled back at her. "I think that sounds wonderful. You'll be a great teacher."

"Thanks. I'll get things squared away here, and then I'll come up to St. Louis," she said. "Then we'll talk."

"About?"

"About a lot of things." She reached over and took Tony's hand. Her touch was like electricity. "I'm no longer a witness," she said. "I'm Kate O'Brien again. Whoever she is. But this time, she's going to be stronger."

"You've always been strong."

"Trying to take your life isn't strength," she said quietly.

"But it isn't weakness, either," he replied. "It's just a strong person who's grown tired. And that's not a crime. It's just finding yourself in a place where you need help."

Kate nodded, and a tear ran down her cheek. "I like that. Thank you. And help came. *You* came. And you pointed me toward God. There's nothing better you could have done for me. He and I are working it out. Day by day."

"Breath by breath," Tony said tenderly. Even though he hadn't planned to do it, he leaned over and kissed her. When he pulled away, her incredible eyes were looking into his. He took a deep breath. "I love you," he said gently.

Kate reached up and rested her hand on his face. "Took you long enough," she said with a smile.

It had only taken a few days to plan Fred's funeral. He didn't have any family, and very few people in Garden City knew him. Leon stopped by the small funeral home the church had picked to handle the details. When Leon went into the office, the director of the mortuary frowned at him.

"I thought you wanted us to handle Mr. Fisher's service," he said.

Leon nodded. "Yes, that's right. Is everything okay?"

"No, it's not." The director, a rotund man named Horace, was obviously upset. His broad face was red with emotion. "Callahan's came by and picked up the body. Said they were in charge."

Leon shook his head. "For crying out loud. That's not right. How could they get that idea?"

"Well, I'm sure I don't know, but you need to talk to them. I can't do anything without the body."

Leon said good-bye and left, driving straight over to Callahan's, the most prestigious and costly funeral home in town. He got out of his car and hurried inside. Marsha Weaver, daughter of the owner, greeted him when he came in the door.

"Marsha, I arranged for Fred Fisher's service to be handled by Peaceful Hills Mortuary. They told me you picked up his body. What's going on?"

"Why don't we talk in my office?" she said. "I think I can explain everything."

Leon followed her down the hall and through a large wooden

door into an office the people at Peaceful Hills would envy. Dark wood furniture, polished wood floors, deep plush chairs. There was no way Leon's small church could afford this place.

"Have a seat," Marsha said, gesturing toward an over-stuffed chair in front of her desk.

With a sigh, Leon sat down.

"Let me look up the details about Fred's service." She riffled through some papers until she removed one from a large file. "Here it is. I remember what happened, but I wanted to make sure of my facts."

"I know the facts," Leon said. "I contacted Peaceful Hills myself. Fred's service was to be conducted there. My church is paying for everything, and unfortunately we can't afford your fees."

Marsha looked over her glasses at Leon. "I don't know why you'd want to pay for a service that's already been covered."

"I . . . I don't understand. Fred was alone. Who would pay this much for his funeral?"

"I wasn't in the office at the time, but our receptionist said a man came by and purchased our deluxe package. Paid cash."

"What was his name?" Leon asked.

"All I have here is . . . Bobby." She cocked her head to the side and studied him. "Do you know this man?"

"No. No, I don't. But as long as the money's good, that's the important thing, I guess."

"Yes, it's good."

"When will the service be held?"

Marsha smiled at him. "Well, that will be up to you. You're listed as the person to contact for details."

Leon gulped. "Are . . . are you sure?"

"Yes. It's right here. Contact Sergeant Leon Shook."

Leon stood up, feeling a little shaky. Who was Bobby? Fred had no living relatives. When Leon had contacted Tally to tell him Fred had passed away, he'd shared his findings about Darrell. That he'd been dead for years. So who was behind the payment? Leon had a feeling he didn't want to know the answer to that question. He definitely had no intention of telling Linda the truth. He'd let her believe some generous Garden City resident had picked up the cost of the service.

"I'll get back to you, Marsha. Okay?"

"Sure, Sergeant. We'll wait to hear from you."

Leon walked out of the building into a bright spring day. Maybe it was enough to know that Fred would have a great funeral with all the typical pomp and circumstance. Perhaps at this point it was best to let sleeping dogs lie. He got into his patrol car and drove back to the station.

EPILOGUE

Richard Batterson, Chief Deputy U.S. Marshal for the District of Missouri's U.S. Marshals' Office, sat looking out his window. It had been raining all day, and his mood matched the weather. Three months had passed since Darrell Fisher, the man behind the Blue-Eyed Killer, had disappeared. Law enforcement across the country had undertaken a huge manhunt, determined to bring an extremely dangerous man to justice. Just two hours ago, Batterson had received a call from Jack Watts, chief of the Marshals' Kansas City office. The manager of a local motel had called to say Fisher was staying in one of his rooms. This wasn't the first time someone had said they'd seen Fisher, but this situation was different. The manager was a retired cop. Someone local law enforcement trusted. Could it really be that easy? Was Fisher finally going to be held accountable for the lives he took and the deaths caused by those he'd manipulated?

As he waited for a follow-up phone call, Batterson tried to think of something else, but every time he did, his mind wandered back to the situation at hand. Batterson had seen a lot of criminals come to justice during his time with the Marshals, but this case was unique. Fisher was responsible for almost twenty deaths. Maybe more. There were a couple dozen other unsolved murders that the FBI and local police and sheriff's departments wanted to lay at Fisher's feet—if they could get him to confess.

When the phone finally rang, Batterson grabbed it like he was dying of thirst and it was a drink of cool water. Since he'd told his assistant not to let any other calls through except the one from Kansas City, once he'd picked up the receiver, he only said, "Yes?"

"It's him," Jack said.

Batterson let out a breath he hadn't realized he was holding. "Are you sure?"

"Yes. But . . ."

"But what? No buts on this one, Jack. Please."

"Sorry, Richard. He must have known we were closing in."

"No."

"Yeah. Shot himself before we could nab him."

Batterson swore under his breath. Not the outcome he'd wanted. Not only would Fisher get away without punishment, they'd never know if he was connected to the other murders.

"All right. Thanks, Jack. At least it's over."

"Maybe."

Batterson rubbed his left temple with his free hand. Another headache. Great. "What are you talking about?"

"He left a letter."

"So?"

"It's addressed to Kate O'Brien."

Anger bubbled up inside of Batterson like lava in a volcano getting ready to erupt. "Listen to me, Jack," he said through gritted teeth. "I don't want the press to know about the letter. Keep it under wraps. I'll talk to the FBI, ask them to do the same. Keep this from the public."

"You can ask them. Not sure if they'll do it."

"All I can do is try. I think they'll work with me. They hate this guy as much as we do."

"You know she'll need to see it someday."

"Maybe. Maybe not. Darrell Fisher's done enough damage. I don't want him messing with O'Brien again. Especially from the grave."

There was silence from the other end. Finally, Jack said, "Okay, Richard, I hear you. Not a word from us."

"Thanks." Batterson put down the phone. If he had anything to say about it, that letter would never see the light of day. It was time to silence the Blue-Eyed Killer for good.

And that was what he intended to do.

Batterson straightened up in his chair and picked up the phone again. When his assistant answered, he asked her to open his door and gave her permission to put other calls through.

It was time to get back to business as usual.

ACKNOWLEDGMENTS

First of all, thank you to God for calling me to write. No matter how fast the deadlines come rushing in or the words don't seem to be rushing out, You come through and get me to "The End." I'm so grateful. May every book glorify You.

My thanks to retired U.S. Deputy Marshal Paul Anderson. Your patience with my clueless questions is appreciated more than I can say. I've learned so much from you. I'm not only grateful for your help with these books, I'm thankful for your service to this country. You and those like you are heroes. God bless you, Paul.

To Officer Darin Hickey with the Training and Community Affairs Division in Cape Girardeau, Missouri: Thank you for all your help. Your input has helped to keep this story on track. Thank you even more for your service to America. I feel blessed to know you.

My medical information came from Dr. Andrea McCarty in Wichita, Kansas. Thanks, Dr. Andy! I miss your great smile.

Thank you to the real Leon Shook who helped me with my

Garden City information. I also want to thank Leon and his wife, Linda, for allowing me to use them in this book. Their honesty, integrity, love for God, and for each other shaped my characters perfectly. Knowing you both has been one of the great blessings in my life.

Thanks so much to my Inner Circle: Zac, Mary, Cheryl, Liz, JoJo, Shirley, Tammy, Bonnie, Lynne, Deanna, Breeze, Mury, Karla, Michelle, and Rhonda for your support. You guys are the best!

Thank you to Candice Prentice for letting me bounce ideas off of her—and for reading through the rough draft of *Dark Deception*. Your help was invaluable.

As always, I appreciate Raela Schoenherr for her great advice. And thanks so much to Sharon Hodge for her editorial assistance. You're awesome!

ABOUT THE AUTHOR

Nancy Mehl is the author of more than twenty-five books, including the ROAD TO KINGDOM and FINDING SANCTUARY series. She received the ACFW Mystery Book of the Year Award in 2009. She has a background in social work and is a member of ACFW. Nancy writes from her home in Missouri, where she lives with her husband, Norman, and their puggle, Watson. To learn more, visit NancyMehl.com.

Sign Up for Nancy's Newsletter!

Keep up to date with news on Nancy's upcoming book releases and events by signing up for her email list at nancymehl.com.

More From Nancy Mehl

The small, primarily Mennonite town of Sanctuary, Missouri, is something of a refuge. In this private community, many secrets dwell undetected. As three young women investigate mysteries centered here, each will unknowingly put her life—and her heart—in jeopardy.

FINDING SANCTUARY: *Gathering Shadows, Deadly Echoes, Rising Darkness*

◊ BETHANYHOUSE

You May Also Like . . .

When Avery Tate's friend disappears, the only lead is a chilling photo of her in a morbid exhibit in which all the models appear dead. As Avery, her ex-boss, Parker, and his friends in law enforcement dig into the mystery, things heat up when their suspect zeroes in on a new target.

Still Life by Dani Pettrey, CHESAPEAKE VALOR #2
danipettrey.com

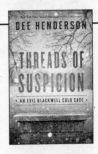

With the public eye fixed on the governor's Missing Persons Task Force, Detective Evie Blackwell and her new partner, David, are under pressure to produce results. While they investigate two missing-persons cases in Chicago, Evie and David's conviction that justice is truly possible for all will be tested to the limit.

Threads of Suspicion by Dee Henderson
AN EVIE BLACKWELL COLD CASE, deehenderson.com

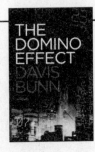

Esther Larsen, a risk analyst at a powerful banking institution, is convinced she has uncovered a ticking bomb with the potential to overshadow 2008's market crash. She has to do something—but *what*? With global markets on the brink, Esther races against the clock to avert a disaster that threatens worldwide financial devastation.

The Domino Effect by Davis Bunn
davisbunn.com